Also by Maurice Edelman

ALL ON A SUMMER'S NIGHT

THE PRIME MINISTER'S DAUGHTER

MAURICE EDELMAN

STEIN AND DAY/*Publishers*/New York

FIRST STEIN AND DAY PAPERBACK EDITION JUNE 1986

The Prime Minister's Daughter is published by arrangement with
David Higham Associates Limited.
Copyright © 1964 by Maurice Edelman
All rights reserved.
Printed in the United States of America

Stein and Day, Incorporated
Scarborough House
Briarcliff Manor, N.Y. 10510

ISBN 0-8128-8266-0

to Natasha

'Is that his head?' said Lady Drayford. Her voice, commanding even as she inquired, overlaid the *allegretto grazioso*.

'No,' said a man, half-visible in the penumbra beyond the projector's beam. 'It's her shoulder.'

A hiss rustled through the drawing-room, starting close to Mayland, who sat in his familiar caricatured position, head sunk on to his chest and hands clasping the tapestry of his chair arms. On the screen at the verge of the Savonnerie carpet below Canaletto's 'Market Place at Verona', obscure images stirred and uncoiled to the accompaniment of the 'cellos on the sound track.

'As long as it's Brahms,' said Lady Drayford, challenging the withheld breath of those around her, 'they can get away with anything.'

'Please!' said the newspaper proprietor, and with the signal given the thirty-nine guests turned hostilely towards Lady Drayford, long enough for disapproval but not to divert themselves from their hope that the screen would lighten to unveil the tangled lovers in their adulterous loft.

'I'm sure it's his head,' said Lady Drayford defiantly.

But the horns now followed the 'cellos, and the glimpses quickened of a hand, a breast, a naked hip, an ambiguous curve, an arching back; and the stereophonic breathing exhaled from among the carved festoons near the fireplace and beneath the *pietra dura* of a Florentine table where Lord Wainley, a Joint Under-Secretary at the Foreign Office, was resting his arm. The gasps and moans came in counterpoint, attended by aspiring chords, till at last the woman's voice burst out, incontinent,

'*Mon amour ... mon amour,*'

and died with the *andantino*.

The film cut to the husband, self-satisfied in his sun-filled Paris office; and the guests uncrossed their legs as if at drill.

Mayland snapped his fingers twice, and for a fraction of a second the darkness became total as the projector was switched off, but almost immediately the chandeliers bloomed into light, the red walls flared and the painted ceiling became alive with gods and chariots. Wainley rubbed his eyes, and said to Lady Drayford,

'Most remarkable. What's it called?'

'*Le Baiser*,' said Lady Drayford. '*Le Baiser* – it's the adaptation – modernized – of *La Nouvelle Héloïse*. Banned in France, of course.'

Wainley looked at the half-moons of his fingernails as if he had just discovered them, and said,

'Yes.'

Mayland sat in silence, and an unease came over the company as his immobility subdued conversation. They waited and he said nothing, his black tie twisted by his chin into a gay attitude which the frown above his thin features contradicted. When he spoke, he said,

'It's hot. Let's have all the windows open.'

He enunciated carefully, his *a*'s and *i*'s ill-defined as if processed.

'Yes, let's have the windows open,' Hunter, his personal solicitor and man of affairs, echoed.

And the others, released, said,

'Let's have the windows open.'

The butler opened the windows wide on to the night, and the summer breeze blew into the drawing-room from the Surrey hills, mingling a faint smell of midden with *Joy*, *Sortilège* and *Nuit de Longchamps*.

'All this and an erotic film show. It's very civilized,' said Lady Drayford's other neighbour, Peter Talbot, a young backbencher.

'What is?' asked Lady Drayford, looking coolly at Talbot's outstretched legs, and then at his arms resting nonchalantly on the back of Mrs. Melville's gilt chair. 'Are you practising for the Front Bench?'

'This museum,' said Talbot, ignoring the second question. 'The tapestries – the Sèvres – all that "rose Pompadour" and the Bartolommeo. It's an extraordinary collection. Where did he get it?'

'He bought it,' said Lady Drayford, 'as a job lot. When you've got eight million pounds, you can buy anything as a job lot.'

'Can you?' said Talbot. 'He was against us at the Castleton by-election.'

'Yes, but you're here – and so are lots of others,' said Lady

8

Drayford. She stood, and the cold silk of her evening dress brushed against Talbot's leg before he could rise and grope for a reply.

Mayland moved towards her with his respectful entourage forming a hemicycle behind him.

'My dear Edwina,' he said, extending his hands, blue-veined and macular under the lights. 'I'm so glad to see you here. You're looking wonderful. But where's Edward?'

'In Ghana,' she said, 'forming that new TV company. Ever since he was High Commissioner—'

'One of our best,' said Hunter, at Mayland's elbow.

'Yes, but I can't keep him away from there.'

'Well,' said Lord Wainley, who had joined the group, 'Africa's gain is our loss.'

Lady Drayford gave him a quick glance, quivering like a white butterfly among blackbirds, and said to Mayland,

'It's certainly not yours, Andrew. You're in the consortium, aren't you?'

'Of course he is,' said Wainley. 'Andrew's in every consortium.'

Mayland smiled deprecatingly, looking down.

'Not every one – only the ones that make profits.'

The blue curves under his eyes seemed to become heavier with responsibility. 'Mind you,' he said, brightening up, 'no one can say I don't spread it—' His voice trailed away.

The half-circle around him had become a circle, and a woman asked,

'Is there a formula for making money?'

'Yes, ma'am,' said Mayland. 'Read the business end of my papers – especially on Sundays.'

There was a guffaw from behind him, and Mayland frowned.

'Yes,' he said. 'Sunday belongs to God, but from time to time we've got to see what Mammon's up to.'

'He's doing all right at the moment,' said Henry Lacey, the Chancellor of the Exchequer, his cavernous voice smothering Mayland's tenor.

A smile fluttered at the left tip of Mayland's mouth, a signal for a general laugh from his attendants.

'You should know,' said Mayland.

'No, you should,' said the woman, who had taken a long glass of whisky from one of the butlers.

9

'Any news of the P.M., Hunter?' Mayland asked in a parenthetic aside.

'Not yet,' said Hunter.

'*She* won't be asked again,' said Lady Drayford, now on the periphery, to Talbot who was fingering a rococo scroll on the panelling of the wall. He smiled to her, accepting her words as a renewal of their acquaintance, and thought that seen *contrejour* she could be thirty-five, but that when the light fell on her delicately tinted hair, she must be over forty.

'Would that be a hardship?'

'Oh, horrible. Mary's one of those who'd rather be neglected than not received. If you look around this room among the antiquities, you'll see four old ladies ranging from twenty-five to sixty.'

'Old?'

'Yes – everything that Mayland touches becomes old as soon as he puts his hands on it. There are some people who make things fresh and young by their contact – Henry Lacey, for example. And others who make them worn and decayed. Keep away from him.'

'Keep away from who?' said Lacey, who had caught her eye and strode with his step towards them. 'Why should this attractive young man keep away from me?'

'Not you, sir,' said Talbot hurriedly. 'Lady Drayford was giving me some excellent financial advice.'

'I wish you'd give me some,' said Lacey, inclining from his height of six foot four to Talbot's five foot eleven, and peering into his face with his short-sighted eyes which he refused to cover with glasses. 'I wish she'd give *me* some.' And his sentence ebbed away in a rumble of laughter which rose from deep inside him without ever reaching his eyes.

'What's happening now?' asked Lady Drayford.

'Renewal, Edwina,' said Lacey. 'Renewal – that's the cry – renewal. Our host's going to tell us all about it.'

The chairs were being rearranged to face Mayland, who had taken up a position behind a small French writing table, replacing the rolled-up cinema screen.

'I'm afraid he must have been detained,' said Elizabeth Melville, taking an imagined strand of hair from her eyes. 'Don't you think so, Sylvia?' she said to her fair-haired daughter, who was standing with an indifferent expression at her side. 'You know Sylvia, of course.'

'Yes,' said Mayland, taking her hand, which Sylvia withdrew abruptly. 'I met you just before you went to America. Where were you – Cincinnati?'

'No – Philadelphia.'

'The city of brotherly love,' said Lacey, leaning over a chair behind Mayland. 'Did you find much brotherly love, Sylvia?'

She looked at him unsmilingly and walked away.

'She hasn't been awfully well,' said Elizabeth. 'I do wish, Henry, she'd get married instead of rushing all over the place preaching sociology.'

'Don't discourage it,' said Lacey. 'At twenty-three or so you need raw material. Any news of Geoffrey?'

Mayland looked at the blue clock on the commode and said, 'Let's give him another ten minutes. Prime Ministers – well, you know better than anyone.'

'Oh, no,' said Elizabeth with her familiar robust laugh. 'Geoffrey's always very punctual. He'll be here any minute – it isn't half past eleven.'

Mayland offered her a chair and she sat next to him, scanning the other guests who were moving into their places. Mayland was preoccupied with the speech he was about to make, and Elizabeth calculated that if a bomb fell on Hedley House, it would cause eight by-elections, eleven successions, two episcopal nominations, and would bring the Chancellor several million pounds in death duties. Edwina's shoulders seemed to her to have become sharper, and she wondered where she had seen the dark young man next to her. Sir Gregory Broome, the Prime Minister's physician, smiled to her and she smiled back. She was glad about his knighthood; he'd liked it, and deserved it, and the film intruded into her mind. The château, the loft, Greystoke, the opera – she felt tired, and shapes and faces, remembered and imagined, wandered in her thoughts like strangers in an open house.

Gregory had been very good, but that was a long time ago when Geoffrey was still Secretary of State, and to Sylvia too. Now he smiled to her, but, strangely, without seeming to look at her. She raised her hand to wipe away the imaginary strand, and her fingers stroked the small scar. They never spoke of it –

almost never, but sometimes Geoffrey touched it with the tips of his fingers. Broome had noticed her hand feeling the smoothness, and turned his head.

Hunter hurried to the table, and said,

'I've just had his secretary on the phone. He can't get away. We'd better make a start.'

'Any message?' said Mayland, his lips unmoving.

'No – that's the lot.'

Elizabeth looked up, and composed her mouth in a smile as if for a photograph, but Mayland's face had fallen into its thin bloodhound's folds.

'Right,' he said, and tapped twice with his gold pencil on the table-top. The conversation which had become a sustained clamour fell immediately, and Mayland rose.

'Ladies and gentlemen,' he began. 'No' – he corrected himself – 'my lords, ladies and gentlemen' – there was an approving murmur and a chuckle – 'the Prime Minister has asked me to give you his apologies. He is detained in London · by urgent political business, but I know you'd like to welcome Elizabeth' – he spoke the name familiarly – 'his very gracious lady, and Miss Melville too.' He paused and examined his notes, putting on his heavy glasses to read them. 'I welcome you all – all eminent men and women in your various walks of life. I'm grateful to you for having made the long journey to Hedley House to dine with me and my friends and to talk about Renewal.' He took his glasses off, and looked around.

'Renewal,' he said, 'has a capital "R". It is a movement which some of us are going to sponsor – without political or party prejudice – I have no politics' – there was a laugh – 'as a programme for Britain. Some of you may wonder why it is that I who come from the Dominions – still trailing an accent' – his audience laughed again – 'perhaps the language of Australia, should have the temerity to sponsor a movement of this kind. Well, I'll tell you.'

He paused, and sipped from a glass of water, and in that moment, as if getting a word in, the clock struck a hurried twelve.

'You saw that film an hour ago.' A few heads in his audience nodded. 'I wanted you to see something of the foul and corrupting stuff that's entering the life-stream of Western Europe – the nauseating material that today passes as art – the flaunting of religion, the prostitution of sex, and the crucifixion of our sacred values.'

There were a few approving nods, and a murmur of 'Hear, hear', quickly subdued as if someone had clapped in church.

'I think we ought to see it again,' Talbot whispered to Lady Drayford. 'How can we make up our minds after only one show?'

'Don't be absurd,' said Lady Drayford crisply.

Mayland was fumbling for his place.

'I'm not really used to this,' he said apologetically. 'Yes ... Some time ago, a leading figure in our public life said, "A gust of lust is blowing through the West End." Enlarge it – multiply it – and we can say with truth that the gust is blowing through the whole of the West.'

'Yes – I like that,' said Talbot. 'But I prefer "the lust of gust" – it's exciting – it's different. Did I tell you that I once wrote adverts for television?'

Lady Drayford half-turned her back on him and listened intently as Mayland delivered his speech. He spoke of the patrons and sponsors of Renewal – eminent figures in politics, industry and the Church. His words, hesitant and somewhat jumbled at first, became more assured.

'I don't make a secret,' said Mayland, 'that I run my newspapers for money. If I didn't, I wouldn't have any newspapers to run.'

Lacey laughed his resounding laugh that made the chandelier's pendants clink.

'The Chancellor relies on me,' said Mayland, gaining confidence. 'But I've reached a stage in life when having gathered what might be thought enough to live on for a year or two, I want to play a part in the rehabilitation of the nation's life. I want to pledge to you tonight that all my newspapers – daily and Sunday – will serve the cause of Renewal.'

There was loud applause. Renewal had become revival.

'More than that,' said Mayland, still in the same monotone, his lips scarcely moving. 'My TV interests will serve the same cause. My aim is to drive out of the nation the corrupt and demoralizing elements that are sapping it. From this meeting, a clarion call will go out – a call to redemption – and national renewal. That's all I have to say. My Lord Bishop—'

13

As the Bishop advanced, dealing benevolence amid the applause, Mayland took his seat again, and said to Hunter,

'I want to see you in my room after the meeting. And keep an eye on Ellen.'

'Yes,' said Hunter, looking at Mrs. Ellen Martin, a sixty-year-old resident at Hedley House, sometimes described as Mayland's fiancée, whose frail features, caked with an outmoded make-up, were moving as if they were being cranked up for speech.

'My friends,' the Bishop began.

'I'll die of it,' said Mrs. Martin in a clear but conversational voice, standing up. 'I tell you I'll die of it.'

Hunter rose swiftly, and led her by the arm through the door.

Mayland sat unstirring and the Bishop went on, flicking a glance at the gold seat which Mrs. Martin had lately occupied.

'I rise to add my support and express my appreciation to our host. The decline . . .'

He spoke for thirty-five minutes, and was warmly received.

At ten to one, the Committee of Renewal, 'non-Party and non-denominational', was formally constituted out of the twenty signatories to the manifesto which had previously been placed on each seat. Two archbishops, a duke and three peers were among the patrons, and Mayland, by acclamation, had been appointed chairman. After the applause had died down, he lifted his hand, and without rising to his feet said in his flat voice, 'There's just a little more, ladies and gentlemen.' They waited, and he said, 'Money! Remember the words of the Proverbs: Wine maketh merry; but money answereth all things. ... No, it's not a laughing matter. We can't fight evil without money, and what we need is a war-chest of, say, £50,000. Now who's going to begin?'

There was an uncomfortable silence as he scanned his audience's faces, and they scanned his.

'God!' said Talbot. 'He's looking at me!'

Hunter whispered in Mayland's ear, and the newspaper proprietor stood up.

'Ladies and gentlemen – here's a good start. Lord Gradwell and his family – two thousand pounds. Reggie – where are you? Thanks very much.'

The audience cheered, and Talbot gave two decisive claps, commendatory but undeferential. Meanwhile, Mayland was already assessing his guests, since many had commercial dealings with his own companies and he knew their resources as well as did a Collector of Taxes.

'Now, electronics,' he said, 'electronics are doing well – Mr. Bridges – Frank – what about five thousand? ... No, not three. Five.'

Bridges smiled through cold teeth, and held up five fingers.

'No applause for him,' said Talbot to Lady Drayford. 'I can't stand indecisiveness. What are you giving?'

'A thousand from Lady Drayford,' said Mayland with a nod, accepting her sign.

'Guineas,' she added. 'From the Drayford Charitable Trust.'

'Guineas,' Hunter said aloud, noting it in his book.

'Why guineas?' Talbot asked.

'It stands out in the subscription list,' said Lady Drayford.

Motor-cars, plastics, chemicals, furniture – the metallic voice was like an auctioneer's, making its own bids and capriciously knocking down the lots.

'We need money for advertising, circularizing, publicizing. ... This is a national campaign. ... What about you, Henry? Come on, printing-machinery's doing nicely.'

By one o'clock he had reached a figure of £36,000.

'The sum total is £36,000,' he said. 'That's a good beginning. You've been a great help, every one of you, and to show my appreciation I'm going to make it into a round figure of £50,000.'

The clapping was now heartfelt, everyone enjoying the release from Mayland's pressure. They pushed their chairs away, and began to move towards the entrance hall and the cloakrooms. Lacey put his heavy arm around Talbot's shoulders and said, booming a secret in his ear,

'Makes me wonder where they stash it! There's a lot of it about. Can I give you a lift back to London?'

'No, thank you,' said Talbot. 'I've got an old beaten-up Rover that I've got to nanny along to Hampstead.'

'Pity,' said Lady Drayford, coming up behind them. 'I was going to offer you a lift myself.'

Talbot looked at her laughing face, which had wakened from its heaviness during the appeal, and said, 'I'll drop you home if you like. You can send your chauffeur on.'

'I'll quarrel with you all the way,' said Lady Drayford. 'I see

15

that you're one of the new, aggressive backbenchers – second-generation Redbrick.'

'Not exactly,' said Talbot, angry with himself both for flushing and explaining. 'I was at Jesus, Oxford – and so was my father.'

'Close enough,' said Lady Drayford calmly. 'Where's your car?'

'On the other side of the fountain. I hid it.'

'You should flaunt your austerity a bit more ostentatiously,' she said. 'In fact, I don't know what you're doing here at all.'

'Observing,' said Talbot.

'Who for?'

'I'm writing an article for the *Spectator* on Renewal.'

'Have you spoken to Mayland?'

'I listened to him.'

'What did you think of it?'

He smiled to her, and she turned her face away.

'Yes,' he said, 'that's what I think, but I don't have to pretend.'

'You have to pretend with Mayland. Where've you been all this time?'

'Is that a serious question?' Talbot asked.

'Yes,' said Lady Drayford.

'Well,' said Talbot, 'until I came into the House I was working for Voluntary Service.'

'As a volunteer?' asked Lady Drayford.

'No,' said Talbot. 'For money. I'm a journalist, you know, and I have to work for a living.'

'Well,' said Lady Drayford, 'you belong to the modern mercenaries.'

'Sorry,' said Talbot, watching her fingers playing with an emerald pendant that drooped between her breasts. 'I'm not rising to that one.'

She touched his hand in reassurance that she only meant half her jibe.

'What did you make of it all, Edwina?' Lacey asked her as they stood at the door with Sylvia Melville close behind, watching the cars manoeuvring in the drive. She drew her white stole closer round her neck in the cool night air, and said,

'What *is* there to make of it? Mayland likes power. Haven't

16

you noticed that as some men get older, their need for power becomes obsessive?'

'Quite right,' said Talbot. 'With men like Mayland, power is a substitute for potency. It's why they're always crusading against sex.'

'And selling it,' said Lacey. 'Like Maria Theresa, they weep and weep, and keep on annexing. Well, there's my car. Good night, Edwina – good night, Peter. We'll have a drink in the smoking-room.'

When most of the waiting guests had been taken up, Lady Drayford and Talbot began to make their way to his car, invisible among the lime-trees. Beyond the radius of the light cast from the large windows, they found themselves in darkness, and Lady Drayford slipped her hand through Talbot's arm.

'It probably won't start,' said Talbot, uneasy at her strange proximity.

'In that case,' said Lady Drayford, 'we'll sit here all night.'

Talbot tugged at the starter, and the engine began to throb at once.

'I hope you're not in a hurry,' he said. 'This thing can't go very fast.'

'Please take a long time,' said Lady Drayford. The light from the dashboard illuminated her face, and he saw that she was looking at him, smiling.

'All right,' said Talbot. 'But you must tell me stories to keep me awake.'

He had turned the car so that, as it circled the small lake, they could see above the stone dolphins and seahorses the whole elevation of the house with its château towers and its brilliantly-lit windows, extinguished one by one, as if by a dowser.

'What a miserable, lonely old man he is!' said Talbot.

'You're very sentimental,' said Lady Drayford. 'It's a comfort for the poor to imagine that being rich makes people unhappy. It doesn't. It makes them happier than they'd be if they were poor. You said it yourself – Mayland likes power and respect. He uses his money to get both.'

'All that charity?'

'Yes, all of it – cancer research, chairs at Cambridge, honorary degrees and all. He isn't a generous man. He's a mean man. The Chancellor pays for most of his philanthropy, and for the rest – well, it's worth it. When he gets a peerage—'

'Will he?'

'Everybody expects it.'

'Well, tell me about the decline of the Upper House.'

'I've just told it to you. . . . This is a very pleasant drive.'

The car was lumbering along a secondary road, and the woods that accompanied them seemed lonely and endless and the light from the rising moon otherworldly.

In the study, Mayland was eating bacon and eggs and re-hearsing the evening's events with Hunter, whose smooth, fiftyish cheeks were now topped by saucered eyes, struggling hard to show interest in his employer's ruminations. This was the hour which Mayland liked best, when his last visitors had left, his pensioners had gone to their rooms, and in the quiet house, an island of silence in the sleeping countryside, he could try out projects, gambits and opinions on the man who for twenty-six years had been his go-between in the world of affairs, finance, board-rooms, lobbies and administration. On these occasions, he used Hunter for exercise as much as for service, the champion trying out punches on a sparring partner who from long experience knew how to absorb them.

'. . . so there it is,' Mayland ended his dissection of the even-ing. 'We've got it moving.'

Hunter sat with his reddened eyes fixed on a marble bust of Mme de Maintenon by Lemoyne, and made no comment.

'Well,' said Mayland, 'what d'you say?'

Hunter pulled up his head, and saw that Mayland was wait-ing for an answer.

'Which account shall we pay from?'

'The Mayland Charities Fund,' said Mayland dismissively.

'It's not a charity,' said Hunter.

'In that case, register it – or affiliate it with something else. Edwina Drayford's paying from her Drayford Charitable Trust. There are others too. You'd better get cracking on it first thing tomorrow.'

'How?' asked Hunter.

'How?' said Mayland, his voice rising. 'You tell me. That's—'

'I know,' said Hunter quickly. 'I know. . . . Unwed mothers, delinquent teenagers, child monsters – all right, we'll affiliate!'

'I don't know why it is,' said Mayland through a mash of rind and hardened yolk, 'I pay you fellows, and have to do your thinking for you.'

It was Mayland's regular formula, and Hunter, unoffended, waited for his next observation, which he knew would be tangential, although Mayland would return to his original grumble. To watch Mayland eating had been one of his permanent duties, since his employer was most at ease in the chairman's Dining Room in Fleet Street or here at Hedley Hall. But Hunter had never quite got over an original distaste dating from their first luncheon meeting when a ribbon of tomato, expelled from between Mayland's teeth, had landed on Sir Edward Holgate's lapel and remained there like a Légion d'Honneur, irresistibly drawing the eye. When Mayland spoke, Hunter had to force himself not to back away – not because of memory alone, as he liked to pretend, but because Mayland created around him an aura of fear which no familiarity could dispel.

Mayland took up the first edition of the newspaper sent from London by special messenger, and began to examine its pages. After a few moments, he said,

'Get me Colson.'

Hunter picked up the green receiver which was on a private line to the newspaper office, and asked for Colson.

'Sorry – the editor's left,' said the operator.

'Get him at home,' said Mayland in a quiet voice without taking his eyes off the page.

Hunter dialled the number on the other telephone, and handed the receiver to Mayland.

'Page two,' said Mayland without a greeting. 'It's no good.'

A sleepy voice answered from the other end, half-defiant.

'I can't see why.'

'That's what I mean – that's why it's no good. That's why you're no good. It's no good. Two stories about strikes side by side. . . . And I told you – I don't want anything on cigarettes. Kill it, Frank.'

Colson began to speak, but Mayland raised his voice in step, overbearing the editor's.

'Never mind that. . . . The page is too black. Let's have a bit of light in it. . . . I don't care what I said. . . . It's too black. And kill that cigarette story. I don't want it.'

He hung up the receiver while Colson was still talking, and turning to Hunter said,

'Colson goes to bed too early. What about that boy in features?'

Hunter shook his head.

'He couldn't do it.'

'We'll see,' said Mayland, pushing the remains of his congealed bacon away from him.

He sat for a few moments in silence and then dialled Colson's number himself.

'Yes!' said Colson, with the emphasis of a man who in the early hours of the morning has had enough.

'Oh Frank,' said Mayland amiably, as if speaking to him for the first time that day, 'why don't you and Mary come to lunch on Sunday? She wanted to see that new porcelain I got.'

'Well—' said Colson, who, prepared to fight, felt himself suddenly disarmed.

'O.K.,' said Mayland, smiling into the receiver, 'try and get down early – half-past twelve. Good night, Frank.'

Mayland began to hum to himself.

'Did the Chancellor say anything?' he asked at last.

'No,' said Hunter calmly.

'I see,' said Mayland, his hands playing with a paperweight while his thoughts seemed abstracted. 'Did he speak to Melville?'

'I think he must have,' said Hunter, still observing his employer's attempt to dilute his concern with calmness. 'Elizabeth—'

'What did she say?'

'She said something about not knowing if it's premature to congratulate you.'

Mayland pushed the paperweight on one side, and said with a twitch of his mouth,

'That sounds like news. Are you sure, Harry?'

'Well,' said Hunter judiciously, 'she might have been congratulating you on your chairmanship of Renewal.'

'It couldn't be that,' said Mayland, walking over to the pedestal clock, and beginning to wind it. 'It couldn't be. When did she say it – before or after?'

The clock began an urgent ticking, and he put the key on top.

'I can't really remember,' said Hunter. 'My God, is that the right time? I've got to get back to town.'

'No, have a drink,' said Mayland with a particular affability.

Hunter looked at Mayland, watchful, unwilling to be left alone and eager to talk, and he sat opposite him, reluctantly answering the order.

'Let's have some more lights on,' said Mayland.

Hunter looked around at the wall-lights and the table-lamps which were all blazing, and said,

'They're on.'

And for a second, remembering the incipient cataracts in Mayland's eyes, he faced him not with sympathy but with a sense of advantage.

Mayland poured himself another whisky and soda, and drank it hurriedly.

'How do you think he's doing?' he asked.

'Melville?'

'Yes – Melville.'

'He's got a majority – for the time being!'

'He's got twenty—'

'It isn't enough. They'll get tired.'

'He's got a lot of tough young men.'

'It's all right to begin with,' said Hunter. 'I've seen it all before. They get into the House ready to change the world. They make their Maiden Speech. It's the best since Pitt. What happens next? They jump up a few times – they don't get called – they find they can get by as long as they vote. It's all the Whips want. They usually settle for a quiet life. But sometimes the boys get restive. Twenty isn't enough.'

'It's just as well,' said Mayland. 'The proper balance of democracy is a Government with a small enough majority to be tamed by the Opposition while a strong Press sees that there's fair play.'

'You mean,' said Hunter, 'a Government weak enough to be thwarted by public opinion.'

'That's another way of putting it,' said Mayland. 'Especially when public opinion coincides with my own.'

They both laughed.

'I believe,' said Mayland with a sudden earnestness, following a private train of thought, 'that in the Lords I'll be able to reinforce the public opinion we create in our papers, and give it an added authority.'

Hunter took note of the collective 'we', and nodded complaisantly.

'There's something about it,' said Mayland, 'a sort of mystique like being a Privy Councillor when you're in the Cabinet. You can't measure it – and yet you can. I'll bet you a shilling, Hunter, that after the Honours lists our Preference go up half a crown.'

'Too risky,' said Hunter, laughing off the uncertainty. 'I think it's in the bag.'

'I want a piece next Sunday,' said Mayland, 'on the Lords – something forward-looking, and linking it with Renewal.'

Hunter said, 'Why not do it the other way? What about a piece on the decline of oratory in the Commons? – you know, "At a time when the Commons is checkmated—"'

'No,' said Mayland. 'Melville wouldn't like it, especially when he's dealing with the Monopoly Bill. He likes to believe that with his twenty he can do anything.'

'Well, make it "At a time when the House of Lords is once again taking its place as a forum of the nation".'

'Not bad,' said Mayland. 'Let's have something with a bite. "A young, healthy Member of Parliament challenges the Commons." What d'you think of Talbot?'

'Can he write?' said Hunter, following his thought.

'We'll teach him,' said Mayland.

'He didn't sign a Renewal form,' said Hunter.

'All the better,' said Mayland. 'It underlines his objectivity.'

'And if he won't?'

'We'll find another M.P. who will. They all fancy themselves as journalists when the fee's a hundred pounds.'

Hunter rose and stretched himself. 'I must be off,' he said.

'You know,' said Mayland, still sitting and unwilling to let Hunter go, 'years ago when I lived in Adelaide, my father took me to the race-course where he had to mend the back axle of a brake. And when we were there – I remember it like today – he pointed out a man with a grey hat and a flower in his buttonhole, and he was walking arm-in-arm with two beautiful women in the paddock – lovely women, big – like that – and he said, "That's Lord Rosser of Wrotham in England."'

Hunter waited for him to continue, but seeing that Mayland had fallen into a reverie, he walked softly to the door. As he put his hand on the knob, he heard Mayland say again,

'Lord Rosser of Wrotham.'

Hunter closed the door gently, but before the lock clicked, the voice said, as if addressing its owner in a looking-glass,

'Lord Mayland – Lord Mayland of Hedley.'

CHAPTER TWO

MELVILLE shut his eyes again and pressed his face into the pillow, excluding the mallard squawk from St. James's Park and the seep of light through the drawn curtains. In half an hour, the overnight boxes would arrive, the curtains part, Harrison would bring him a cup of scalding tea, and his day minutely parcelled – papers, breakfast, Chief Whip, meetings, luncheon, the House – would begin. After an uneasy night, he felt that he would like to sleep for another six hours, or at least doze among his drifting fantasies. The moons of Jupiter. Once, many years before – perhaps thirty-two, he had only just come down from Cambridge – he had looked through a telescope in an observatory. It wasn't what he had expected. No lunar landscapes. *L'épouvante sidérale.* From a million light-years away, stars long dead still shone down on earth, and perhaps a million generations still turned somewhere in the endless, repetitive universe. Ten tons of dynamite for every living person, and Geneva had entered its ten-thousandth session. Before he had gone to bed, he had read the telegrams from East Africa about the attacks on the bases. Holdsworth, the Minister of Defence, had wanted to send reinforcements, but he had asked him to wait till morning, so that the Soviet Note with its incantations about neo-colonialism could be discussed at the Cabinet. Sixty-eight British casualties, including three nursing sisters. The figures had kept him awake for long stretches of the night.

Then he remembered that his daughter had returned, and his sense of oppression ebbed away.

After the three years that she had spent in America, Sylvia had come back thinner, harder-featured, brighter-eyed, abstracted in an enigmatic moroseness that changed with an effort into a demonstrative affection. She wouldn't live in their flat at Number Ten, but had taken rooms in Holland Park. Nor had she invited either Melville or Elizabeth to visit her there, and all that he knew of her life were the cautious references to her independence in the gossip columns. Yet, when he imagined her face, it was rarely of the adult woman; more often of the smiling twelve-year-old schoolgirl on her pony, the prefect in uniform home from Cheltenham, or the student of nineteen talking anxiously of commitment, engagement, identity and communication and marching in anti-apartheid demonstrations; and there was the memory of her last vacation from Oxford, before his predecessor Collard died, when she held Melville's arm as they walked together at the Zoo, and she had begun to speak of her mother.

Melville changed his position. Questions at 3.15. The usual roustabout with the self-appointed Parliamentary wits, Crawford, Jones, Budd and Radley-Baker. That was all right. In the twenty years he had been in the House, they had always been there under one name or other, fervent for truth or publicity, alternately useful and tiresome. Budd with his aggressive, porcine face snuffling for scandals as if they were truffles. Budd, a former schoolteacher, disappointed of a headmastership, who specialized in a tenacious and pedantic malice which never forgave a snub, and elevated his private resentments into a crusader's altruism. Melville's thoughts sharpened. He would have to read his brief more carefully on the second report of the Committee of Estimates on Military Stores. Two days earlier, he had just managed to turn Budd's supplementary question with a quip, after the Speaker had intervened with his standby formula for lowering the temperature – 'We must get on.' He wouldn't be able to do it again quite like that.

But in the main Commonwealth debate, which he had chosen to wind up, things had been different. Whenever he now spoke he had the feeling that he commanded the House and that he was sustained not only by the collective braying automatically at the disposal of Front Bench spokesmen, but by the confidence of the Government supporters in his mastery over Alfred Yates, the Opposition Leader. The Opposition hadn't merely lost the vote of censure; they had lost the argument too. During the whole time he had been in politics, Melville couldn't recall a debate in which the mood of the Party had been so elated, the Press quite so unanimous in praising a speech or he himself more confident in his own vigour and the strength of his case. Melville stretched himself, well content to remember.

Harrison came in quietly and drew the curtains fast so that the yellow sunlight came charging into the room. Melville greeted him, and Harrison replied with his invariable, 'Cup of tea, sir.'

Melville opened the boxes which Harrison had brought in, and began to study the telegrams and reports, pencilling marginal notes. The Paper which held his attention dealt with his intended visit to the United States President the following month; Cuba, gold reserves, Indonesia, the Middle East, Geneva Disarmament Conference. It was the usual agenda, the same pack reshuffled. Melville wrote 'Desalination by nuclear power'. For several weeks, he had been absorbed by a project which Henry Granger, the Minister of Technical Co-operation, had casually mentioned to him for the desalination of sea-water by nuclear power. The practical experiments were still embryonic, but the scheme's potential effect was enormous. Instead of a few rivers trickling their water into the deserts of the Middle East and Africa, the sea itself would be harnessed to irrigation. Again, as he thought of its effect, Melville became excited by the possibilities of cheap desalination. The U.S.A. and Great Britain could together give a lead in Overseas Aid through vast enterprises of enlightened self-interest, stimulating consumption and redirecting trade towards the West.

In his bath at ten past seven, Melville continued to think of desalination till it became a fetish word. As he sponged his chest and back, he imagined great murmuring plants rising like temples on the Mediterranean coast, pumping huge volumes of fresh water into transformed deserts. He dried himself cheerfully, and in the bedroom looked quickly at the clock, impatient to talk again to Granger.

The house-telephone buzzed, and when he lifted it Elizabeth said from her room,

'Geoffrey, can we have breakfast together?'

He frowned, reluctant to change the established pattern of his day, and said,

'Of course – but aren't we lunching at Lancaster House?'

'Yes,' she insisted, 'but it's important. I won't disturb you – it's something to do with Sylvia.'

'All right,' he said quickly. 'Let's have breakfast in my room. In ten minutes, so that I can look through the newspapers.'

Harrison had stacked them on an étagère, and Melville sat in his dressing-gown by the window, performing an old ritual of newspaper reading. To begin with, the obituaries in The Times, then the letters, the foreign news headlines, the Political Notes, the leading article. The gossip and cartoons in Gradwell's newspapers. Then the front page and editorials of the tabloids. And last of all, the Mayland Press – the 'Papers that Everyone Reads' – the classless common denominator, lucid, informative and optimistic. Sixty per cent of Government supporters read the Mayland Press. But a hundred per cent was affected by its opinions and prejudices. Mocked at in the Smoking Room, the Mayland Press remained immune from public attack, except by two or three politicians who had decided in any case to retire at the next Election. Brash, self-praising and dogmatic, it had discovered that the only thing the public won't forgive in a newspaper is uncertainty. The Mayland Press was always decisive. When it was right, it never tired of drawing attention to its prescience; when it was wrong, it changed the subject.

As Secretary of State for Commonwealth Relations, Melville had sometimes dined with Mayland at Hedley House or at one or other of his London clubs; and during the anxious flurry of uncertainty when Collard was dying and Ormston, the Home Secretary and Old Pretender, as he was sometimes called, had seemed the natural heir to the Premiership, Mayland had given his support to Melville, at first with an unfamiliar daintiness but, after the Queen had sent for Melville, with a banner headline, 'Melville's the Man'. Mayland had exaggerated his role of king-maker; but his intervention had finally destroyed any hope within the Cabinet of a rally in support of Ormston who, after his defeat, became so hangdog and melancholy that even his backers felt a retrospective embarrassment at their fancy.

Melville left the Mayland Press till last. Its news pages were crisp, their headlines conclusive. 'Dead Man in Bank Drama', 'Fiddler Faints on Stage', 'Envoy's Wife Says Sorry', 'Police Chief Sacked'. Melville turned the page and read, 'New Force in Nation's Life: Primate'. Without mentioning Mayland's name, the story of Renewal spread over three columns, including quotations and comment from four peers, a Test cricketer, an industrialist and two Members of Parliament.

On the leader page there was an article by a popular boxer, headed 'What a Flop! K.O. the New Morality', with a short editorial comment on moral laxity in schools, entitled 'Teach the Teachers'. Melville turned the page to the serial story by Alvin Long, a writer described as the greatest thriller writer

27

since Buchan. Under the drawing of a monstrous bespectacled scientist bending against a background of retorts over a terrified, big-breasted girl in a bikini, he read, 'Chort looked at her fingernails, and said, "Pliers, I think" . . .' Melville let the paper drop to the ground. The Mayland Press, bulging with euphoria, always managed to depress him.

He stood and looked through the open window at the early summer green.

After a light and formal knock at the door, Elizabeth, wearing a grey silk dressing-gown with pink rosebuds, came into the room, and turned her cheek for him to kiss. 'Good morning, Elizabeth,' he said, looking at her with an affectionate and embarrassed curiosity. It was a long time, perhaps three years, since she had come into his room like this, and he felt the same ill-ease as he might have felt if he had met a stranger dressed only in a pyjama top walking through a corridor late at night.

'I'm sorry, Geoffrey,' she said, avoiding his glance. 'I know you hate these things.'

She was wearing a black hairnet, and she took it off with her left hand. Melville didn't answer, and she said,

'Will you ring?'

'What would you like?' he asked.

'Oh, me? You know what I like – just coffee. But you must have a good breakfast yourself.'

She spoke rapidly and cheerfully, adjusting chairs and edging the small table towards the window as she spoke. A lock of hair, disengaged when she took off her net, now fell over her eyes, and Melville noticed with irritation that she still wiped it furtively away with the back of her hand.

Melville ordered breakfast, and Elizabéth said to Harrison with a smile,

'We'll be a quarter of an hour. Aren't you going to have eggs, Geoffrey?'

Melville answered, 'No.'

With a comfortable familiarity she had taken the seat he usually occupied at breakfast, and Melville, after a hesitation, drew up another chair, watching her arms baring themselves as she poured the coffee. He had wanted to do it himself, but she had taken charge.

'They were all asking after you at Andrew's last night,' she said.

'Yes,' said Melville.

'He's a strange man,' said Elizabeth. 'The sweetest man – despite all that money. He couldn't have been nicer to us.'

Melville raised his cup to his mouth without comment.

'They made £50,000,' said Elizabeth.

'That's very interesting,' said Melville. 'What are you going to do with it – found hostels for prostitutes?'

'Oh, no,' said Elizabeth. 'Nothing like that. We're going to do propaganda – support prosecutions where necessary – all that sort of thing.'

'What sort of thing?'

'Well, we're against pornography.'

'I see – all the "p's" – "pornography, propaganda and prosecutions".'

'No, you mustn't laugh. It's all very serious.'

'That may be,' said Melville. 'But I'd prefer it if you don't get too involved in it.'

'Why not?' said Elizabeth. 'They wanted me to be a patron.'

'I hope you had the good sense to refuse.'

'I don't know about good sense. I said I couldn't because it would mean being invidious about all sorts of good causes.'

Relieved, Melville said good-humouredly,

'That's a perfect politician's answer.'

'It comes of being married to a politician,' said Elizabeth. Melville became silent again, and she went on,

'Sylvia loathed it, of course.'

'I'm not surprised,' said Melville.

'Why not?'

'I imagine—' Melville began, but he stopped and said,

'You wanted to tell me something about Sylvia. Would you like to tell me now, Elizabeth?'

She put down her cup of coffee which she had barely sipped, and said,

'Geoffrey, I don't want to worry you. You've got such a lot on your mind – I heard about the East Africa base on the seven o'clock news – I don't want to worry you . . .'

Melville waited impatiently, watching the flush on her cheek-bones with a faint distaste.

'You see,' she said, 'since Sylvia's been back, she's been behaving so strangely.'

'What has she done?' Melville asked crisply.

'It isn't what she's done, but how she is,' said Elizabeth. 'Last night was really the first time I've been with her for any real time since she came back. It was dreadful. I could hardly get a word out of her. I tried to be gay, but she simply sat there – every now and again she'd say a word or two. At Hedley Hall, it was most embarrassing. I introduced her to everyone, but she was positively rude. And she looks so strange – no make-up – nothing.'

She paused for breath, and Melville, who had twice looked at the clock while she was speaking, said,

'Well, that isn't very serious. You haven't any make-up yourself.'

Elizabeth looked at herself quickly in a wall looking-glass, and said,

'It doesn't matter for me. But it does for her. She's young. She ought to get married.'

'Perhaps,' said Melville, 'what she's seen of marriage doesn't encourage her.'

'That may be,' said Elizabeth. 'But it's still worth trying. Oh, Geoffrey – don't try to score points this morning. It's much too early, and I'm much too worried. She just sits and looks into space.'

'We all do,' said Melville.

'Please, Geoffrey,' said Elizabeth urgently. 'It's desperately serious. I'm telling you – there's something wrong with Sylvia. I met the Corwins the other night – you know, the ones we gave Sylvia an introduction to in Philadelphia. They were terribly strange. When I wanted to talk about her, they changed the subject.'

'Well, what does all this add up to?' said Melville, rising. Suddenly he felt that Elizabeth's concern for Sylvia wasn't disinterested, that she was merely using the occasion to change the basis and mode of her own life.

'I'm trying to tell you,' said Elizabeth in a defeated voice. 'But you won't listen. I think Sylvia's a very sick girl.'

Melville stood looking down at her, and at the scar on her temple. Restraining the rage which had leapt into his mind as if released from a pit, he said,

'In that case, you'd better take her to a doctor.'

He saw the tears prickle her eyes, and turned to the door

where Frobisher, his Private Secretary, was standing with his hand on the knob.

'I knocked, sir,' he said. 'Good morning, Mrs. Melville.'

'Good morning, Eric,' she said, averting her face.

'They're all waiting, sir,' said Frobisher apologetically.

'Is the Chief Whip there?' Melville asked. Frobisher nodded.

'Tell him I'll be down in a few minutes,' Melville said. He turned to Elizabeth, but she had hurried to the door, and he watched it close.

At about twenty past ten, after the Chief Whip, Charles Scott-Bower, had analysed for the Prime Minister 'the business for next week', he added as an afterthought,

'By the way, how's Mayland coming along? I had him on the phone this morning. Complained you hadn't turned up last night. And then asked point blank.'

He squared his large shoulders, and said in his clipped voice,

'They usually beat about the bush a bit more.'

'We sent it up,' said Melville absently, fingering the menu card with his list of engagements. 'He'll have to be patient.'

'They've been exceptionally slow,' said Scott-Bower.

'Let's see what Henry has to say,' said Melville. He pressed a button on his desk, and Henry Loring, the Secretary for Appointments, came rapidly into the room from his private office.

'Well, Henry,' said the Prime Minister, 'have you appointed any new deans lately?'

Loring laughed, and said,

'No, sir. But I feel a couple coming on.'

'What about Mayland?'

Loring looked straight at him, and said with a change of expression,

'I'm afraid there's bad news, sir.'

Melville waited for him to continue, and Loring said,

'I didn't want to trouble you with it before the Cabinet. The Honours Scrutiny Committee have recommended against him. Something in his background.'

The Chief Whip looked at the clock, and said,

'I think we'd better get along, Geoffrey.'

'They're getting very sticky,' said the Prime Minister. 'At that rate, we'll never have any new peers.'

Loring maintained his earnest expression.

'It's a bit more concrete than that. He was in gaol in Australia in 1923 and 1924 – under a different name – fraud of some kind.'

'There you are,' said the Chief Whip with a shrug. 'Nothing clean like highway robbery. Fraud!'

He became thoughtful.

'Somehow or other,' he said, 'I think we've lost the Mayland Press. It's difficult, though. We promised it to him.'

'He should have told us,' said Melville. 'He had no business to put us in this embarrassment.'

'How shall we deal with it?' asked the Chief Whip.

Melville took up his papers, and said,

'The Chancellor brought us the nomination. He'd better tell Mayland.'

'Don't you think, sir,' said Loring, 'it might be better just to let it die in the usual way?'

'I don't think so,' said Melville. 'Mayland doesn't let things die. I think we've got to give it to him straight, and see what happens.'

Loring opened the door, and the Prime Minister, followed by the Chief Whip, began to walk in the direction of the Cabinet Room.

'I can understand his passion for Renewal,' said the Chief Whip.

'I don't hold that against him,' said Melville. 'Haven't you ever wanted to shake off something that happened to you?'

'Often,' said the Chief Whip. 'But, then, I've not yet applied for a peerage.'

'It's very irritating,' said Melville as they entered the long room with its curtains, dark green against the buff-coloured walls. The Cabinet Secretary rose from his place beneath the portrait of Walpole to greet him, and Melville nodded to a number of Ministers already there. Then he took his armchair at the centre of the table whose coffin shape had been decided on by one of his predecessors, so that he could see more easily who was speaking at its ends. Melville turned to Frobisher, his Private Secretary, still standing behind him, and said,

'Tell Works to get rid of this table, Eric. It makes me feel I'm at a wake.'

Towards three o'clock, the Chamber began to fill with Members who drifted in from the lobbies in ones and twos for

'Questions to the Prime Minister'. Crawford, a Queen's Counsel, was putting a long meandering supplementary question to the Minister of Agriculture and Fisheries about the herring industry in Scotland, and his involved sentences were punctuated by cries of 'Speech! Speech!' from the Government Benches. The mutter of uninterested conversation on both sides of the House combined with the interruptions to make his words inaudible, and the Speaker rose to say, 'Order! Order! I can't hear what the hon. Gentleman is saying.'

Crawford, short and pugnacious, adjusted his stiff collar, and in the silence that followed began to read in his high voice some statistics about the Continental Shelf. 'Reading! Reading!' some of the younger Government supporters below the gangway began to chant. Crawford-baiting was one of their established sports.

'On a Point of Order,' said Mulligan, a public relations consultant who had found that the readiest way to gain the ear of a crowded House was to raise a Point of Order, 'Is it in order for the hon. Gentleman to read his supplementary question?'

The Speaker stood impatiently, his Roman face flushed underneath his wig.

'It wouldn't be,' he said, 'but I understand that the Honourable Gentleman is merely quoting from copious notes. We must get on!'

As Melville, followed by Waters, his Parliamentary Private Secretary, entered the Chamber, picking his way between the Table and the legs of his colleagues on the Front Bench, he heard an Opposition Member say,

'Well, will the Minister say exactly what he has done for the farmers in the last three years?' and the Minister's triumphant reply, 'What we've done can be told in a very few seconds—'

The Opposition roared its delight at the bewildered Minister; and his friends at his side and behind him smiled sportingly, delighted that they hadn't made the gaffe themselves. Melville settled himself in his place in front of the despatch-box, and gave a quick glance around the Chamber. As always at this time, the Public Gallery was crowded with visitors looking down on the proceedings as if on a bear-pit. Today there was a whole row of nurses and Westminster schoolboys. A group of peers, a line of ambassadors above the clock, Mrs. Speaker with a green hat in her own gallery, the attendants, ex-N.C.O.'s digni-fied in their tailcoats and chains of office; and opposite him, Yates with his Shadow Cabinet and their dismal feet on the Table; the jesters below the gangway, Budd with his sheaves of references garnered from the research assistants in the lib-rary, and the Serjeant-at-Arms at the Bar handing out admission orders with the portentousness of a man who makes grave decisions. The mace on its bracket, the Clerks at the Table, the easy and turbulent exchanges within the respected rules – all combined to give Melville a feeling of ease.

Through long familiarity, he had become accustomed to ignore the Visitors' Gallery in fact as well as in Parliamentary theory. But in his rapid scrutiny he thought that he had seen Elizabeth, sitting next to the Speaker's wife and bending over the rail to the right above his head. Elizabeth hadn't come for Questions for nearly three years, and her presence disquieted him. His brief lay open on his knees with the answers drafted by his staff to the questions, and a series of contingent replies to supplementary questions. He read the papers rapidly, and cleared his mind for 'Question Number One to the Prime Min-ister', which was coming up as the two clocks at the front and rear of the Chamber, cocooned in a green twilight, recorded 3.15.

'Mr. Bowater!' the Speaker called. Bowater rose in his place, and said, 'Number One, sir, to the Prime Minister.'

The first two questions dealt with Ministerial co-ordination, and Melville answered them briefly. In the interval between the second and third questions, Sylvia's face obtruded itself irrelevantly but insistently into his thoughts. Once, about twelve years before, he had visited her alone at school – Elizabeth had had to go somewhere else with his brother, Robert – and to-gether they had walked across the playing-fields to the river, and Sylvia, shy at first, had taken his arm, looking very proud as she passed her school friends, and told him that Miss Foun-tain had said he was very good-looking; and when it was time for him to go, she had clung to his hand, not wishing him to leave; but then, recovering from the single tear that crept along her nose, she said she'd had a super time. She'd had a super time, and a whisper of a smile went over his lips, then and now. But now, it passed as he remembered her before she left for America – anxious, self-absorbed and apart. Elizabeth's discouraged voice when she spoke of Sylvia stayed in his mind.

'Wake up,' someone called out from the other side, and the cry was taken up on the back benches. 'Number Three,' murmured his P.P.S., leaning forward from the bench behind him, and the Prime Minister, lifting his head at the amused faces opposite him, fumbled for his brief, apologizing as he rose. The question read:

'To ask the Prime Minister what are his proposals for the reorganization of the Ministry of Defence.'

'None, sir,' he said, and sat down.

Budd rose ponderously from his place below the gangway, clutching his papers under his left arm.

'In the light of the Minister's failure to get reinforcements to East Africa at the right time, in the right numbers – and for the right reasons' – there was laughter from the Opposition benches and a rumble of 'Hear, hear!' – 'is the Prime Minister satisfied that the Minister of Defence is doing his job adequately?'

'Without accepting the first part of the hon. Gentleman's observations,' said Melville, 'my reply to his supplementary question is, "Yes, sir." '

His backbenchers cheered loudly, but Budd stood his ground till the Government cheers died down.

'Is the Prime Minister aware,' he said, 'that the terrible happenings at N'dola camp, involving a heavy loss of British life, is directly attributable to the intervention of the Ministry of Defence, for whom the Prime Minister must take full responsibility in view of—'

The rest of his speech was lost in the clamour of cheers and counter-cheers.

Melville stood again, and without looking at Budd said contemptuously,

'All I know is that the hon. Member never fails to use the occasion of a British difficulty in order to aggravate it.'

From the Opposition Benches came a roar of protest and dissent, dashing itself against the cheering from the Government side. For a second or two, Budd relapsed like a boxer taking a quick count. but then he was on his feet again while the clamour continued.

'On a Point of Order, sir!' he called out. His demand was taken up by those around him, until it penetrated through the uproar to the Speaker.

'Point of Order,' he echoed, standing. 'Mr. Budd!'

'My Point of Order, sir,' said Budd, 'is that the Prime Minister by his statement has impugned my patriotism. I'd like to say that my own record will measure up to his at any time. I'm asking your protection, sir, and ask you to call on him to withdraw a disgraceful aspersion.'

He sat down with an aggrieved air, and the Opposition immediately took up the word 'Withdraw', chanting it in a disciplined chorus.

Melville sat with his ankles crossed, smiling at the indignant smouldering faces in front of him.

'They don't like it,' said the Chief Whip at his side.

The Speaker, troubled by the sudden storm, got up again and said,

'I heard the Prime Minister's observation, and didn't think there was anything in it which could bear the construction the hon. Member has put on it.'

A series of Points of Order now began on both sides of the House, but the Speaker brought them to an end.

'I can't allow my ruling to be debated,' he said. 'If it is disputed, hon. Gentlemen know that their recourse is to put down a substantive Motion.'

Melville exchanged a quick smile with the Chief Whip. He was conscious that his reply to Budd had been sharpened by his totally unconnected anxiety about Sylvia. He was sorry he'd been quite so offensive. But there it was. It was too late to do anything about it. Anyhow, Budd needed to be slapped down on principle. And then again, the backbenchers loved it.

The Prime Minister's questions were over, and followed by his Parliamentary Private Secretary Melville picked his way over the legs of his colleagues towards his room, attended by the Speaker's iambic command:

'The Clerk will now proceed to read the Orders of the Day.'

Throughout the afternoon, he received a series of callers – a High Commissioner from Africa, a deputation from the North-East Regional Development Council, the Mayor of West Berlin and the Chairman of his Constituency Association, who visited him once every two months. Melville had decided to spend the rest of the day at the House, since, with a majority of only twenty, the Chief Whip was anxious to have every possible vote available for the Committee Stage of the Town Centres

Betterment) Bill which the Opposition was harrying. Besides, he usually enjoyed the slow shuffle through the voting lobbies, the casual meetings and disengagements and the contact with the younger Members.

Shortly before seven, the Division Bell ended his interview with the Constituency Chairman, who had prolonged it in the hope of being invited to dinner. But Melville shook his hand, and hurried into the lobby.

'Slapped him down!' said Parfitt, a businessman who specialized in plunging from the middle of his own thoughts into the privacy of anyone he chose to accost.

'Who?' said the Prime Minister, unsmiling.

'Budd!' said Parfitt, surprised that Melville hadn't responded with his usual friendliness.

Melville pushed forward through the Members crowding around the Clerks' Table where the registers were being marked.

'What's bitten the P.M.?' Parfitt asked.

'Showing strain,' came the reply from a tall Member, a Chamberlain of the Household, whose duties included a report of the day's proceedings to the monarch. 'I had to paraphrase him a bit yesterday.'

But Parfitt, the snub forgotten, had already taken the arm of a younger Member, and was repeating to him in detail a speech he had made earlier in the week.

'Sir,' said a Lobby Correspondent, waiting outside the Members' Lobby in the Library Corridor.

'I'm sorry,' said Melville curtly.

'What's the matter with him?' said the journalist to a colleague standing near by.

'East Africa, I suppose,' said the other.

On the way to his room, Melville, with his head down, hurried past a stream of Opposition Members coming from the No' lobby. Usually he greeted those who had come into the House with him when he was a new Member; now, he passed them with a blinkered air as they neared him, half-openmouthed.

In the outer office, his secretaries stood, and Melville said, 'Get me this number, please.'

He gave a number, scribbled on a piece of paper, to a typist, and went into his room without speaking. For a few minutes he sat, tired and preoccupied. Throughout the afternoon his

anxiety about Sylvia had mounted until, during his last inter
views and his walk through the Lobbies, his mind had become
obsessively fixed on the thought of his daughter. He remem
bered his panic once at Le Lavandou with Elizabeth when Sylvia
was nine and she had gone bathing alone and then he had looked
for her, and all he could see beyond the *plage* crowded with
sunbathers under the bright umbrellas was the vast, deserted
sea. And then the frantic joy of finding her again, slim and fair
carrying an ice-cream in her hand, and escorted by a French
schoolboy.

'I'm sorry, sir, there's no reply,' said the typist on the tele
phone.

The anxiety welled again.

'Try the number every quarter of an hour,' said Melville, 'till
you get an answer. It's important.'

He looked at the clock, and then through the Gothic window
at the stir of evening traffic and the lamps in New Palace Yard
glowing against the blue-dusted sky. He returned to his desk
switched on the reading-light, and waited with his chin resting
on his clasped hands.

At half past eight, Melville's bell rang, and the telephonist
said,

'Your number, sir.'

'Sylvia,' said Melville eagerly. 'I've been trying to get you
all the evening.'

'Well, here I am,' she said. Her voice was flat and seemed to
come from afar.

'How are you?' he asked.

'I'm well,' she said, and their conversation halted.

'Such a long time since I've seen you,' Melville said.

'Yes.'

Their conversation paused again.

'Have you dined yet?'

'No.'

'I wonder if you'd like to dine with me at the House – or at
home?'

'No, thank you, daddy. I'm terribly tired. I think I'll go to
bed early.'

'I'd very much like to see you,' said Melville. 'Wouldn't you
care to jump in a taxi and come to Number Ten? We'll have

dinner quietly in the flat. I'm sure your mother would like to see you too.'

'No, thank you,' she replied, her voice firmer.

'Why not?'

'I don't really want to.'

'Can I come and see you?'

His voice had become suppliant, and he resented his own humility. There was a silence at the other end, and then Sylvia said,

'I'm very tired, daddy.'

'But I do want to see you. Don't you want to see me?'

Again the supplication, and the surge of resentment.

'I do, but—'

'Please!'

'I look a terrible mess.'

'It doesn't matter. Tell me your address again.'

She told him, her voice dragging and reluctant. Melville wrote it down, and spoke to Frobisher in the outer office.

'I'm going out for an hour or two. Tell the Chief to see that I'm paired.'

A summer rain began to fall as the Prime Minister's car with its windscreen wipers swishing like a metronome groped its way through the streets and squares of Holland Park. Hodges, the Ministry of Works chauffeur who had been seconded to Melville ever since he had been a senior Minister, pulled up outside a house, once the property of a Victorian merchant-banker, which after falling into a scabrous decay had been reconstituted by a property developer, and now described itself as an apartment block. The door was open, and Melville said to Hodges,

'Is this number seventy-one?'

'Yes, sir,' said Hodges dubiously. The Prime Minister had abandoned his personal detective at the House, and Hodges had an additional sense of responsibility. 'Shall I come in with you, sir?'

'Have you some pressing reason to visit my daughter, Hodges?' Melville asked curtly.

Hodges held the door open, and didn't reply. Melville touched him apologetically on the arm, and ran through the rain into the entrance hall of the house.

He pressed the electric light switch, and looked with a quick distaste at the worn carpet and at the water-stain on the ceiling. The stairs had a lingering dankness untouched by the changing seasons. Melville climbed the first six steps, two at a time, but his pace dwindled as the stairs curled steeply at the landings. When he reached the second floor, the light, operated by a time-switch, went out, and he was left standing angrily in a total darkness.

He swore and lit his cigarette lighter while he groped for the switch. 14a. The 'a' depressed him. He imagined the developer examining the cubby-hole of a flatlet and deciding that he could add a sink and sub-divide it. For a few seconds, he felt anger at Sylvia for being the occasion of a visit which made him feel undignified and furtive.

But at that moment, a door opened and he saw Sylvia wearing a shirt and trousers, and heard her say,

'I thought it was you. Come in.'

He closed the door behind him, and took her in his arms, and briefly she held him tightly so that her long hair fell against his face and he was conscious of her whole body pressed against his. Then she drew away from him as suddenly as she had clasped him, and said,

'You are an old silly, coming out here.'

'Why?' said Melville, looking around at the small room with its book-case facing the narrow bed, the kitchenette trailing pipes into the sitting-room, the bathroom door half ajar so that he could see the bath and lavatory in a dovetailed congestion, and the *passe-partout*-ed reproductions of 'La Source' and 'Sunflowers' on the wall.

'They're not mine,' said Sylvia, observing his glance.

'How long have you been here?' Melville asked.

'Just a few weeks – after I left Cornford's.'

'You've left them?'

'Yes,' she said casually. 'Like some coffee, daddy – or a whisky and soda? ... I left them because—' She threw up her hands.

'Why, Sylvia?' asked Melville, sitting on her bed.

'Oh, I don't know,' she answered. 'I went there to develop their sociology department. But all they wanted was – oh, you know, books by established dons and American professors.'

'But they're very good publishers,' said Melville.

'Yes,' said Sylvia. 'But I've given up publishing.'

She sat in the armchair opposite him, and lit a cigarette.

'What have you been doing?' he asked.

'I've been writing my diary,' she replied. 'Did you say you'd like coffee?'

'No, thanks,' said Melville. 'Why don't we go out and have dinner properly?'

For the first time he could see how pale she was in contrast with the darkness of her eyes. Her voice too seemed to have changed. It was, he thought to himself, an avoiding voice.

'I don't like going out,' said Sylvia. 'But thank you.'

She forced herself to smile, and then stood and poured herself a cup of coffee from the percolator.

'Why did you come here tonight?' she asked.

'I want you to come and live with us, Sylvia,' he said.

'Do I embarrass you?' she asked tauntingly.

'It's possible that you might,' said Melville. 'But you know that isn't the reason. We want you to come home. This' – he waved his hand around the small room – 'is very unsatisfactory.'

Sylvia took a small tablet from her handbag and swallowed it with a gulp of coffee. She saw that Melville was watching her closely, and she said with a laugh,

'My saccharine, daddy.'

She found another cup for him, and for more than an hour they sat talking, and gradually her fingers stopped tugging at the buckle of her belt. When Melville spoke to her of her personal life, she became silent. But when he spoke of Africa, she asked him questions, her eyes bright and her cheeks colouring. He told her how he had spent his day, and looking at the clock, switched on the news.

' ... the Commons today,' said the announcer, 'the Prime Minister said ...'

Sylvia turned the knob to lower the volume.

'I've got the Prime Minister here. I'll ask him myself,' she said.

Suddenly she had become gay and excited. She came and sat on the bed beside her father, and said,

'You know, daddy, I've got a splendid idea.'

'What's that?'

'Why don't you come and live here?'

She was laughing, and he said, 'You're absurd,' and she said, 'I'm not,' and he said, 'Yes, you are.'

Laughing, she pushed him on to the pillow and said,
'You're absurd – you're absurd – you're absurd.'

But her laughter as she wrestled with him went on and on till
Melville took her wrists and said sharply,

'Sylvia – that's enough.'

'It's not enough – not enough,' she said, still laughing.

Then suddenly she buried her face in his chest, and said,

'Oh, God, I'm so unhappy,' and burst into tears.

He held her head with his left hand, and with his right he
stroked her wet face. From the radio came a ghostly voice.

'The programme of meetings in Washington ... the Prime
Minister ... the Prime Minister ... the Prime Minister ...'

TALBOT stood at the vast bow-window that occupied one side of Mayland's office on the twelfth floor, and examined the panorama – the street with its toy motor-cars endlessly running, steeples seen as pin-points, people and machines too remote to be heard. The previous day, he had received a telephone call from Hunter, whom he had met briefly at the Renewal meeting, asking him if he would call and see Mayland about a 'proposition', and now he had arrived at the Mayland Building, with curiosity and the pleasurable conviction that he was going to say 'no'.

Hunter's message had surprised him, since he had made no pretence of sympathy with Renewal, and Mayland, even as he offered Talbot a cold-fingered hand in farewell, was already glancing over his shoulder in search of someone more important. Talbot couldn't understand why Mayland had sent for him – he frowned at his own description, and changed it mentally to 'invited him' – but whatever the reason, it was interesting to find himself in the office with its thick blue carpet, its throne-like chair and dominating view of London. The room itself, apart from its desk, a book-case, two telephones, a green cigarette-case and a large Douanier Rousseau called 'Le Deuxième Octroi', had no other furnishings or decorations. It had the austerity of a sentence reduced to a noun and a verb. Talbot liked it. Mayland at work could afford to discard the ornate flourishes of Mayland at leisure.

'Well, what d'you think of it?' said a voice behind him.

Mayland had entered the office in a cat-step, and had been standing watching him.

'Oh, good evening,' said Talbot without extending his hand. He still remembered Mayland's frozen grip and had no wish to experience it again. 'It's a superb view. Bismarck said—'

'Sit down!' said Mayland, pointing to the green leather armchair, and Talbot, thrown off his line and not sure whether it was Bismarck or Blücher who had said 'What a city to sack!' sat. Yielding beneath his weight, the leather cushion gave out a sigh like a winded man, and Talbot, realizing that Mayland intended to stand, felt at an immediate disadvantage.

'I sent for you—'

Talbot winced.

'I sent for you, Talbot—'

Talbot winced again. He had been brought up in a middle-class world where strangers of equal status added the prefix Mister to their names, and he had never got used to a different convention.

'—because I've got a—'

Talbot waited for the word 'proposition', but Mayland went on to say,

'—a job I want you to do.'

The newspaper proprietor had begun to walk about the room as he talked, and now was standing directly behind Talbot's chair, giving him the choice either of squirming around or of staring ahead at the empty desk. Talbot compromised by seating himself diagonally, and trying to keep Mayland in sight from the corner of his eye.

Mayland was silent, and Talbot waited for him to speak. Instead, he went to the window, and looking out at the evening sky, began to hum abstractedly. After a long minute, Mayland said,

'You're thirty-one.'

'Yes,' said Talbot, glad to have found a voice, and the word came out explosively.

'You taught at a grammar school. You've been in the army, and you've worked for Voluntary Service in the publicity department. You've done some journalism.'

'That's it,' said Talbot more confidently.

'You live in Hampstead, and pay £420 a year excluding rates for a two-bedroomed flat, and you send your mother, a widow—'

'I don't think we need go into all that,' said Talbot. He had wanted to raise himself in a quick heave from his armchair, but his fingers had sunk into the soft sides, and before he could stand, Mayland had continued,

'—and you've made a number of first-class speeches since you've been in the House.'

Talbot felt an involuntary smirk come over his mouth, and sinking back into the leather cushions, said,

44

'Thank you.'

'Yes,' said Mayland, walking in front of him. 'I read Hansard every day – I don't rely on our own reports—'

Talbot began to smile.

'—or on anyone else's,' said Mayland before the smile could develop.

'The trouble with democracy today,' said Mayland, 'is the decline of controversy. I'm not talking about parish-pump arguments, or the politicians biting at each other's jugulars. I'm talking about real debate – debate about the big issues of our time – the sort of issue that one man can champion and another man attack. I want to see debate personalized – that's it, personalized.'

'You mean,' said Talbot, 'you want to see debates in the form of personal attack?'

'No,' said Mayland impatiently. 'You're not with me, Talbot. I mean that democracy must work through public spokesmen – controversialists. We haven't got them today.'

'What about Yates?' asked Talbot.

'Yates,' said Mayland contemptuously. 'That fellow thinks more of the cut of his hair than his job as Leader of the Opposition. I'll tell you something, Talbot – if you see a policitian look at himself twice as he passes a shop-window, you can write him off. He'll stay small. Yates is a small man – for all his size.'

Mayland stretched himself, and drummed with his fingers on the table where he had paused.

'Well, what about Lacey?' said Talbot.

'Lacey?' Mayland echoed. 'Just a loud voice. . . . He's no good. Look at the way he behaved over Bank Rate. At the first whiff of trouble, put it up to six per cent. He's no good.'

'The P.M.?' Talbot put in quickly. He could see that Mayland was enjoying his session of abuse, and he wanted to encourage him.

'Melville,' said Mayland, softening. 'Melville – he's different. There's a man – how can I put it? – a man who's never hesitated to do the unpopular thing, and to argue it out till he's convinced his opponent or been convinced himself. If he hadn't become Prime Minister, he could have been one of my editors.'

'That's a very great compliment,' said Talbot.

'Yes,' said Mayland simply. 'It is . . . How would you like to work for the Mayland Press, Talbot?'

Talbot had prepared the manner and tone of his refusal. Instead he heard himself say,

'What sort of work?'

Mayland spoke to his secretary on the internal telephone.

'Bring us some drinks, Mary, and some sandwiches.'

He turned to Talbot, and said, 'I want to create a new kind of journalist – or better still, I want to resurrect an old kind. We've all got too many correspondents – special correspondents, our own correspondents – and God knows what else. It's got to change. I want a controversialist – a tip-top controversialist who'll become a national figure in a month.'

'You'll have to find him,' said Talbot. Watching the absorption in Mayland's face, he himself felt the excitement and complicity of a *voyeur*.

'I won't find him,' said Mayland. 'I'll make him. I'll make my controversialist into the best-known name in England.'

'Why?' asked Talbot.

'Why?' said Mayland, as without asking he poured out a whisky for Talbot. 'To sell papers!'

Talbot stood, and held his glass while Mayland squirted the siphon. To his surprise, his own hand was trembling slightly, and he said 'Thank you' quickly so that he could withdraw from Mayland's scrutiny. The conversation, despite its impersonal form, was about a *Doppelgänger* of himself.

'I'm not sure he could rise to this – this—' said Talbot.

'He doesn't have to,' said Mayland. 'We'll do it for him. Have a sandwich.'

'No, thanks,' said Talbot, shaking his head. The interview hadn't gone as he'd expected.

'Pass me one,' said Mayland. And Talbot handed him the plate, from which Mayland carefully made his choice.

'What exactly is your proposal?' asked Talbot. Mayland waved him back to his seat, and said,

'I don't know yet. No one knows.'

'Then how—?'

'It will have to work itself out. Obviously there'd be a big weekly article – you know, "Talbot Thinks" – no, "Talbot Talks" – something like that. Then I'd want you to have a weekly meeting with the lobby men—'

'I couldn't—'

'—give them ideas – keep them informed – and I'd like you

to go about more – meet people – entertain and be entertained – keep your ear to the ground – that's the job. A backbencher is nothing if he hasn't got an outlet.'

'It's all very interesting,' said Talbot thoughtfully. 'But there are just two points I'd like to ask you about.'

Mayland looked at his watch, and said,

'I'm going to the theatre – you'd better be quick.'

'Well,' said Talbot, 'I'm flattered you've asked me. But why me?'

'Why you?' said Mayland, raising his eyebrows. 'Because you're the man for the job – young, intelligent, not bad-looking, enthusiastic, ambitious – I want an M.P., and you need the money.'

'We all do. But I'm a bachelor. I can manage very well,' said Talbot.

'You need some capital. £3,000 will make all the difference. The only problem is that first three thousand. Look at all those fellows I employ to give tips on making money. If they had that first three thousand, they wouldn't be working for me.'

He sat himself at his chair behind the table, and said,

'I'll tell you something. I made my first three thousand by luck – just by chance. I was a mechanic – nineteen – and I was sent to fix an electric switch for a small printer in a little place near Adelaide. He took a liking to me, and I started to work for him – odd jobs around the place. He had a newspaper – all advertising and births and deaths and Rotary – and I began to sell space for him and see that the copy came in on time.'

Mayland pondered for a few moments with the tips of his fingers making an arch in front of his face.

'Well, anyway,' he said, 'that's how I started in journalism. The old man died – his widow wanted to sell – so I bought it from her, and after I bought it I borrowed the money from the bank to pay for it – on the security of the printing press. You see, Talbot, I knew what it was worth.'

'Yes,' said Talbot.

Mayland chuckled.

'I saw for the first time,' he said, 'that to get rich, you must use other people's money. Do you know anything about money?'

'Not much.'

47

Mayland went to the bookshelf and took down a collected edition of Shakespeare's plays.

'Listen,' he said, 'I keep this book for people like you. Here we are.

> 'Gold! Yellow, glittering precious gold! . . .
> Thus much of this will make black, white; foul, fair;
> Wrong, right; base, noble; old, young; coward, valiant.'

He looked at Talbot and said,

'It's still true. . . . What was your second question?'

'You've answered it.'

'Yes – I said £3,000. What do you say?'

'I'd like to think about it. It's a novel idea.'

'Mind you,' said Mayland, 'there are one or two conditions – or perhaps assumptions.'

'What are they?'

Talbot's reluctance was now struggling with fear that Mayland might withdraw his offer.

'I'd want you to live up to the picture.'

'What does that mean?'

'It means to begin with that you'll have to dress better' – Talbot glanced indignantly at his suit, which he had had made in Kensington and which he thought fitted him rather well – 'and I'd expect you to live somewhere nearer and a bit smarter than Hampstead.'

'That's rather difficult. I—'

'You'd get £2,000 of your salary in advance – as a loan – on recall, of course.' Mayland took another sandwich. 'Hunter will put you in touch with our business manager, and he'll find you a flat not too far from here on a short lease, paying a year's rent in advance. Your work, Talbot, as an editorial consultant will of course, be confidential and you'll receive certain expenses.'

He swallowed the rest of his whisky, and added,

'You should arrange to be available when I want to discuss public affairs with you.'

'I haven't yet decided—'

'Hunter will settle the details. One other thing – there's the Albert Hall Rally – the Annual Rally.'

'I'm afraid I'm not—'

'It doesn't matter. I want a piece on your impressions – not of the speeches but the audience. Treat them like a football crowd. Ask yourself whether they're for it or not. After that, just answer the question "Yes" or "No" – in seven hundred words.'

'What about the editor?'

'Frank Colson and I see eye to eye on all these matters. Hello, here's Hunter. You two had better have a little chat.'

Talbot shook hands with Hunter, who had come into the room after knocking quietly.

'Hello, Mr. Talbot,' said Hunter, relaxing as Mayland left. 'You're coming into a terrible organization.'

He rolled his r's with an artificial solemnity.

'Why?' asked Talbot.

'He eats M.P.'s,' said Hunter.

'Has he eaten many?' asked Talbot.

'A lot – it's an addiction. He likes them young.'

'He's always eating,' said Talbot, looking at the empty plate.

'Basic insecurity,' said Hunter. 'Never had enough to eat in his youth. One day, he'll be eating, and he'll drop dead.'

His jovial tone had disappeared, and when Talbot looked him in the face, he lowered his eyes.

Walking through St. James's Park on the way to the House of Commons, Talbot decided that on balance the interview hadn't gone as unsatisfactorily as he had thought when he was talking to Mayland. He hadn't definitely committed himself, and from what he had gathered at a short meeting with the editor, whom he liked, all that he would be required to do would be to write a weekly article, its theme to be agreed at the Thursday editorial conference. Hunter had offered to draft a contract, but Talbot had said neither 'yes' nor 'no', and pausing by the bridge to look at the ducks, he thought that there was merit in his indecision. If Mayland had taken the trouble to *send* for him – he succumbed to the word – he must have wanted him urgently. It wouldn't harm to leave him in doubt.

The evening was warm, and the park was crowded with sauntering couples, and as Talbot walked by the lakeside he remembered that the business of Parliament was non-controversial that day, and there's be no votes. The thought that his evening was free, that he was alone, and that he had been offered a job for an extra £3,000 a year elated him; he thought of the friends to whom he could confide, but disqualified them on the grounds that they might try and dissuade him. He decided finally that he would go to a concert in the Festival Hall and ruminate while he listened. When he reached Parliament Square, he hailed a taxi, but after glancing inside his wallet, he waved the taxi away, and continued to walk. The sun was striking Westminster Bridge, and as he crossed towards it on foot, he felt free and independent.

In the foyer at the first interval, Talbot, carrying a glass of gin and tonic, was walking away from the bar when he came face to face with Sylvia Melville. He didn't recognize her at once, but as she hesitated, he said, 'Renewal!'

'Hello,' she said casually. 'What was that you said?'

'Renewal!' said Talbot. 'Remember Mayland? The password's Renewal.'

'All right,' said Sylvia, laughing. 'Renewal to you! What happens next?'

'Have a drink,' said Talbot. 'I just got this for you.'

'And you?'

'I never drink before Schoenberg.'

She took the glass from him, and made a face as she tasted it.

'You finish it,' she said. 'They've laced the tonic with sugar.'

'Revolting,' said Talbot, swallowing the drink.

'I don't think I know your name,' said Sylvia, and without waiting for him to answer, she said, 'What a heavenly evening! Look out there.'

They looked together through the wide windows at the night, pricked with lights along the river, and she said,

'Do you really want to hear the Quintet for Wind Instruments?'

Talbot examined her excited face from which she had pushed aside her long, pale hair, holding it with both hands so that the oval was carefully defined. It was an act of coquetry, and he liked it.

'What shall we do instead?' he asked.

'Well,' she said thoughtfully, 'it's nine o'clock or so. Why don't we drive right into the country – to the Chilterns or somewhere? Or find some cave – somewhere absolutely black and hidden away in the earth?'

She saw that his expression had changed and she added quickly,

'That's just a private joke. What about a drive? My Mini's outside.'

'Wonderful!' said Talbot.

'But what's your name?' she asked.

'Talbot,' he said, 'Peter Talbot. I'm one of your father's more obscure back-benchers.'

'Yes,' said Sylvia, as they hurried down the steps towards the car park. 'Actually, I know your name. I asked mother at Hedley House. I felt you might get conceited if you thought I knew it too quickly.'

Talbot said, 'I'm flattered you asked. Does your mother know the names of all Members?'

Sylvia frowned.

'She gets to know the names of Members quickly,' she said. 'She's very interested in other people.'

'I like your mother,' said Talbot.

'Do you?' said Sylvia casually, as she got into the driving seat of her red Mini-Cooper. 'I don't.'

Before he could comment she switched on the engine, put the car into gear, and drove it in a dashing sweep from the car park.

'What I couldn't stand,' said Sylvia as they moved at an easy pace along Western Avenue in the direction of the A40, 'was the way they all took it for granted that there's an equation between sexual behaviour and morality.'

'There can be,' said Talbot judiciously.

'Yes, of course there can be,' said Sylvia. 'But it's only part of it. They never think that cruelty and exploitation and ordinary commercial lying have anything to do with morals. All those people at Hedley House were busy with sex as a source of immorality just because they wanted to gloat over it – or because they were past it.'

'What do you think of Mayland?' Talbot asked, looking at her profile in the light of a passing car.

'Mayland?' she repeated. 'He's made medocrity into a cult.'

'You dislike Mayland?'

'Yes, I do. He corrupts good causes, and then pimps for them.'

'I'm going to hire you as my speech writer,' said Talbot.

'Just a hangover from the time when I wrote blurbs,' said Sylvia. She looked at the road streaming ahead of them, and said, 'This car heads for Oxford like a horse. Shall I go right?'

'Yes,' said Talbot. 'Let's drive on to Aylesbury.'

He watched the speedometer rise to fifty miles an hour, and his hand tightened on the edge of his seat as the car seemed to rear into the hedges turned white by the headlamps.

'Are you nervous?' Sylvia asked.

'You're a very good driver,' Talbot answered.

The speedometer was still rising, and Sylvia's expression was concentrated. She drove without speaking for about five minutes till they saw the lights of Chalfont St. Peter.

'I think you'd better slow down,' said Talbot. 'It's a village. Like a drink?'

The time was twenty to ten.

'Yes, why not?' she said, braking gradually. His knuckles unclenched and he said,

'You're very docile.'

She turned her face to him and smiled.

'Yes,' she replied. 'It's what I like most – when I can get it.'

Her assertiveness had changed into a kind of modesty and Talbot said nothing.

At the Relay, an old coaching inn, they found a bar that opened on to an orchard where people were drinking under the lanterned trees. They took a table set apart from the others, and Talbot ordered beer.

'It's lovely here,' said Sylvia, looking around. 'Everyone is so absorbed and private and self-important.'

A sudden laughter came from inside the bar, and she said,

'I like that too.'

'Mayland's readers getting this morning's point,' said Talbot.

'That's all right,' said Sylvia. 'As long as they stay in the bar. It's such a warm night. It reminds me of Connecticut.'

'How long were you there?'

'I was a year in New York – after Philadelphia – but I often used to go to Connecticut. There was a place there called *L'Equipe* or *La Crémaillère* or something. Strange how one forgets! I used to think it the most wonderful place on earth.'

'Why?' He asked the question hesitantly, reluctant to hear the answer. She bent her head forwards, and folded her arms over her knees so that her hair trailed in front of her. Without looking up, she said,

'I was in love.'

'I imagined that,' said Talbot.

'I loved him so much,' said Sylvia. 'He was an assistant professor – he taught in Columbia – and he lived in Connecticut – his house was there.'

'You used to stay with him in Connecticut?'

'Oh, no,' said Sylvia quickly. 'I'd just go out there with him for the ride. I was always riding with him – in trains and car and subways. Just to be with him. You see, he had a very nice wife and two children.'

'I see.'

'He never would have left them – he wasn't like that.'

'Oh, yes.'

'He was very devoted to his family. ... The hours I spent following him around!'

She smiled to herself in recollection.

'And this place reminds you of Connecticut?'

'The trees,' Sylvia said, looking upwards. 'The maples – the beeches – they're wonderful in that part of America.'

Talbot hesitated.

'What happened with this man?'

'Nothing,' she said.

'What do you mean?' Talbot asked.

'It's a long time ago,' said Sylvia.

'How long? A year?'

'Just about. It was my twenty-second birthday.'

Talbot sipped his beer, and said, 'Perhaps we ought to go back to London.'

'I'm not in a hurry,' said Sylvia. 'Tell me about you. What were you doing on May 17th last year?'

'Last year? I forget.'

'The year before?'

Talbot said, 'On May 17th two years ago I was writing reports on other people's voluntary service.'

'It sounds pretty deadly,' said Sylvia.

Talbot stiffened.

'I did a year of voluntary service of my own though – in Morocco. I ran a camp for orphaned children – most of them sub-normal – after Agadir.'

'Did you enjoy that?'

'No,' said Talbot. 'I hated it. But it was what I chose. I believe that everything one does is an act of choice.'

'Even when you don't choose the circumstances?'

'Yes – we make our choice within those circumstances.'

'Is it choice,' asked Sylvia, her face remote, 'when you wake in the morning with your heart thumping, knowing it's going to be like that till your last pill at night? And that after four hours' sleep it's going to start again the next day?'

'Yes,' said Talbot, rising and guiding her to the car park. 'You choose the person who makes you feel like that.'

Her face was pale, and her eyes dark-ringed under the strip of neon lighting that contrasted with the pseudo-antique inn-sign creaking above it. Talbot half-regretted that he had ex-changed the concert for this pointless flight into the country with a self-absorbed girl. What he now wanted was to get back to town so that he could work on the speech for the Technical Co-operation debate. He opened the door of her car with a slight resentment. With its special engine, it stood for a pose of modesty with built-in privilege.

After a long silence as they drove back to London, Sylvia said, 'You know, I've always wanted to do Voluntary Service.'

'Why don't you?' Talbot asked crisply. 'What's stopping you?'

'I don't know,' said Sylvia, accelerating till, on the main Lon-don road, the car was travelling at sixty-seven miles an hour. 'Perhaps it's because I never really want to do anything. I al-ways feel I want to do it. And then, when it's right there, in front of me – I no longer want it. . . . Do tell me. How did you get into politics?'

'By luck,' said Talbot. 'Just by chance.'

And he smiled to himself as he realized that he had echoed Mayland's words to him earlier in the day.

'What happened?' she asked.

Talbot stretched himself and said,

'The B.B.C. asked me to do a round-up of opinion at Framp-ton when they were looking for a candidate – you remember, there was all that row between the Mayor who thought he ought to get it, Brian Young who thought he'd like to come back into politics, and that dreadful fellow Tomlinson. Well, when I was rounding up opinion, I rounded up the opinion of the

Party chairman, who said, "You're a nice chap. Will you let your name go forward?" and I said "Yes," and they chose me and that's how I'm here.'

'Do you call that an act of choice?'

'Of course I do. I did everything I had to.'

'And are you glad?'

'Yes,' said Talbot. 'Parliament's a good place to be in.'

'Did you meet Enid Blakely?'

'Yes,' said Talbot, 'she's the Constituency Chairman – she helped me a lot –why?'

'Nothing,' said Sylvia. 'I just wondered. Don't look so hostile. I'm glad I met you.'

'Can we meet again?' he asked. She turned her head to him, and examined him for a moment, and said,

'I don't know you.'

'I want to see you again,' he said affirmatively.

She didn't reply. At last she said,

'I'd like to live and work somewhere very far away.'

'Where?'

'Anywhere – but very far away.'

'Perhaps we'll go there one day,' he said.

'That would be very nice,' she said, and took his hand in hers, gradually slowing down as the arc of London's lights grew in front of them.

Talbot bent inside the door of his flat and picked up the large bundle of letters redirected from the House of Commons. Constituents' letters, circulars, news-sheets and a few buff envelopes, most of them containing bills. One letter was from his bank manager, telling him that his 'accommodation' was limited to £500, and he would be obliged if he would reduce his drawings. He put the constituents' letters – always the same careful handwriting – on a tray with the previous day's bills, and recalled that his part-time secretary would be working for one of her three other employers the next day. He took from the floor a separate letter addressed to him at the flat by his mother. The usual monthly letter, containing a number of reminiscences and recalling that her allowance was due, and suggesting that if she had another £250 a year her difficult life would be, if not exactly transformed, at least made endurable. After reading some of his constituency correspondence, he got into bed and re-read the personal letters that had turned the day's satisfaction sour. His mother's letter was insistent. 'In my unfortunate circumstances . . .' The phrase recurred every time, adding guilt to each of his private pleasures. He ought to send her his bank manager's demand. But it wouldn't help. 'In my unfortunate circumstances . . .'

He reached out his hand for the telephone book and looked up the number of the Mayland Press. He'd talk to Mayland in the morning.

CHAPTER FOUR

THE strait-jacket enveloped her, paralysed her arms, held her clamped in the darkness under the restrainers, cowls, smothers, the heart panting for air, up and down, up and down, smother and bobbin, and Robert the cowled face unclad, the horror, paralysed, uncle, uncle, till unclad she screamed smother, and the scream was a groan into her bare arm lying across her face.

Sylvia lay with her heart racing, her eyes shut in consciousness, unwilling to be dragged again towards the nightmares. 'Why don't you sleep?' Dr. Kron asked her in New York. And she'd answered, 'Because I'm afraid.' And that had been the truth.

Soon after she had arrived in New York it had begun again – the stifling fear when she turned the light out, and the dreams, barely remembered, that left her trembling and trapped in an endless squalor. Sometimes, afraid to sleep, she would sit for hours at her window of the apartment lent to her by Mrs. Alice Rinehart on the eighteenth floor in West 72nd Street, surveying the city until she became cold, and after taking a tablet fell into an exhausted morning sleep. And sometimes she dozed all night with the lights full on till the sky faded into dawn and she could sleep with the assurance that day had returned.

Sylvia lay on her back and looked through the half-drawn curtains. The sleeping pill marked the time. After three hours, it wore off, and now it must be six o'clock, a London summer morning of sparrows and empty streets. Three hours. It was enough. From now on, she would lie listening to the city stretching itself, to the voices of the BBC announcers through thin walls, and the running and gurgling of water.

Sylvia examined the sunlight on her bed, and noticed that the lamp in the bathroom was still lit. She had no wish to move and switch it off; no wish to do anything except lie still like a corpse in a coffin. She put her arms to her sides, and looked up at the ceiling where the leaking pipe had left an arabesque tracery. She became as absorbed in it as she used to be at school when she found faces in the grain of her desk.

In the Museum of Modern Art on West 56th Street there was an optical machine that made patterns of endless variety, billowing clouds assembling and dissociating and re-forming through the spectrum; and there she had stood watching the shapes and the watchers, the grey, the tense, the hard and the cold, all gentled in curiosity by art, as if by death. He had stood next to her, and said,

'It makes us innocent.'

She had wanted to walk away, but instead she answered,

'It makes us *feel* innocent.'

He laughed, and said,

'That's right. That's how we saw the world – all shape and colour and no meaning – when we were infants.'

A press of students pushed them away from the machine, and they walked together towards the garden.

'My name is Don Cullen,' he said hesitantly. 'I teach at Columbia.'

She glanced at his friendly, sunburnt face, the solemn eyes and his slightly askew mouth, and decided that she liked this mature man – he must be nearly forty – half-brash, half-diffident.

'I'm Sylvia Melville,' she said. 'I'm a postgraduate researcher.'

'British, of course.'

'English,' she said. 'Have you ever been to England?'

'No,' he answered. 'Next year's my sabbatical. I hope to come then. Would you like tea or something?'

'No,' she said, taking a chair on the edge of the café. 'Do you think the English are always drinking tea?'

'Yes,' he replied. 'I'll get you a Coke.'

She watched him return, awkwardly carrying two glasses, carefully balanced, through the crush of girls in sleeveless dresses which the hot spring sunshine had brought out, and the young men in cotton shirts. He looked anxious to please, like a dog wagging its tail, and she felt a patronizing benevolence towards him. She decided that she would finish her drink, look at the sculpture in the garden, and leave.

'After Korea,' he said, 'I went to Japan. Long before abstracts, they had stone gardens – lovely zen gardens with a few rocks and white gravel raked in great swirling lines.'

'Why can't we have them in London or New York?' she asked.

'Someone would shift the rocks and scramble the gravel,' Cullen replied. 'You can't have a public art without a public faith. In Japan, they're Shintoists – animists. Their art is limited, but it's part of their way of life. Everywhere's a potential shrine, and everyone lives in contact with the spirits of the place.' He leaned against a massive Lehmbruck sculpture, and said,

'I'm sorry. I'm in a teaching mood.'

She laughed, and said,

'I'm a permanent student. I like it. You know, I'm in a state of constant rage because there are places in the world where I haven't been – places like Kyoto, and Rabat, and—'

'We're lucky,' said Cullen. 'Some people have been to them all. They've got nothing to look forward to.'

'Have you been to Kyoto?'

'Yes,' said Cullen. 'And I've stood on the Emperor's moon-viewing porch and watched the moon on the lake.'

'That was very sentimental of you,' said Sylvia. 'What do you teach?'

'Modern history.'

'And what about the Zaibatsu?' she asked serenely.

He took her arm, and said,

'I thought I'd leave them till my next visit.'

They walked as far as Central Park with the dust from the hot, dry sidewalks stinging their eyes, and by the time they were eating an ice-cream at the Tavern on the Green, Sylvia knew that Cullen lived in Connecticut, and that he had taken part in a Civil Rights sit-in but hadn't liked it because he had been kept in gaol for forty-eight hours and been hit over the shoulder with a night-stick. She told him that her father was in politics in England, and Cullen, either out of discretion or a failure of association, hadn't pressed her to talk about her family. She liked that too, because immediately after her arrival in the United States she had been pursued by invitations which she had only thrown off by the plea that to accept them would disturb her studies. In the end, with only a few exceptions, her would-be hostesses left her alone, comforted in their own minds by the thought that where everyone was rejected no

59

one was spurned, and that anyway, Sylvia Melville was an eccentric and someone at the Embassy who knew her family well had said that she had always been difficult, and that there'd been some sort of trouble between her and her mother.

That night, Sylvia fell asleep with Cullen's face in her mind, her cheeks warmed by the sun, her body tired by their long walk, and the sound of his voice on the telephone saying, 'I'll call you tomorrow.'

After that, they met twice each day, early in the morning and in the evenings when he finished his seminars. Sometimes they visited theatres off Broadway, but usually they walked together for endless miles through the streets, talking and watching the city quieten and the Manhattan lights festoon the high buildings while the breeze blew in from the Atlantic. At the end of the first week, they were sitting together late at night in a café near Washington Square, enclosed by two sets of chess players, hard young men intent over their boards.

'I won't be able to see you tomorrow evening,' Cullen said.

'I'm sorry,' she answered.

'You see,' he said, and hesitated. 'You see, my wife's been visiting her mother in Cincinnati.'

'Oh, yes.'

'She's coming back tomorrow – with Anne and Naomi – Anne's twelve—'

'Oh, yes, and how old's Naomi?'

'Ten. Would you like to see their photographs?'

'Very much,' said Sylvia, and she finished her coffee. 'Perhaps later.'

'Yes,' he answered. 'Later – you see—'

Sylvia had risen, and he paid the bill.

In the street, he walked at her side for a few minutes without speaking. Then he said,

'That's how it is.'

'Why should it be otherwise?' she asked. 'How old are you?'

'Forty-one. Old enough to be your father.'

He waited for her contradiction, but she said,

'Yes. But it's too late.'

'What is?'

'Nothing. Let's take a taxi.'

They drove fast uptown through the almost deserted streets,

and at the canopy of the apartments he took her hand as he had done each night to say goodbye. But Sylvia said,

'Come in and talk to me. I don't want to sleep yet.'

The night janitor in his shirt sleeves looked up at them thoughtfully, and said, 'Good night, Miss Melville,' and Cullen averted his face.

When she opened the door and switched on the lights, the gauze curtains of the living-room billowed towards them, and Cullen said,

'Shall I pull the curtains?'

'No,' said Sylvia. 'Let's be like the Japanese – all open to the sky. You see those windows over there?' She pointed across the street. 'We never draw our curtains. It would seem rude. Would you like a drink?'

'No,' said Cullen. 'Let's sit on your sofa and talk.'

'I'll get myself a glass of water,' said Sylvia, and went into the kitchen. As she returned, Cullen switched off the light, and took her in his arms and led her to the couch. He kissed her mouth, and her lips were tight, and in the light from the windows across the street, he saw that her eyes were watchful.

'Sylvia,' he said, 'Sylvia.'

Her hands moved to the back of his neck, and her mouth opened, but when his fingers touched her body, she said, 'No.'

The following day when Cullen drove to Connecticut, Sylvia went with him as far as Greenwich, the nearest commuters' station to his home. The traffic was heavy, and Cullen apologized and Sylvia said she wished it were heavier so that she might stay with him longer.

The evening journey became ritual, and when she returned alone in the train she felt the tranquillity of a celebrant who has discharged her office. Sometimes they went by the 5.50 train, and the train itself, overcrowded with tired and anxious faces, became 'their' train, a special benevolent train that gave them privacy and shelter. Their partings were often as anguished as if they were about to be separated for ever instead of meeting again the next day. And then, Sylvia would return to Manhattan self-absorbed in a corner seat, flicking away her tears and insensitive to the jostling crowds.

At first she used occasionally to meet some of her friends at their homes or visit galleries in the afternoons. But when she met Cullen in the evening he would inquire carefully where she had been during the day, and once she had told him he would stand sulkily, his eyes hooded, till after much bewilderment she realized that he was jealous of her world in which he had no part. And so, very soon, she divested herself of her acquaintances, never returned the telephone calls of Mary Renwick whom she had roomed with in Philadelphia and who was now working for a literary agency, and regarded her days as the gap between her meetings with Cullen.

Now they often spoke of politics, and what Cullen liked best was to hear Sylvia talk of her father and the men around him in a tone of inconclusive banter which they reserved for serious matters.

'I adore politics,' Sylvia said to him one afternoon at her apartment shortly before he was due to make a TV broadcast. 'What I can't stand are politicians.'

'Why not?'

'Well, politics is all about ideas—'

'—and power.'

'Exactly, but the people best equipped to get power usually have no ideas.'

'Isn't that just as well? Anyhow, what about your own father?'

'My own father,' she echoed. 'He's got ideas and he's got power.' Then she added, 'I'm not sure, though, whether he's got the right sort of power for his ideas.'

The telephone began to ring, and Sylvia continued to sit on the sofa with her head against Cullen's shoulder.

'I'm not going to answer it,' she said.

'Why not?' said Cullen, raising himself against the cushions. 'It might be important – perhaps it's one of your boy-friends.'

'Oh, don't be absurd,' Sylvia said, nestling herself against him. The telephone droned on, and Cullen said,

'You've got to answer it.'

He put out his hand, and gave her the white receiver.

'Hullo,' said Sylvia wearily.

'Miss Melville?' said a man's voice. She saw Cullen stiffen and his mouth became more askew.

'Yes,' she confirmed.

'Sylvia,' said the voice, 'this is Henry – I'm talking from Washington.'

'Henry,' she said with delight. 'Why aren't you drafting diplomatic notes or something?'

'What sort of something?'

'Oh, you know – whatever you do in Washington on hot afternoons. Addressing the English-Speaking Union, or receiving visiting M.P.s.'

'I did all that yesterday. How are you, Sylvia?'

'Oh, fine.'

'Working hard?'

'Very.'

Sylvia had seen Cullen rise and turn his back to her as he looked out through the window. Her answers were monosyllabic.

'I met Elinor Curtis – she told me you don't go out very much.'

'Don't go out at all. So much to do.'

'Any chance of your coming down for a weekend with us?'

'Well, it's very hard to get away.'

There was a pause, and Sylvia heard his uneasy determination at the other end of the line.

'Why don't you take a plane and come for the night?'

Sylvia cast a rapid glance at Cullen, and said,

'I'd like to. It's really very nice of you, Henry, but I've made a self-denying ordinance for myself while I'm working. How is Isabel?'

'She's fine. Actually, Sylvia, I was talking to your father yesterday.'

'Lucky you. I can't afford it.'

'Well, H.M.G. can, so we speak from time to time.'

'How is he?'

'Oh, he's flourishing. He asked me if I'd seen anything of you. It was a bit embarrassing for me to tell him you staunchly turn down all our invitations.'

'I'm sorry,' said Sylvia. 'I'll write and tell him you couldn't have been kinder.'

'George Morrow – the Shadow Minister of Defence I think they call him – is out here. We're having him to lunch on Wednesday week with Senator Porter and a few others. Your father was particularly anxious for you to join us – as, of course, I am myself.'

'That's very good of you, Henry. Does your father arrange *your* social activities?'

The voice at the other end of the line became sharper.

'I believe, Sylvia,' the Ambassador said, 'that if you think about it, you'll see it's not the point. Your father wanted you to be present at the luncheon because it would be helpful – a mark of goodwill – for you to meet the chairman of an important Senate Committee while Morrow is visiting here on behalf of the Opposition – a sort of social bi-partisanship.'

Sylvia hesitated.

'At any rate,' he went on, 'I've delivered the message, and I'll send you an invitation. Could you let me know by tomorrow?'

'Yes, I will,' she said. 'Thank you,' and put the receiver down.

'Who was that?' Cullen asked, turning round sharply.

'Henry Claymore,' said Sylvia miserably. 'He wants me to come to lunch in Washington on Wednesday.'

'Wants you to?'

'Well, invited me to.'

'I hope you enjoy it.'

'But I don't want to go.'

'You will.'

She went up to him, and put her arms around his shoulders, but he shrugged himself away from her.

'Why didn't you say "no" – just like that?'

'I couldn't – my father wants me to meet Senator Porter.'

'Porter?' he said. 'That's a laugh. Porter – the wickedest old buzzard on the Hill.'

'He's about eighty, isn't he?'

'He's sixty-five, and suffers from satyriasis.'

'Oh, Don,' she said, and they stood for a few moments with their foreheads touching.

'What do you expect?' he said at last. 'I'm jealous – of everyone who looks at you or speaks your name or shakes hands with you.'

'Haven't you noticed,' she asked brightly, 'I never shake hands nowadays?'

'No,' he answered glumly. 'But people look at you.'

'And what do you think I feel when you leave me each night?' she asked.

Suddenly he laughed and kissed her.

'If you've got to go, don't fall for anyone there,' he said.

Two days later, he was surprised to find among his university mail an invitation to luncheon at the British Embassy in Washington.

They flew down together, but Cullen went to a small hotel while Sylvia spent the night at the Embassy. Isabel came to meet her at the airport, and Sylvia drove away with a sense of injury which she knew to be irrational. But at dinner, she began to recover. She enjoyed the sound of English voices, the familiar references, the gossip about names and people she knew, the manner which seemed different from the American style. Henry was as careful about her comfort as any of her hosts in New York. But he was more casual, more relaxed. And so was Isabel, with her six children who kept appearing with escorts of nannies – or was it the same one recurring like a stage army? – well behaved and restrained and utterly unlike the American children of her acquaintances who took automatic precedence over adults.

In the morning, she telephoned Cullen from her bed. The line to his room was engaged, and for a few moments she had a panic that he was talking to some woman. But when at last she got through, and asked, with her first words, whom he'd been talking to, he said,

'I've been talking to room service.'

Her eyes prickled with tears of relief, and she said,

'I love you.'

'That's very interesting,' he said. 'You've never said that before.'

'No,' she answered. 'But I'm telling you now. Put it in your diary.'

'I will,' said Cullen. 'Wait a minute while I write it down. . . . What are you doing?'

'Guess.'

'Not that, I hope.'

'You're absurd. I'm drinking tea.'

'I told you the English are always drinking tea.'

'Yes, it's all come back.'

'You've forgotten me.'

'No, I love you. Don't be late.'

'I'm a bit worried about all those British.'

65

'Don't worry about the British,' she said. 'You just worry about the Americans.'

As soon as Sylvia saw the table-placings, she regretted that she had pressed the Ambassadress to invite Cullen. Already, before the luncheon began, the Ambassadress and the Counsellor, Peter Hazelton, had made it clear that they had no intention of going beyond the minimal limits of hospitality towards Cullen, and Senator Porter's wife, having established that he was an assistant professor at Columbia, quickly absorbed herself in conversation with Morrow about friends in England. The Ambassadress, after a few polite comments on the humidity in Washington, interrupted by lateral sorties among her other guests, left him standing at the far end of the room with an empty Martini glass. He would gladly have refilled it, but Hillyard the butler was preoccupied with Mrs. Porter, who explained to Morrow that a Martini, unlike brandy, lost its virtue by being held in the hand for more than five minutes, and that ideally the glass should be discarded and not replenished. The butler had already given her two substitutes for her original drink, and the Ambassadress, glancing surreptitiously at her watch, was wondering how she could tell Hillyard not to offer her another.

Cullen listened attentively to Mrs. Porter's lecture. At any moment now, he thought, she'll turn from dry Martinis to the agricultural question in Cambodia, and she'll be equally emphatic.

'They don't know how to make them there,' she ended.

('Where?' thought Cullen. 'At the St. Pierre, the Savoy or in Cambodia?' His mind had wandered, and he had lost her drift.)

Morrow nodded sympathetically.

'Indeed they don't,' he said. 'It's a great pity.'

The butler passed with the tray, and gave a message to the Ambassadress. There would be a delay of ten minutes before they could eat. She frowned, and reluctantly sent him back to Mrs. Porter, who after a moment's doubt took a fourth Martini.

'What an attractive girl she is!' she said, indicating Sylvia with her glass. Cullen wondered how she would ever get her rings back over her swollen joints.

'Yes, very,' he said.

'Are you a family friend?' Mrs. Porter went on.

'No, Miss Melville and I met in New York.'

'Her father's an attractive man too,' said Mrs. Porter. 'Very attractive. You ought to meet him. Isn't he an attractive man, Mr. Morrow?'

'So they say.'

She put her arm on his. 'You British are terribly polite. It's what kills me about you. Why don't you politicians hate each other's guts? Don't tell me. I know. It's your public-school system. You all love each other – all love each other from boyhood.'

She had begun to giggle.

Senator Porter joined their group, and said,

'Well, Mary-Jane – I see you're making a hit with this young man.'

He took Morrow by the arm, and said,

'She tells it to all the boys.'

Cullen walked to a side table and put down the glass. He sensed that he had made a mistake in coming, but surely no luncheon party would go on beyond half past three at the latest.

At the other end of the room, Sylvia was hemmed in by the Ambassador, Senator Porter and the Senator's aide, Walter Anderson, a corporation lawyer. She saw that there was no chance of rescuing Cullen till luncheon, and she waited anxiously for the movement from the drawing-room to the table. But when she saw that Mrs. Oake-Gordon, the Ambassador's widowed sister-in-law, was on one side of Cullen and Joan Felton, the principal of a women's college in England, on the other, she realized that Cullen was in for a difficult hour.

By chance, his two neighbours, immediately they sat down, turned as if at a command in opposite directions, leaving Cullen in the isolation of a man who to retain his dignity must pretend either to be obsessed by the table-ware or to be blandly indifferent to small talk. From the left of the Ambassador, Sylvia tried to catch his eye, but Cullen had occupied himself with his *œufs lulglère*, and all that she could see was the side of his domed forehead, sweating.

Morrow was at ease. As an undergraduate he had learnt that the quickest way of attracting an audience was to affirm the opposite of an accepted idea, to claim that all who held it were outdated, and if the argument became too involved, abandon it as if it had never been advanced. His rumbling voice soon subdued the conversations around the table.

'Oh, no,' he said, 'there's no East and West any more.'

'China?' said Miss Felton.

He ignored her.

'Among the sophisticated peoples, there are only the ideasmen and the technique-men. The problem of politics is to keep the technique-men from getting ideas.'

'But they run things anyhow,' said Mrs. Oake-Gordon. 'Everything's run by officials nowadays. We just don't admit it.'

'The French do,' said Cullen. 'The technocrats have been running France since 1945.'

'Not a bit,' said Miss Felton, a loyal francophile. 'They still keep democracy.'

'Yes,' said Cullen. 'As they might keep a woman. I don't go for a kept democracy.'

The other guests waited for Senator Porter to comment, but he turned to the Ambassadress, and said,

'This is an excellent wine, ma'am. Mary-Jane and I own a small château near Bordeaux—'

'Of course you do,' said the Ambassadress. 'Château Ducreuil-Nevers.'

'Yes,' said the Senator, flattered. 'Our product is small – not so flinty as this—' he sipped – 'but adequate. I'd be honoured if you'd accept a few bottles, ma'am.'

He bowed to the Ambassadress, and she smiled, fingering her pearls with pleasure.

Morrow, who disliked conversation about wine, looked across at Cullen and said,

'But it's been a sham in the West ever since the Party system began. Once you have parties, you get government by caucus. The democracy thing is dead as Gladstone. What we've got in Britain is a kind of Venetian oligarchy, and it runs right through the democracy.'

'But you're always being elected, George,' said the Ambassadress. 'Weren't you just elected to the Parliamentary Committee or something?'

'Not elected,' said Morrow. 'Picked. It's like a rugger fifteen. First you're picked and then you're approved. I've been a politician for twenty-three years, and I've never known a time when decisions weren't made by a caucus.'

'What exactly is a caucus?' asked Mrs. Porter from the other end of the table in her slow, dragging voice that seemed to leave her lungs and nasal passages stuffed with tired and alcoholic vowels. 'If government by caucus means government by Caucasians – why, sirs, we're all for it. Aren't we, William?'

'Yes, my dear,' said the Senator.

Morrow led the laughter with a quivering ho-ho in which the Ambassador and most of the other guests quickly joined. The edge of Cullen's mouth twitched in a guilty complaisance, but Sylvia sat unsmiling.

At intervals during the remainder of the luncheon, the word 'caucus' recurred, till it became a catchword useful for an automatic guffaw when the conversation dwindled. During the early part of the meal, neither the Senator nor Anderson addressed a single word to Cullen, ignoring the interjections or allowing the subjects which others initiated for his benefit to float away.

At the *bombe surprise*, Anderson suddenly looked across the table and said,

'Will you be coming South again this year, Mr. Cullen?'

'I haven't any plans at the moment,' said Cullen. He stuck his spoon into the ice-cream, and for the first time felt comfortable. 'Why do you ask?'

'Well, I was looking at you,' said Anderson, 'and I thought, "Now, we've met before."'

'Yes,' said Cullen calmly, his mouth full of ice-cream. 'We may well have met at Nashville.'

The Senator, his face sallow except for the cheekbones where two crimson spots stimulated by Bloody Marys and Haut-Brion had been deepened by some endogenous emotion, turned his pale blue eyes towards Cullen.

'Have you been to Nashville, sir?' he asked.

Morrow began a sentence, but stopped in the silence that had spontaneously fallen on the table. Cullen glanced quickly at Sylvia, and said,

'Yes – very briefly.'

'I've never been to Nashville,' Sylvia said hurriedly. 'What's it like?'

'I'll tell you, Miss Melville,' said the Senator in his courteous, metallic voice. 'Nashville is a city where we – the Americans – fought a great battle in the Civil War. The Confederates were overwhelmed, and two thousand of them lie buried on the slopes of the hills.'

'And a lot more Federals,' said Cullen.

The Senator again turned his pale eyes towards him, and said, 'My ancestors were among the Confederates. I think that explains why we are a bit sensitive in the South when we get radicals and trouble-makers from the North who come to stir up mischief with the nigras.'

'That's right, William,' said Mrs. Porter.

'Shall we have coffee outside?' said the Ambassadress. 'It's such a lovely day.'

As the other guests followed her on to the terrace outside the dining-room, Cullen, Anderson and the Senator spoke rapidly in undertones.

'What did he say?' Sylvia asked, coming up to Cullen at the door.

'The Senator didn't say anything,' said Cullen. 'I told him I didn't like the word "nigras", and Anderson said he didn't like kikes either.'

'Perhaps that's why they're leaving so soon,' said Sylvia.

'Perhaps I'd better go too,' said Cullen.

'Yes – with me,' said Sylvia.

In New York, they had dinner at La Potinière, and then strolled together through the streets. Sylvia took his arm as they walked across town past the small, closed-up shops, the deserted offices with only the cleaners' lights still on, the bars and the purposeful hurry of people. They had exhausted the subject of the luncheon party, the Ambassador's chilled farewell and Morrow's confusion at the Senator's sudden departure, but from time to time they returned to the Washington events, half in guilt and half in gratification.

'Where are you supposed to be tonight?' Sylvia asked Cullen.

'In Washington.'

'And where will you be at three o'clock tomorrow morning?'

'In your apartment – with you.'

'Why don't we go there now? It's past ten.'

'Are you sure – are you sure you want to?'

'Yes – let's take a taxi.'

At half past three in the morning, the telephone burred at

her bedside. Awake, she picked it up quickly and gave her number. The operator said, 'Is that Miss Melville? Can she take a long-distance call from London, England?' And when she said, 'Yes,' she heard her father's voice, which she hadn't heard for several months.

'Daddy!' she said.

Cullen stirred at her side, and she looked anxiously around her, panicked by her father's presence in the room.

'Can you speak up?' she heard him say.

'Who is it?' Cullen growled, half-asleep.

She shook him, her hand over the receiver, and put her other hand to her mouth. Cullen switched on the light, and sat up, watching her.

'I'm so sorry,' Sylvia said into the telephone. 'We were cut off for a moment.'

'You sound agitated.'

'No, just surprised. Do you know what time it is here?'

'Yes, I do. I imagine it's early in the morning. How are you, Sylvia?'

'Oh, fine – fine. It's lovely hearing from you. Is everything all right?'

'I don't know. I hope so. How are you?'

'I just told you. I'm fine.'

'I thought you were in Washington.'

'I was.'

'Henry telephoned me.'

'That was quick of him.'

'I gather the luncheon wasn't a great success.'

'No – it wasn't.'

There was a pause.

'Sylvia.'

'Yes.'

'Who is this fellow you took down to Washington?'

'You mean Don Cullen?'

'If that's his name.'

'He's a friend of mine.'

'I believe he's married.'

'That's right.'

There was a pause, and she began to breathe more quickly as Cullen passed his arm round her waist and laid his head on her breasts.

71

'Do you think it wise – or courteous to me or your mother, Sylvia – to take him to an official luncheon?'

'I didn't want to go. I went to please you.'

'But how could it please me for you to take this man?' His voice became harder. 'Your behaviour—'

'Oh, for God's sake don't start talking about behaviour. I'm an adult woman. I don't need to be told how to behave.'

Melville's voice fell again. She could hear his effort at constraint.

'We all need to be told some time. I think, Sylvia, you'd better come back to England.'

'No – I won't.'

'You must think about it.'

Her arm tightened around Cullen's head.

'I don't need to. I'm not coming back.'

'I think we'll have to see.'

A silence fell between them again. At last the Prime Minister said,

'Please, Sylvia –please think about it.'

She wiped the moisture from her forehead with the back of her arm, and said,

'No, I'm very sorry.'

'Well' – she could hear the shrug in his voice – 'take care of yourself. See that you eat regularly.'

She softened.

'I do, daddy. I'm getting fat.'

She felt Cullen's fingers moving over her back, and she giggled.

'Take care of yourself,' said Melville. 'I don't want you to come to harm.'

For the next few weeks Sylvia and Cullen resumed their old habit of meeting, but now he contrived to stay late with her instead of returning in the early evening to Connecticut. They ate quickly in drugstores, or made improvised meals in her apartment, and twice, on the pretext of staying in Manhattan for academic dinners, Cullen spent the night with her.

At eight in the morning on the second occasion, there was a sharp buzz at the door. Neither of them moved from their position with the bedclothes flung back in the room already breathless despite the air-conditioning in the living-room.

'The mail,' said Cullen languidly.

'It's already been,' said Sylvia, her mouth on his.

'The janitor,' said Cullen.

'He always uses the other door.'

The buzzer went again, urgently, then again.

'You'd better answer,' said Cullen.

'No, I'm busy.'

The buzzer insisted, and Sylvia slowly rose, drawing on a dressing-gown.

'Yes?' she said through the door.

An English voice answered,

'Miss Melville? I'm an Embassy messenger. I've got a letter for you.'

'Well, I'm not dressed. Put it through the door.'

'I need a signature.'

She opened the door, leaving it on the chain, and took the crested envelope with the acknowledgment slip in her left hand. She signed, and hurriedly closed and locked the door. Cullen looked up anxiously when she returned.

'A letter from the Embassy,' she said.

'Good,' he said flippantly. 'I thought it might be someone from the D.A.'s office.'

While she read the letter, he switched on the television set with the large screen that faced the bed.

'. . . news from the Hill,' said the announcer. 'And on this bright morning, we're collecting the views of a few Senators concerned with the new legislation. Here is Senator Porter, who has been very much involved in the Civil Rights Bill. Now, Senator . . .'

'In my view,' the Senator began reasonably, and the camera zoomed so that his face swelled to fill out the screen.

'Oh, no,' said Cullen, switching off the set. 'Not at eight o'clock. What do they want, sweetie?'

Sylvia laughed, and said,

'Actually, it's from daddy. He's sent me an open ticket home.'

Wearing only his pyjama trousers, Cullen went to the washbasin and began to shave.

'Why should he want to do that?' he asked.

She went behind him, and put her face on his strongly muscled, sunburnt back.

'My father,' she said, 'is a very kind man – a very considerate man. Wouldn't you send your daughter an air ticket in a similar situation?'

In her ear she could hear the scratch of his razor blade as he thought of the answer.

'Wouldn't you?' she insisted.

'If I were your father,' Cullen said, 'I'd come and take you right home.'

She kissed the centre of his spine, and he yelped.

'Now you've drawn blood,' he said. 'That makes us quits.'

She sat him on the bed, and staunched the cut on his chin with a towel. When it stopped, she said,

'Why not skip your lecture?'

He kissed her cheek, and said,

'Listen, darling. I'm as anxious to become a full professor as your father was to be Prime Minister. Skipping lectures isn't the quickest way there.'

'You know,' she said, 'you remind me a lot of my father.'

'In what way?'

'Sometimes even the way you look. But chiefly I think, the way you always seem to be struggling with your angel – and always getting the better of him.'

'Not always,' said Cullen, standing. He had the same look as in the garden of the Museum.

'No – I'm sorry – not always,' she said. 'You were wonderful with Porter.'

'No,' said Cullen. 'It was touch and go. I'm still not sure if I was right.'

'You *were* right – of course you were. I'd have despised you if you'd done anything different. And it's the same with my father. I've only once known him—' She stopped.

'Known him what?'

'Known him make a decision that I thought opportunistic.'

Cullen went into the bathroom, and turned on the shower. After he had bathed, he came back wearing a towelling coat and said,

'I've been thinking about that word "opportunistic". It's a hell of a schoolgirl's word. Don't you realize that all civilized life is based on compromise?'

'I don't believe it. If people could always live by principles, life would be really civilized.'

He dried himself, and said,

74

'What are we doing? Are we living by principle or compromise?'

'How do you want your eggs?' she asked.

'Boiled,' he said. 'Five minutes.'

Over breakfast she said to him,

'I've forgotten your wife's name.'

'You never knew it.'

'Well, what is it?'

'Emma.'

'Emma,' she repeated, 'Emma.' The face had acquired a name.

One night, later that summer, they were leaving Carnegie Hall, spilling into the street with the audience which, released from silence, was now loudly discussing the concert.

'The *andante*,' Sylvia began, and caught sight of his absorbed and anxious expression. 'Is there anything wrong?' she asked.

He took a press cutting from his pocket book and handed it to her. It contained a marked extract from a tabloid column which Sylvia read, standing on the sidewalk at a street intersection. The lights changed, and she was swept forward into the road by the presence of those around her.

Holding hands in public places. British politico's only daughter and Columbia egg-head. Wedding bells? Uh-huh, says Embassy. M'm, m'm, says wife.

Sylvia screwed up the paper, and said,

'I'm sorry. I suppose it was bound to happen. The Press have been on to me for days.'

'Why didn't you tell me?' he asked sullenly.

'I didn't want to worry you.'

'What did you tell them?'

'I told them what I always tell journalists when they ask about my private life. I tell them to go to hell.'

'Well, this is bound to start something.'

'Is there anything you'd like me to do?'

'Like what?'

'Like not seeing you, for example, for a bit?'

He took her arm as they reached the other side of the street, and said,

'It wouldn't help. Anyhow, Emma showed it to me first.'

'What did you say?'

'I said you're a very nice girl – she knew I'd been to

75

Washington – and she asked me to ask you back to Connecticut.'

'You said "no", of course.'

'No, I didn't. I said I'd ask you.'

She stopped and looked him in the face, and he looked away.

'I think it might be a good idea,' he went on. 'This thing is bound to get around unless it's sat on. Besides, Emma wanted to ask one of the senior members of the University – the President himself – well, he'd come if he knew that you'd be there. After all—'

He had become humble, and Sylvia listened uneasily.

'I think I'll hate it,' she said.

'So will I,' said Cullen. 'But it'll kill all that tabloid stuff – in the faculty, at any rate.'

At the weekend, they drove together to Connecticut, relaxed and almost ostentatious, in Cullen's convertible, and the summer breeze blew through Sylvia's shoulder-length hair.

'Let's drive on like this and never stop,' she said.

'No, we're nearly there,' he answered.

She had expected that Cullen would live in a fairly small house, set apart in one of the open-planned estates. Instead, he drove into a nineteenth-century modernized mill-house, surrounded by lawns, a swimming-pool and stretches of pasture, with a lake and a landscaped garden. Emma and the two children were waiting to greet them, and Naomi dashed through the sprinkler's spray to open her father's door. He kissed her, hurried to help Sylvia out of the car, put his cheek against his wife's, and with his arms around his two daughters introduced the visitor.

Emma gave Sylvia a warm smile, and Sylvia observed how her smile irradiated her face, transforming her commonplace features.

'Well, hello,' she said, and her voice was resonant and forthright. 'Welcome! I've heard so much about you.'

She was wearing a bathing-suit under a gaily-coloured housecoat, and she said,

'They're all at the pool. Why don't you get changed and have some drinks? Don – why don't you help Sylvia with her bags?'

He showed her to her room, and put down the suitcases next to the chintz-covered bed.

'Don,' she said.

He paused at the door before leaving.

'What?'

'Oh, nothing. I'll be down soon.'

She sat on the edge of the bed, absorbed in thought, and then went to the window which looked on to the blue-painted swimming-pool about a hundred yards away. About fifteen people were sitting on striped chaises-longues at its side; from the pool itself came the splashing and shouting of children. Everyone seemed relaxed in the afternoon sun, intimate friends, and after a few minutes she saw Cullen, wearing linen trousers with a bright yellow sports-shirt, open at the chest, moving from chair to chair and greeting his guests.

She changed, and joined them by the pool. Naomi was standing near the mattress where Emma guided her, and Sylvia asked,

'Can you dive?'

Naomi looked at her from beneath her dark eyelashes, and said 'Yes,' and moved away quickly.

'She's awfully shy,' Cullen said apologetically.

Later on, while Emma was standing on the diving-board for her last swim of the day, Edgar Probert, a New York publisher who was the Cullens' nearest neighbour, said,

'She's a handsome woman, isn't she?'

Sylvia looked at Emma's heavy breasts, raised up by the posture of diving, and her mature hips, and said,

'Yes – very handsome.'

'She's a Wollheim, you know.'

'Wollheim?'

'Yes – the Wollheim Auditorium – her father gave it to New York – you pass it on the way out from Brooklyn. He had four daughters and an art collection, and Emma got the Manets and Rouaults. You must see them.'

'Yes, I'd like to,' said Sylvia.

Probert was leaning on his elbow, looking at the curve of her shoulder, and Sylvia sat up with a resentment against Cullen that he had told her so little about Emma, transferred against this man with the thatch of red hair on his chest who was lying near her in such a peculiar intimacy. She finished the glass of lime-juice at her side, and rose. As she did so there was a general stirring and the guests moved to the changing-rooms to prepare for the evening. Before she could go indoors, Cullen came over to her with a tall, middle-aged, lean man who had just arrived, and introduced him as 'Professor Lovell, the head of our faculty'.

'I've only dropped in to greet you, Miss Melville,' he said.

'Me too, I hope, Stephen,' said Emma, who joined them and took his arm.

'Oh, you,' said Lovell slowly. 'I only come to see you when no one's looking.'

They all laughed.

'All right,' said Emma. 'Only a small daiquiri for you.'

'No, Scotch on the rocks. Seriously, Miss Melville, I wanted to meet you because I think your father – well, it's an impertinence to say so – but I think he's a great man.'

Sylvia smiled.

'I think so too.'

'No, really. His work for the underdeveloped countries – I came across it personally when we were working for the Government on the cultural expansion programme – it was quite remarkable, and I just wanted to thank him at second hand.'

'Thank you very much,' said Sylvia. She was moved by his enthusiasm, and added, 'I'll tell him what you said. And if you're ever in England—'

'Well, you'll let us know, and we'll tell Sylvia,' Emma interrupted.

'I'll be glad to,' said Lovell. 'Thank you, Emma – Don. You've got a charming house-guest. I must be off.'

On the way back to her room, Sylvia turned left instead of right, and found herself in a large bedroom, warm with the afternoon's sun, where a pair of blue pyjamas and a white nightdress had been laid out for the night. They were artfully spread as if in a window display, and for a second Sylvia looked at them against the silk-padded headrest of the large bed.

'It's the wrong room, darling. It's ours,' said Emma who came up behind her. 'But you must look at this little Guardi while you're here.'

She led Sylvia by the arm across the room, and showed her the small painting of a Venetian scene.

'Guardi the younger,' she said. 'Don simply loves it. Do you like painting?'

'Yes,' said Sylvia. 'I think I'd better get changed.'

When at last she went to bed, she had been introduced to at least a dozen people and listened for five hours to a din of conversation that left her longing for privacy. Cullen, acting as host, eager to please, sharing himself among his guests, obeying his wife's orders for a drink here, a telephone call there, seemed an exotic figure despite his occasional visits to her for reassurance. She watched him in his dark suit, now related by familiarity to a wholly different world, and she felt free in proportion as he felt tied to it. But her freedom was a barren one, and as dinner wore on and the anecdotes and exchanges about plays and books and faculty gossip multiplied she felt more and more isolated, shrivelled and reduced by the clanship in which she felt no place.

When at last she went to bed and switched off the light, and the house had fallen quiet except for the intermittent cries of a nocturnal bird among the willows by the lake, she was disturbed by the sound of an insect buzzing in her room. She switched the light on again, and saw that the biggest wasp she had ever seen was staggering drunkenly from side to side of her dressing-table, sometimes rising with a whirring and then lying still like a companion by her bedside. She got out of bed, and backed away and fumbled to remove the wire mesh from the window to let the wasp out. But a drift of mayfly blew in, and she shut the window quickly. She went to the door and opened it, but the house had fallen into sleep and she had heard the Cullens' bedroom door close a quarter of an hour before, after Emma's loud 'Good night'.

The wasp now lay on the bedside table, droning from time to time like someone snoring in sleep. Sylvia picked up a glass weight with periwinkles inside, took aim and slowly pressed it on the wasp. It crackled as the weight descended, and when she released it the wings stirred. She pressed the weight again till the wasp became an obscene mess, still as the glass, as the silent house.

'I'm going to be sick,' said Sylvia, as she had often said when she was a child. And, afraid only that they might hear her, she went into the bathroom and vomited her undigested dinner.

The following day, after she returned to New York – Emma drove her to the station because Cullen had to get back early – she went to bed and stayed there for three days. She saw no one, and left a number of messages for Cullen at Columbia, but he didn't return her call. She wrote a letter of thanks and telephoned to Emma on a number of occasions, but Emma was only available once and said, 'We must meet again.' At about the same time, Mrs. Rinehart wrote to say she was sorry, but she would require her apartment at the end of the month.

'If there's anything I've done . . .' 'If I've hurt you in any way . . .' Sylvia's letters to Cullen remained unanswered.

Eventually, the Counsellor came from Washington. Mary Renwick had telephoned to say that she wouldn't leave her apartment, that she just stayed in bed staring, and they'd simply have to do something about it. The Counsellor sent for Dr. Kron, and he put her on dexedrine for the day and sodium amytal for the night.

And for a few months, she worked for Milford's Art Gallery. Each day when she walked down Fifth Avenue with his image in front of her, she walked with the hope that one of the faces might be his, that miraculously he might emerge from the crowd, that she might see him scrutinizing a painting, or that one morning, early, the telephone would ring and he would say, 'I'm sorry, Sylvia darling, I'll explain it all when I see you,' and she would say, 'It doesn't matter. Just come here now – straight away.'

But it didn't happen like that. She heard from Probert the publisher who came into the gallery that Cullen had taken an exchange professorship in the University of Florida, and that his family had followed him there for the summer. At about the same time, she had to leave her apartment and Palfrey, her employer, who to begin with had put high hopes on having the Prime Minister's daughter in the gallery, became dissatisfied with her apparent apathy and late arrival for work. Then in July she had a letter from England offering her a job with a publisher. She accepted, and returned home.

But it was no good – no good at all. To move from her bed was such a terrible effort; to confront people, to talk, to answer, to justify herself. In the flat in Holland Park it was the same as those last months in New York. They were back, the nightmares, the dexedrine dawns that began in the afternoons.

Sylvia moved her hand to the capsule by her bedside when the telephone rang. She let it ring seven, eight, nine times, and decided that she'd answer if it rang another twice. It continued to ring, and heavily, as if her arm were weighted, she picked up the receiver.

'Yes,' she said.

'Hello, Sylvia,' said Talbot, his voice crisp and delighted. 'How are you?'

'I don't know,' she said and sat up. 'I haven't considered it.'

'In that case consider it.'

She smiled faintly.

'I think I'm bearable.'

'Will you have dinner with me tonight?'

She hesitated.

'I'd like you to,' he said.

She sat up higher and said,

'All right – I'd better start getting up, or I won't be ready.'

'I meant dinner, not lunch.'

'So did I. I'm a slow dresser.'

She heard him laugh, and say, 'I'll call for you at half past seven.'

'Half past seven,' she repeated. She got out of bed, and drew the curtains wide. The sky was a blue wash over the chimney-pots, and Sylvia raised the window sash to look out. In the street a barrow-boy had turned his pitch into a brilliant garden. Sylvia looked from her room into her sitting-room and decided that before Talbot came she would fill it with flowers.

CHAPTER FIVE

THE Chief Whip shaded his eyes against the sun, and said to Melville,

'I think that ball was out.'

'Yes,' said Melville, propping himself on his elbow. 'You don't think he's going to let himself beat the Chancellor of the Exchequer?'

Lacey prepared to serve. Despite his height, he gave an impression of smallness because as he struck the ball he crouched, bending his arm in order not to over-hit. Talbot had moved up from the base-line to take the weak service, but then withdrew. To approach too closely would have been to undervalue his opponent. The ball waddled over the net and fell flabbily out of his reach.

'Oh, good service, sir,' said Talbot.

'That, I suppose,' said Scott-Bower, 'is what you meant.'

'Yes, Charles,' said Melville. 'There's a certain kind of young man – you get them in every big organization – the army, politics, everywhere – who's a dedicated squire. If he isn't hanging around the boss, he's hanging around your wife. What takes some people years to do, he does in weeks. Never pushes – he's always pushed.'

Melville plucked a dried stalk from the sloping lawn that led down to the Hedley House tennis courts and watched a ladybird that was slowly balancing its way along it.

'I suppose,' he said, 'you've got to be really young for all that climbing to seem worth while.'

The Chief Whip laughed, and said,

'Oh, come on, Geoffrey. You've got to be Prime Minister before you can really despise patronage. When you were young—'

'I'm only forty-six, you know.'

'Yes, I do. But Talbot—'

Talbot volleyed at the net, and Lacey put his hands on his hips in mock chagrin as the red dust spurted from the court.

'He's very good,' said the Prime Minister. 'It's amazing how Mayland brings his young men along.'

'It's always the same technique,' said the Chief Whip. 'After all, we've seen it for years. He pays them top prices so that he can use them, insult them and make them feel that it's worth while to be paid and insulted, especially if they can become national figures overnight. ... In the last month, he's put Talbot's name on practically every bus in London – on the hoardings, and Edwina's got him on Table Talk twice a week after the news.'

Melville laughed.

'Lady Drayford,' he said, 'always reminds me of Catherine the Great, except that she prefers young politicians to young hussars.'

'She once told me that soldiers make her sneeze – a sort of allergy.'

'What a ghastly life it must have been to have been a Queen's favourite!' said Melville, rolling on to his back and looking up at the unclouded blue sky. 'So exhausting!' Then he shut his eyes to show the Chief Whip that he didn't want to talk, and lay listening to the sound of the tennis balls, the occasional voices of the other guests who had been spending Ascot week with Mayland, and the distant barking of the Afghan hounds in the kennels. He himself had arrived early that Sunday morning, and intended leaving the following day, but first he had to perform what the Chief Whip called 'political surgery'.

The loss of the Canley by-election had been a shock. The Opposition attacks on the Government's handling of the N'dola incidents had worried him because he felt their substance to be justified, not because there seemed any electoral disadvantage in a tragedy which to the voters of Canley was remote and to their material affairs, at any rate, irrelevant. The Government had lost the by-election because the unseasonal rise in unemployment after Lacey's restrictionist Budget, followed only a few weeks later by yet another increase in Bank Rate, had affected some of the engineering firms, like those in Canley, more rapidly and drastically than anywhere else. The last Gallup Polls had confirmed the sense of grievance sweeping the industrial constituencies. 'If there were an Election tomorrow,' Lord Endersley, the Party Chairman, had told him, 'we'd be out by fifty seats.'

'Fortunately,' Melville had answered, 'we don't have to test your judgment for another two years.'

But it was troubling. What had made matters worse was Lacey's off-the-cuff comment to a TV interviewer before a Guildhall dinner when, stepping in white tie and tails out of his car, he said in connection with a new redundancy of nearly ten thousand aircraft workers,

'In time of change, we must all make a few sacrifices and put up with some transitional inconvenience.'

'A few sacrifices!' 'Transitional inconvenience!' For the last few weeks, Lacey had been greeted, each time he appeared in the House, with incantations from the Opposition Benches, which lost their good-nature as the percentage of unemployed rose steadily. Nor had the Ascot pictures of Lacey done anything except help the cartoonists. Lacey had once told him that arithmetic made him tired, and that the only way he could sleep was by working out taxation formulae to reduce the trade gap. Melville had smiled, and quickly regretted the smile.

There was no doubt about it. Lacey, despite his Parliamentary nonchalance, his impressive voice and his mastery of the esoteric language of economics, was a political liability. Beneath his public braggadocio lay a network of private fears, reaching out beyond his political self-doubts into obscure personal involvements with an ephebic court which Melville wanted to know nothing about. With his outstanding experience as an academic economist and then as a banker, Lacey had been the inevitable choice as Chancellor of the Exchequer when Ormston, defeated by Melville for the Premiership, had refused to serve under him. But he had tired quickly. The backbenchers' Committee who had sent a deputation, led by Laurence Gore, to see the Prime Minister the previous week, had spoken brutally. Lacey, they had said, was now a handicap, and what was needed was a strong Chancellor ready to tackle unemployment. It was the same inside the Cabinet. At least three Cabinet Ministers and six Junior Ministers had been urging that Lacey should go, and Ormston take his place. Ormston. What a strange return! After losing the battle for the Premiership, he had accepted a peerage rather than serve under Melville in the Lower House. Since then he had never commented on the events, though he often spoke of loyalty.

The game was over, and Lacey was walking towards the gate with his heavy sweating arm on Talbot's shoulder. He had won; but he and his opponent both seemed pleased with themselves.

'What did Ormston say?' Melville asked the Chief Whip.

'He said "Yes" – if asked. He wants to be Deputy, too.'

'We'll have to see,' said Melville slowly. 'We'll have to see.'

'He nearly had me,' said Lacey in his rolling voice as they approached. He was panting a little, and he flung himself on the grass.

'Made me run,' said Talbot, but Melville and the Chief Whip had already turned to Lady Drayford, who had come up behind them with Mayland and two of his honey-coloured Afghan hounds.

'Really,' she said to Lacey, 'it's too much. So unbecoming – all that running around.'

'I like it,' said Lacey.

'I don't mean you, Henry. You're suitably dressed. I mean Peter. No politician should be seen in shorts after the age of twenty-five.'

She examined his legs, and one of the Afghan hounds began to lick his knees ingratiatingly.

'I told you,' said Lady Drayford. 'It's unseemly. Did you see his piece on Renewal yesterday?' she asked the Prime Minister.

Melville ignored her question, and said to Mayland,

'You were going to show me your cattleyas.'

'Oh, yes,' said Lady Drayford. 'He's got the most wonderful ones. Is it true that there are thousands of different species?'

'Yes,' said Mayland, pulling his Panama hat over his eyes and groping with his other hand inside the pocket of his tropical suit. 'But for the time being, I can't find my glasses.'

Talbot helped Lacey into his jacket, and had begun to pull a sweater over his head when Mayland said,

'I must have left them on the study table.'

'Oh, never mind,' said Melville, 'you can show us the orchids some other time.'

'No,' said Mayland. 'Young Peter here will run up and get them for me.'

Melville and the Chief Whip halted in their slow walk towards the greenhouses whose glass was leaping in the dazzling sun, and waited for Talbot's reply. He glanced quickly at Lady Drayford, and said,

'Why don't we see the orchids some other time?'

Mayland, his voice now sharp, said,

'Because we want to see them now. Be a good chap, Talbot, and get me my glasses.'

Lacey walked on quickly, unwilling to be involved in a domestic disagreement, but Lady Drayford took Talbot's arm and said,

'Yes, Peter. I have to go up to the house for a few minutes. You see me back.'

The hounds jumped happily around Mayland as he hurried to catch up with Lacey.

'What you must understand,' said Lady Drayford, 'is that he's a bastard. He likes it that way, and you're paid to like it too.'

Talbot struck fiercely with his racket at a low-hanging branch, and said,

'It was deliberate.'

'Of course it was deliberate. Everything Mayland does is deliberate.'

'But in front of the P.M.—!'

Lady Drayford pressed his arm against hers.

'You mustn't take it personally,' she said. 'He just wanted to show Geoffrey and Henry that whoever else makes the motions, he himself has the last word.'

Talbot smiled.

'Not with Mrs. Martin. Who on earth is she?'

'She's a left-over mistress who knows Mayland too well to be sacked. She drifts about the place like an old ghost that can't have peace till she's told all. It's very creepy. When the time comes for her to speak, she'll have forgotten what she wanted to say.'

'Mayland never talks to her.'

'No – never. Is she on the Renewal Committee?'

'I don't know. I think he's getting tired of it already. I wrote three pieces on Renewal and two got killed.'

'I think he'll keep it going till he gets his peerage. After today, perhaps—'

'What about his glasses?' said Talbot as they neared the idling groups on the terrace. 'Shall we forget them?'

'No,' said Lady Drayford. 'That would be very unwise. The thing to do is to get his glasses – but slowly. . . . Do you know

Helen Langdale?' she said, introducing him to a tall, strikingly beautiful woman who was walking alone from the house.

'I saw you in *Ariadne*,' said Talbot.

'Yes,' said Helen. 'What a lovely play! Where's Geoffrey?' she asked Lady Drayford.

'He's lost among the orchids,' she replied.

Helen moved on towards the tennis courts, and Talbot asked, 'Is she an old friend?'

'Of mine?'

'No – of Melville's?'

'Oh, yes, we're all old friends – all of us. You'd better get those glasses.'

On the way back after the visit to the orchid houses, Mayland went ahead with Lacey who had begun to feel chilled after the game, and Scott-Bower, who, as Chief Whip, had developed a dislike of dawdlers. Melville and Helen walked behind slowly, alone for the first time since she had joined them.

'How many years is it, Geoffrey, since we met?'

'That's like a statement in one of your plays to establish the characters.'

'It's exactly what I'm doing,' she said.

'It's three years and two months,' he said.

'I'm flattered that you remember so exactly.'

Melville smiled to her, raising a tree branch that lay across her path so that she could pass.

'You'll think me ungallant,' he said. 'I remember it because it was a few days before Collard died.'

'Yes,' said Helen. 'What a sad summer!'

'It was a very sad summer,' he repeated, and they walked without talking.

'Have you had any regrets?' she asked. They had begun to talk of different things.

'Many,' said Melville. 'Many. But I'm not sure that I would behave differently if it all – God help me – had to happen again.'

'What about Elizabeth?'

'What about her?'

'Is she happy?'

'I don't know. I've never asked her.'

Helen persisted.

'But you must know.'

'She likes being my wife.'

'I see. What about Sylvia?'

'Oh, she's fine.'

He spoke airily, but Helen insisted.

'I often wish I'd met her. I once saw you both walking together, and I thought how alike you both were. She must be how old now – twenty-three, twenty-four?'

'Twenty-three.'

'That makes me feel so old.'

'How old are you?'

'You know perfectly well – thirty-six.'

'Thirty-eight.'

'All right, thirty-eight – it's awful.'

'You were splendid in *Ariadne* – you looked twenty-three – I swear it.'

For a second, her eyes became luminous with pleasure. Then she said,

'That's not important. I—'

'It wouldn't have worked, Helen,' said Melville dismissively. 'It wouldn't have worked.'

'I wouldn't have minded anything. I would have hidden myself away in the north of Scotland. I would never have wanted to appear in public.'

'It wouldn't have worked,' Melville said stubbornly, and he walked with his face turned to the flagstones lining the avenue of eighteenth-century Italianate sculpture where they were alone. She took his arm, and said,

'When you became Prime Minister, I cried for a whole week.'

'You were probably thinking of the nation.'

She stopped, and faced him, and looked at his eyes.

'You can be as flippant as you like, Geoffrey. It doesn't matter. I've always loved you, and you know it.'

'Are you staying tonight?'

'Yes,' she answered quickly. 'What about you?'

'I'm leaving after dinner,' he said. 'Elizabeth's coming up to London from Suffolk – she's spent the weekend with the Grangers.'

'I'm sorry,' Helen answered. 'I would like you to have stayed. I only came to see you.'

'When did Mayland ask you?'

'He told me an old friend of mine was coming for the week-end, and then he said it was you. Are you angry?'

Melville had begun to walk on.

'No,' he said, 'not a bit. Mayland's a considerate host.'

'Is that all?'

'Not all. Be careful of him.'

'I'd never cause you difficulties, Geoffrey. You know it.'

Melville touched her bare arm above her elbow as they walked, and said,

'No – you wouldn't. But in any case, it's too late.'

They had come out near the terrace, and seeing them the other guests who had been preparing to go in moved towards them in a surge.

After dinner, Mayland beckoned to Melville, inviting him to lead the way from the candled dining-room so that they could join Lady Drayford and the others in the salon. But Melville, still cupping his brandy glass, asked his permission to stay and discuss an administrative matter with Lacey. Mayland said, 'Most certainly, Geoffrey,' addressing Melville by his Christian name for the first time, and led the men into the other room. General Bowles, who had lately returned from East Africa, tried to linger, but Mayland waved him on together with Carson, the property developer, who had been trying to engage the Chancellor in conversation. Melville nodded to him, and Mayland closed the door.

'Our host,' said Lacey comfortably, 'would make a very good traffic policeman.' He sipped his brandy, and said, 'I can't say I enjoyed being so close to Carson.'

'No,' said Melville thoughtfully.

'Kept trying to pump me about our development plans for South-east England, and the Leeds traffic replanning.'

'That's how he made five million.'

'Not by talking to me,' said Lacey quickly.

'No – by listening. Strange man, Carson. Why does he want to spend so much time falling off horses and missing partridge?'

'Ah,' said Lacey, 'they've got to catch up. It's hard in middle age. You know they wouldn't have him at White's?'

'I didn't know,' said Melville, making a pattern of three glasses on the table. He finished his own brandy, and took up his cigar which had gone out. 'I've been thinking, Henry, about the situation generally. You know, I thought Carson was right when he said that the public wants a change of faces much more than a change of policies.'

Lacey laughed a booming laugh that made his eyes disappear, and he passed his hand over his shining forehead.

'I don't know about the public – the cartoonists, perhaps. But one does get tired of our colleagues' faces.'

'I'm worried, Henry, about the public mood – there's a sort of apathy, a sense of indifference – I mean among our own people even. We lost Canley, and I've got a nasty feeling we're going to lose Edgeworth.'

'Will you stay for the result? Mayland's got a TV set laid on.'

'What time will it be through?'

'About half past eleven – quarter to twelve. There are only forty-five thousand voters. It's a quarter past already.'

'Yes – I'll stay,' said Melville. 'There's something important I want to discuss with you.'

He rose, and walked carefully past the disordered chairs.

'You see,' he said, 'I've come to the conclusion that I must make certain changes in the Government, and I would like your help.'

'I can tell you right away,' said Lacey, throwing back his large head, 'that we want changes at the top and at the junior levels. Ardrossan is really past it – and quite frankly, I think that Charles might consider going to the other place. Then there's the Minister of Labour – he's singularly querulous. He rings me every Friday, keening like a banshee about what he calls "the figures".'

'They are, of course, serious.'

'But temporary. Stour-Benson's too anxious. Had you thought of Francis Waters? – Chairman of the Trade Union Committee – first-class man – your P.P.S., I believe, when you were at Commonwealth Relations.'

'I don't think he'd do at all,' said Melville. 'Waters is unreliable.'

'Well, that's an epitaph on any aspirant. Pity. I think he's able. On the other hand, Stour-Benson ought to go. And I think you ought to think seriously of the Board of Trade as well. Barton's not up to it. He's on the edge of my team, and I want someone younger – someone with more guts who can stand up to those damned French and Germans.'

'What about the Economic and Financial Secretaries?'

'Oh, I wouldn't touch those,' said Lacey firmly. 'It's been my policy to encourage the younger men – Mackintosh and Hardy are excellent. No, you can't touch them.'

The expression on Melville's face as he continued to stand disturbed him, and he said,

'Is anything worrying you, Geoffrey?'

Melville took the back of a chair in both his hands, and rocked it reflectively.

'We're going to lose Edgeworth,' he said. 'It's going to be difficult.'

'Yes,' said the Chancellor. ' "Not moribund, but decomposing" – I must say I don't like Yates' description of the Government. Shall we go in?'

He rose, but Melville detained him.

'There is something I wanted to say to you, Henry. I must make some major changes.'

Lacey waited for him to continue.

'You've been a very loyal friend and colleague, Henry. But I have to make some changes.'

Lacey's permanent smile stayed imposed on his mouth, but his cheeks hollowed. He stood facing Melville in stupefaction. He tried to articulate, but no sound came. He swallowed, and put his hand on Melville's shoulder as if for reassurance that he was there.

'I'm sorry,' said the Prime Minister. 'There must be changes. We'll talk about it tomorrow.'

The Chancellor of the Exchequer turned away, and picked up at random a half-empty brandy glass from the littered table.

'Who do you want instead?' he asked.

'Ormston,' said Melville.

'Ormston,' Lacey repeated. 'Ormston. Remember what you said, Geoffrey, about Ormston – "that hangdog face frightening the pound" or something like that?'

'I remember,' said Melville frigidly. 'We'll have to see whether a little gravity at the Exchequer mightn't help after all.'

Lacey drank the brandy quickly, and opened the door, through which they could already hear the voice of the television commentators. A melancholy psephologist with a cowlick was assessing the result as the group gathered round the TV set turned their heads towards Lacey and Melville.

'... the swing of five point four per cent against the Government at Edgeworth,' said the obituary voice, 'shows that the Opposition is still gaining ground. Local unemployment ...'

'Oh, switch it off!' said a woman's voice.

Carson stood watching the programme enigmatically.

'What do you make of it?' he asked the Prime Minister.

'Just a head cold,' said Melville. 'We'll recover.'

Everyone laughed except Lacey, who asked the butler to get him a whisky and soda.

'... the protest vote as I anticipated,' said another commentator on the screen, and Mayland turned the set off.

'You really mustn't be so upset,' said Mrs. Martin in a thin voice. 'Everything goes in threes. This is the second, isn't it?'

Mayland, standing with his back to her, said,

'When the public reads the result tomorrow, Geoffrey, you'll think it was a victory.'

His secretary arrived to tell him that his car was waiting, and with a quick handshake to his host and a comprehensive nod, Melville left.

Mayland went to bed early, and gradually the party broke up, some returning to London and elsewhere, leaving only Lacey, Talbot, and Lady Drayford. Lacey drank whisky steadily, abstractedly, preserving his mood on a plateau of euphoria. Lady Drayford sat on an armchair opposite Talbot and Lacey at ease on the sofa. Lacey had reached the stage when he was conducting a mellow monologue, controlled and rational and unwilling to suffer interruption.

'Yes,' he went on, 'there comes a time when I want to go far away to write my memoirs – far from all that creeping through division lobbies and those dismal faces on the Front Bench and looking at the unsoled shoes of the Opposition. I sometimes feel' -- he smiled with a saintly expression – 'that I'd like to consign arithmetic to the darkest hell, and spend my time reading the Georgian poets – you're too young, Peter, too young – the Georgians are greatly underrated.'

'You look tired,' said Lady Drayford.

'Arithmetic,' said Lacey, sitting up and bending his head forward so that his nose was almost touching hers, 'makes me tired; it doesn't make me sleep.'

'I sleep,' said Talbot, 'as soon as my head touches the pillow.'

'You have an easy conscience,' said Lacey. 'You write and speak about virtue, do you not? That's a splendid vocation.'

'A profession,' said Lady Drayford.

'Yes,' said Lacey sleepily. 'And how is it with Renewal?'

'Renewal,' said Talbot, 'is having its day – rather fast, I suspect.'

'And you, dear boy, like a soldier in action, will then be transferred to other theatres of national activity. ... Yes, a personable young man like you – well, this is the hour when a young man like you dreams – yes, dreams of the future while a – a man of my age must think of the past.'

His chin drooped a little, and as his sadness rose, he reached for his whisky glass to restore the balance of his mood.

'Yes,' he said irrelevantly, 'after ten years – at five minutes' notice.'

He had his hand on the back of the sofa behind Talbot's head, and stroked his hair. Talbot rose quickly and said,

'I think I'll have another drink.'

'Yes,' said Lacey, heaving himself from the sofa and stretching himself to his great height. 'Yes – there is nothing to do, Edwina, but wait for the morning.'

She laughed, and said,

'Things always look worse after a good night's sleep. One can see what's wrong.'

'I will write an Ode to Insomnia,' said Lacey. He walked carefully from the room.

At a quarter-past six the next morning, Talbot was awakened by the sunlight through the window and a tumult of birds. After talking to Edwina for a few minutes about the new political series called Dialogue in which he was to take part weekly with Anthony Guest, the Opposition's best backbench controversialist – Edwina had thought of the programme, insisted on its presentation and nominated the spokesmen – they had set out for a walk to the temple on the other side of the lake; but despite the warm night Edwina had shivered and they had come back and finished the whisky decanter. And at her door, she'd said, 'Stay and talk to me.'

Talbot's head swam, and he closed his eyes. A faint snore awoke him, a sound that trembled at its peak, twittered and glugged before it expired. Edwina lay on her back, her mouth half-open, a map of red veins on her cheeks illuminated by the brilliant light, and one flaccid breast revealed where the sheet had slipped. Talbot looked around the room at the discarded pile of clothes on the floor, the cream silk dress crumpled at the bottom of the bed, the clock with its exposed circular movement, and his own unshaven reflection in the wall looking-glass with its gilt *putti* gambolling on a see-saw.

'Christ!' he said, and averting his face, pulled the sheet over Edwina's naked shoulders. He dressed quickly in his dinner jacket, and cautiously opened the door, looking to right and left down the corridors.

As he was about to turn the door knob of his own room, he heard a scamper of feet and Mayland's brisk voice.

'That's what I like to see. Up before breakfast – ready for a walk.'

Mayland, spruce and closely shaved, was wearing a tweed suit, heavy shoes, and was holding his two Afghan hounds on a leash.

'I always walk for an hour before breakfast. Started in Australia. Had to walk four miles to work. Not in Brisbane. Before then.'

He guided Talbot to the entrance and stood for a few seconds surveying the magnificent, sun-tipped landscape, and ignoring Talbot's dress.

'Let's walk,' he said.

'I think I'd like to ch—' said Talbot.

'Let's not be formal,' Mayland interrupted him. 'There's something I want to discuss with you.'

Talbot looked with distaste at his patent-leather shoes and began to walk. Mayland chose a pathway that led across the farm to Hedley church, rising with its saxon tower above the hillock known as Boadicea's Mount. They met no one on the way but the air was full of a rural polyphony – cocks crowing, machines starting up and cows ruminating – which, combined with the rasp of Mayland's voice, made Talbot feel that his brain was being relentlessly sandpapered. He had only slept for an hour or two and as he stumbled across ruts following Mayland's dapper step, and the exultant dogs, he said aloud,

'Khrushchev dancing the gopak for Stalin.'

'What's that?' said Mayland turning his head.

'Nothing – I was just trying out a phrase for a piece I want to write on Russia.'

'Russia?' said Mayland. 'Leave it alone. No one's really bothered about foreigners. Home affairs. That's when people get interested. If Melville gave more attention to home affairs, he wouldn't have lost Edgeworth. Here, Fariz!'

He called one of the dogs that had started after a sheep, and it came bounding back to him with a guilty and docile air.

'He took it very well,' said Talbot.

'No option,' said Mayland. 'It's like a drought in the outbacks. It's there. It's yours, and you've got to do your best with it. Remember, my boy, what the Psalmist said of the men who turn evil to good. "Who going through the vale of misery use it for a well, They will go from strength to strength." '

'Yes,' said Talbot. They were walking up the flinty side of Boadicea's Mount, and he could feel the sharp stones cutting into his thin soles.

Mayland paused, and looking down on Hedley House, neat as an architect's drawing in the carefully planned landscape, said as if to himself,

' "The Lord Himself is thy keeper; the Lord is thy defence upon thy right hand, So that the sun shall not burn thee by day, neither the moon by night." '

Talbot's shirt was sticking to his back after the exertion of the climb, and his head was reeling, but Mayland with his dried skin seemed unaffected by the long walk.

'Perhaps I ought to get back,' said Talbot.

'In a minute,' said Mayland. They had reached the main road where a man in an estate car had pulled up. When Mayland approached, he got out respectfully and touched his cap.

'Oh, Peter,' said Mayland, 'this is O'Shea, my farm manager – this is Mr. Talbot, one of Her Majesty's Members of Parliament.'

O'Shea, who was wearing a dog-tooth suit and a neat check shirt, looked with bewilderment at Talbot's black tie and silk lapels and dust-caked patent shoes.

'I wanted to see the church,' said Talbot.

'Ah, yes,' said O' Shea. He had heard of white tie and tails at the Vatican, but he'd never thought that Anglicans were quite so ceremonial.

On their return Hunter, who had been watching from his window, came down to greet Mayland. He could see that his employer was in high spirits from the way he allowed the dogs to leap up against him, and from Talbot's scowl.

'Breakfast!' said Mayland, slapping his hands together. 'Kippers! Is the Chancellor up yet?'

'Yes,' said Hunter. 'He left for London about half an hour ago. He made a telephone call and left. Asked me to apologize to you.'

'Oh well, we'll have to do without him. What's the time?'

'Just after eight. He asked me to give you this note.'

Mayland glanced at the envelope that was marked Private and Confidential, and said,

'All right. What are you holding on to it for? Let's have it.'

He began to hum to himself as he started to tear the flap open, and Talbot walked away. Mayland began to read, then remembered that he hadn't brought his glasses with him.

'Read it,' he said to Hunter.

' "My dear Mayland," ' Hunter read, ' "I'm sorry to leave in such an awful rush but I've been recalled to London by urgent affairs. Before leaving, though, I am writing to thank you for your most agreeable hospitality.'

Mayland grunted.

'Is that the lot?'

'No, he goes on, "I wish, however, that I had more grateful news to offer you about the matter we first discussed some months ago. I spoke to the P.M. about it, and he has asked me to tell you – and this must be in the strictest confidence – that my recommendation has not been accepted. I know you will be as disappointed as is

Yours ever,
H.L." '

Hunter finished the letter, and offered it to Mayland, who didn't take it. Instead, addressing the hills and the day that had so suddenly darkened, Mayland said,

'The bastard – the dirty, bloody bastard.'

Fariz had begun to lick his hand, but he flung the dog away from him and half-walking, half-running, went into the house.

CHAPTER SIX

AFTER Questions and the announcement by Brook –
Leader of the House – of the business for the following week,
the Members' Lobby began to fill with M.P.s, who stood in
groups, some arranging pairs, others talking to Lobby Correspondents, while the policemen at the entrance closely scrutin-
ized the traffic of visitors to and from the galleries. At the door
leading to Westminster Hall, a Government Whip sat like a
bonze occasionally challenging Members who seemed about to
leave furtively. No one was greatly concerned with the Public
Service Vehicles (Concessionary Fares) Bill, but the Chief Whip
had sent out a special three-line Whip in view of the Opposition's threat to support some unofficial amendments, put down
by what he called 'backbench headline-hunters'. The disciplin-
ary threat had provoked some muttering among the private
Members, a short leader in the *Daily Express* on the value of
independence, a longer leader in the *Daily Telegraph* on the
merits of loyalty, and a still longer second leader in *The Times*
on 'The Party System'. The Mayland Press, with its headline,
'Backbenchers in Clash', for once seemed irresolute. 'Clash' was
a word without anger, and the Mayland Press took no sides over
the three-line Whip which had frustrated the dissidents.

A small paragraph by Talbot, hidden away near the bottom
of the column, had diverted attention from the Party dispute.

'The Chancellor of the Exchequer's indisposition, which kept
him from the adjournment debate on the Balance of Payments
and Unemployment, was a convenience to the Prime Minister,
who wound up for the Government. But his continued absence
from the House is causing speculation. The question both on
the Government and the Opposition Benches is, "What's become of Lacey?"'

In the Members' Lobby on his way from the Chamber to the
library, Talbot was halted by Budd, who stood in his customary
buttonholing posture with his legs apart and his gaze bracketed
on his target. 'Well, Talbot,' he began in a loud voice, and the
other Members who were crossing the Lobby moved past him

like water around a stone. To be detained by Budd was usually to be involved in at least twenty minutes of free association, souvenirs and ruminations, interspersed with references to petty victories in mediocre skirmishes.

'Well, Talbot,' he said, his eyes invisible behind his glasses, 'that's a bit of a hare you've started.'

'Which one?' said Talbot. 'I'm always starting hares nowadays.'

'Come off it!' said Budd. 'Everyone knows about it.'

'About what?' said Talbot. 'Why am I the last to know? Owen!' he called out to an M.P. who was passing. 'What about a pair on Wednesday?'

Owen Armstrong stopped and fingered the blue scar on his nose.

'I never pair, boy,' he said. 'You ought to know that. What d'you think they pay you for?'

He winked to Budd.

'I've been working overtime,' said Talbot. 'Two morning committees – constituency all last weekend. Come on, Owen.'

'All right,' said Armstrong, grudgingly. 'But it's an exception. What's all this about Lacey?'

'Honestly, I don't know,' said Talbot. 'All I know is that he's cleared off somewhere, and Ormston's been seeing the P.M.'

Budd squared his shoulders, and put his fingers in his waistcoat pocket.

'It reminds me,' he said, 'of the time when I was still in local politics. We had a borough treasurer – a nice lad but he thought he knew the lot. Well, he didn't. He had a chief clerk who was fiddling with the departmental salaries, and at the . . .'

Talbot settled his mind on the fact that in five minutes' time he would see Sylvia in the Central Lobby, and meanwhile he interrupted Budd at appropriate pauses with words like 'Yes, indeed,' and 'Yes . . . yes.'

'. . . they never found him,' Budd ended.

'Of course!' said Talbot.

'Why of course?' said Budd, his mouth tightening.

'Because,' said Talbot, improvising a foothold, 'a politician who wants to disappear can do it more easily than anyone. There's only the Whips who care – and they're always weeks too late when there's no three-liner. Look at Victor Grayson – Trebitsch Lincoln. That other chap who disappeared in Scotland when he got beaten.'

'I know, I know,' said Budd, resenting this encroachment on his historical expertise. 'Took to the hills—'

'Where's Lacey, boy?' said Armstrong. 'That's the point. Where're you hiding him?'

'Melville's given him his cards, if you ask me,' said Budd. 'Five minutes' notice.'

'No,' said Armstrong, suddenly in earnest. 'He wouldn't do it like that. Not Melville.'

'Why not?' said Talbot.

'Well, Peter,' Armstrong answered, 'I've been three years in the House, and I've known Geoffrey Melville nearly all that time. He's one of the straightest men you could ever meet. If he sacked Lacey he wouldn't hide it. He'd come right out with it.'

'I don't see that,' said Talbot, moving towards the brass-grilled doors. 'There might be a gap between getting rid of Lacey and finding someone to put in his place.'

'He'd never have Ormston,' said Budd flatly, and two Lobby Correspondents turned to listen.

'Why not?' Armstrong asked.

'They hate each other,' said Budd. 'When Melville beat him to it for Number Ten, Ormston swore he'd never serve under him. That's why he went to the Lords.'

'He can come back,' said Talbot.

'Like hell he will,' said Budd. 'He'll only come back if he's P.M.'

Brian Guest, an Opposition Whip, joined them near the exit. 'Corrupting the trade union core?' he asked.

'No,' said Talbot, 'we were wondering what's become of Ormston.'

'He was at Number Ten this morning,' said Guest. 'It's on the tape.'

'Taking over from Melville?'

'Not yet,' said Guest. 'The P.M. looked quite happy at the Wallace Collection lunch.'

'He probably got himself a suit of armour,' said Budd.

'With Ormston behind him, he'll need it, boy,' said Armstrong.

'In our Party,' said Talbot, 'we all love one another.'

They laughed, and Talbot thanked the attendant who held the heavy door for him to pass.

Sylvia was already waiting at the barrier, talking to the policeman who with a handful of green cards apologized to her as he interrupted himself to call the names of unavailable Members. Talbot shook hands with her formally, and she said,

'It's very kind of you to see me, Mr. Talbot. I have a problem.'

'Well, let's sit for a moment, and I'll do my best to help you.'

They sat on the green benches in the Gothic lobby, and Talbot said,

'What can I do to help you, Miss – Miss—?'

'Melville.'

'That's it – Melville.'

'I want to take an M.P. for a walk. Do you think I could persuade him to spend an hour with me in St. James's Park?'

'There's only one available, I'm afraid. Will he do?'

'Yes,' said Sylvia. 'He's the only one I want.'

Talbot laughed aloud, and a group of people, waiting as anxiously for their Member as if he were a doctor, turned towards him with severe expressions.

'Did the curtains come?' Sylvia asked.

'Yes,' said Talbot. 'Harrods dumped them this morning, and they're waiting to be hung. I couldn't stay there.'

'You're silly,' said Sylvia. 'If you'd let me have a key I could arrange the whole thing and be there while they're doing the curtains, and the carpets too.'

'I wouldn't bother you—'

'I'd love to,' said Sylvia. 'Oh, do let me!'

'Do you think it would cause a sensation in Hill Street if the P.M.'s daughter—?'

Sylvia framed her mouth in a short, derogatory expression, and Talbot said,

'Don't say it. . . . I'd be terribly glad if you would, darling. And anyhow, I paid the landlord a year's rent in advance.'

'You must be rich.'

'Not a bit,' said Talbot. 'Hunter arranged it all. Mayland advanced me £1,000 for the rent and rates, and £500 for the fittings and another £500 for curtains and carpets. So you see, I'm hooked.'

'Yes, indeed,' said Sylvia reflectively.

'On the other hand,' said Talbot more cheerfully, 'with TV, the column and my Parliamentary salary, I reckon I'll earn this coming year at least £8,000.'

'What about income-tax?'

'Oh, I'll deal with that when it comes.'

'And your mother?'

'Well, I've promised her another £500 a year.'

'Tax free?'

'Oh, yes,' said Talbot lightly.

'In that case, Peter,' said Sylvia, 'you are hooked.'

'Hooked but happy,' said Talbot. 'Will you really take the key?'

'Yes,' she replied.

'Well, Sylvia,' said a ponderous voice, and they both looked up guiltily at Scott-Bower, who stood over them with a censorious expression. 'Your father said – if you have a moment, would you come to his room?'

'How did he know I was here?' Sylvia asked.

'He saw your Mini from the window – it's hard to miss, you know. It stands out in New Palace Yard like a fire-engine. And you know you're not to park there.'

'Come on,' said Sylvia to Talbot. 'Let's go and see him.'

Talbot looked quickly at Scott-Bower and said,

'I don't think your father wants to see me particularly.'

'Indeed he does,' said Scott-Bower. 'He's got something to tell you about your Lacey piece.'

'About the Chancellor?'

'No, about yourself,' said Scott-Bower. 'Perhaps you'll see Sylvia to his room. I've got to get back to the Bench.'

He smiled to Sylvia, and lumbered away.

'I don't think he really likes you,' said Sylvia, watching him go.

'No,' said Talbot. 'Whips like their backbenchers docile. And they hate M.P.-journalists automatically.'

'Why?'

'Why? Because if you're an honest journalist, you're independent. You don't suck up to the Whips. It's simple.'

'Are you independent?'

'Yes,' said Talbot. 'Mayland's pretty tough, but he gives me a free hand. That's what I like about journalism – why I believe

I'm more a journalist than a politician. In politics, it's all black and white. You're either in the Aye Lobby or the No Lobby. In journalism you can see around a subject. And besides, when I speak in the House, my speech is heard by – how many people? If I'm lucky, by a hundred. When I write my column, it's read by five million. When I speak on TV, I'm heard by twelve million more.'

He paused to take breath.

'That's a long speech,' said Sylvia. 'But you've left something out. You may be independent in a sense. But what if you disagree with Mayland?'

'That's like my income tax,' said Talbot. 'I'll deal with it when it comes.'

He changed the subject.

'Do you know what's happened to Lacey?'

'I've no idea.'

'Would you tell me if you knew?'

'Of course I would.'

'Is there anything you wouldn't tell me?'

'I don't know. I haven't been tested. Come on, I want to see daddy.'

When they reached the Prime Minister's room with its simple inscription, Room Number One, Eric Frobisher came out and asked them to wait. Lord Ormston, he explained, had just gone in, and might be with the Prime Minister for half an hour or so.

'Will you tell my father I've an appointment and that I'll see him some other time?'

Frobisher studied her doubtfully, and said,

'I know he's very anxious to see you.'

He knocked at the inner door, and entered. After a few moments he came out, and said,

'This way, please.'

Ormston, standing by the window on the other side of the long green table, turned when he heard Melville greet Sylvia, and said,

'Good afternoon, Sylvia. I insisted on seeing you.'

She smiled to him, and thought what a pleasant man he was with his sad St. Bernard eyes, his solemn voice, and the smile, full of *Weltschmerz*, that occasionally opened in his otherwise monolithic face. She shook hansd with him, and said,

'You know Peter, of course.'

Talbot, who had stood hesitantly at the door, came forward, and Ormston said with a quick chuckle,

'I read him rather than know him.'

Talbot said to the Prime Minister,

'Sylvia—'

'Oh, no,' Melville interrupted him, 'I'm delighted.'

Sylvia said,

'I just wanted to say "hello", daddy. I don't want to keep you.'

Ormston and Melville glanced at each other and then at Talbot, and Melville said,

'You're not keeping us a bit. We're only gossiping. . . . That reminds me, Talbot. Heard anything about Lacey?'

Talbot looked from the dark panelling at Sylvia, who hadn't heard the question and was idly turning the pages of *Fortune*, and from her to Ormston who was wearing an expression of bland interest. Melville himself was unsmiling.

'No, sir,' he said. 'I hoped you might be able to tell me.'

'No,' said Melville, shaking his head. 'We have nothing to tell you – except perhaps that you might care to do the Party a service.'

'How, sir?' Talbot asked.

'By a little reticence. Especially about matters on which you're not fully informed.'

At the new sound in her father's voice, Sylvia looked up from the magazine, and Ormston took his watch from its fob. Talbot flushed, and said,

'I'm at a disadvantage. Perhaps we can continue our talk another time.'

He turned his back on the Prime Minister, and left.

A few seconds later, Sylvia caught him up in the Library Corridor.

'Peter,' she said. 'I'm sorry. It's so unlike him.'

He didn't answer but walked faster, past the Smoking Room and the stuttering tape, through the Central Lobby and into St. Stephen's Hall, with Sylvia stumbling behind him.

'Peter,' she said, 'do say something.'

He paused by the policeman, and said,

'I'd better not. I might get run in.'

'I'm so sorry,' she said again.

He looked into her contrite face, and suddenly he said,
'I've just realized something.'

'What?'

'Don't tell anyone.'

'I don't. What have you just realized?'

'Your father doesn't like me, either.'

They burst out laughing, and together they walked arm-in-arm through Westminster Hall, their laughter echoing over the great flagstones, the Norman walls and the plaques remembering dead kings.

'You were a bit severe, I thought,' said Ormston, extending his legs lazily under the table in the Prime Minister's room.

'Not severe enough,' said Melville. 'The fellow's a concoction – nothing. Mayland decided he wanted a national figure – and that's what he made. You know, Gerald, the problem of modern democracy is to identify where power lies. It's no longer in the hands of the monarch. Parliament makes laws – but under pressures. One man one vote doesn't add up to a democracy. Not when you've got great concentrations of power like Mayland's. Between him and Lady Drayford, they create images for twenty million people every night. Imagine it – twenty million!'

'It's a reality.'

'But it means the end of democracy by suffrage unless it's tamed.'

'Once you start taming, you start caging.'

'Caging what?'

'Well – you know – liberty.'

'Not liberty – tigers.'

'I still think you were hard on Talbot. Do you read his stuff?'

'Yes – it's very ordinary.'

'I think it's very good, Geoffrey. Never mind, we've differed before. If I need help, I'll call for Sylvia.'

Melville picked up the copy of *Fortune* magazine which she had dropped on the floor when Talbot left.

'She's a very determined girl,' said Melville.

'She isn't unlike her father,' said Ormston, lighting a cigarette. 'Has Lacey's letter arrived?'

'This morning. It was very curt.'

'And your reply?'

104

'Rather longer and more friendly. You know – "My dear Henry" – first names – all that.'

'Well, what is the time-table to be?'

'The Chief's outside. Perhaps he can tell us.'

Scott-Bower joined them, and went through the procedure by which Ormston would renounce his peerage and fight the Wendover by-election for which the writ had already been issued, Hibbert, the prospective candidate, having agreed to stand down for Ormston.

'With a majority of 14,000,' he said, 'you can't miss.'

'Not even I,' said Ormston wryly. 'And Hibbert?'

'It's all change,' said the Chief Whip. 'He'll strengthen us in the Lords, as he put it when he volunteered.'

'Why should he want to do that?' said Ormston languidly. 'It really is a mausoleum nowadays. The only advantage of being in the Lords is that you lose your constituents.'

'It's a matter of taste,' said the Chief Whip to Melville. 'He's waiting outside – twenty minutes early.'

'Let him wait,' said Melville. 'I think it's good for their souls to make men like Mayland wait. I think you had something else to say, Gerald.'

'Why, yes,' said Ormston, uncrossing his legs, 'I want an undertaking from you, Geoffrey, that in the event of your retirement for any reason, you will automatically recommend to the monarch that I should succeed you.'

'That,' said Melville calmly, 'is impossible.'

'It would be unconstitutional to give an undertaking of that kind,' said the Chief Whip. 'You know it, Gerald. Apart from that, the whole procedure – you know we want to revise it.'

'There's no procedure – no constitutional objection – only precedents. Precedents are made by Prime Ministers,' said Ormston, his large face pale, his lips hardly moving. 'Three years ago, Collard chose his own precedents from the past and made his own for the future. He chose you, Geoffrey. He left you like a legacy to the nation. That's all I'm asking you to do.'

Melville stood and walked to the window. Then he turned, standing in silhouette against the leaded lights, and smiled.

'I'm feeling singularly well, Gerald. I wouldn't want to disappoint you.'

'I must explain to you,' said Ormston unsmilingly, 'what I'm asking isn't for myself. Not for myself at all. It's for Cynthia.

She suffered greatly three years ago. I don't want her ever to go through those anxieties again.'

'Of course, of course,' said Scott-Bower hurriedly. 'But quite apart from the proprieties, it wouldn't make for a happy situation. A sort of blank cheque—'

'Only for this Parliament,' said Ormston doggedly. 'I'm sorry.'

He rose, and Melville and Scott-Bower rose reluctantly too.

'I don't want you to feel any sort of obligation, Geoffrey,' said Ormston, walking heavily to the door. 'You've got a lot of very good younger men in the Government – perhaps lacking a little in experience here and there. But they'll learn. The Chancellor of the Exchequer has often been a youngish man. I'll understand if that's how you want to do it. And you can count on my support. From the Peers' Gallery.'

He nodded to Melville and Scott-Bower, and left.

'It's impossible,' said Melville when the door closed behind him.

'You're in very good health,' said the Chief Whip, 'and as you said, it's good for their souls to make some people wait. It's only another two years or so.'

'He'll become a nuisance.'

'We'll deal with that when it happens. At the moment, there's a hell of a leak in the boat. Does it really matter what name we give the bung?'

'The Bung,' said the Prime Minister in a bright voice. 'We will give him the public title of Deputy Prime Minister. To you and me, he'll be the Bung.'

'That should satisfy everyone,' said the Chief Whip.

When Mayland entered the room, the Prime Minister was sitting formally at the head of the long table. He rose, waved Mayland to an armchair on his right, and said to Frobisher who had introduced him,

'I don't want to be disturbed, Eric, for the next half-hour.'

'I won't keep you that long,' said Mayland as the Private Secretary withdrew. 'My business is very brief.'

He tugged at the cuffs of his brilliantly white shirt, exposing his gold links. When he spoke, he spoke hurriedly, looking at a point a little to the side of Melville who, putting both hands on the desk, watched Mayland steadily.

'I needn't tell you,' Mayland began, 'that Lacey's letter was a great disappointment to me.'

'Which letter?' Melville asked. 'He's been writing quite a few letters in the last few days.'

'I am only concerned with one,' said Mayland. 'He wrote to me before he left Hedley House that his recommendation – his recommendation of me for an honour which I have long looked forward to – I'll make no bones about it – has been turned down.'

He waited for Melville to speak, but he was silent.

'I haven't come here,' said Mayland, 'to ask for favours. If ever political services meant anything, I can say that for the last thirty years I've helped the Party – supported it with my newspapers, backed Ministers when they were in trouble, helped politicians by giving them jobs – do you disagree, Mister Prime Minister?'

Melville didn't answer. Mayland waited a moment; then he said, 'The answer's self-evident. . . . My reward for this is a snub. Why?'

Melville picked up a desk calendar which was out of date, and rolled the cylinder till the month and the day were accurate.

'First of all,' he said, 'I want you to know that we value what you've done. I'll go farther and say that no single person in the world of journalism has done more for the Party than you yourself. You've instructed the middle classes – you've created their political mood. We are deeply grateful.'

Mayland now looked at him fixedly, his pale blue eyes like glass marbles.

'I had hoped,' said Melville '—it was on my own initiative – I wanted you in the Lords. It would have been right and fitting for you to be there with the others. I wanted it.'

Mayland sat rigid, only his jaw muscles moving.

'I put your name up in the usual way according to the Privy Council rules. It went to the Honours Scrutiny Committee, and I'm telling you this in the strictest confidence. They recommended against it.'

'Why?'

Melville hesitated, and Mayland said,

'I'd rather have it straight.'

'It isn't as simple as that,' said the Prime Minister. 'It would be at least unusual if I were to answer your question.'

'In that case,' said Mayland, his face parchment dry, 'let it be unusual.'

Melville took up a file that lay in front of him, and opened it at a red tab.

'The Honours Scrutiny Committee – you know its membership – it's an all-Party body, and its job is to see that there is no impropriety in the award of an honour.'

'I've offered nothing except myself,' said Mayland.

'The Committee has also to consider – if I can put it that way – the character of the candidate.'

Mayland looked him full in the eyes.

'Is mine in doubt?'

The Prime Minister glanced at the tabbed page, and said, closing the file,

'I'm afraid that the Committee has taken an adverse view of your trial and conviction at Broken Hill.'

Mayland stood up, and said,

'That's an old, dead story. It was a conviction based on a perjury by a man I sacked. It was a tainted case, tried by a corrupt judge with a verdict by a bribed jury. I'm telling you, Melville, it was the most vicious mistrial known to justice – a travesty. And I was its victim. Are you telling me that over forty years after this – this miscarriage – you're going to hold it against me?'

'I'm not holding it against you,' said Melville. 'The Committee can't reject a nomination, but equally I can't ignore its advice.'

'But you can ask them to reconsider it,' said Mayland. 'You can send it back to them. I know each one of them – Benchley, Fox, and Grantham – I know them personally. They've stayed at Hedley. You send it back to them. I'll talk to them.'

His voice had become plaintive.

'I'm afraid not,' said Melville, putting his fingertips together. 'I can't do it.'

'Why not?' said Mayland.

'Because,' Melville said slowly, 'they've made an independent recommendation. That's what they're there for. Because you're a friend of mine and they of you – I can't for that reason – perhaps specially for that reason – interfere. I'm terribly sorry, Mayland – I really am.'

'Are you saying,' said Mayland, 'that because a man at some

time in his life – in my early youth – got involved in a misdemeanour, innocently or even guiltily, that in your judgment he should for ever after carry it like an albatross through his life – never able to stand erect, always to be pointed at however much he seeks redemption?'

Big Ben chimed the hour, and Melville paused till the trembling tones faded away.

'I don't say that,' he answered. 'I'm only saying that the Honours Scrutiny Committee has terms of reference, settled by the Privy Council, and makes recommendations. I can't ignore them.'

The Prime Minister felt that the interview had gone on too long, and he stood. Mayland continued to sit, absorbed in some inward reflection.

'Tell me, Mister Prime Minister,' he said, 'if you could have ignored them, would you have done so?'

Melville studied the thin, hunched-up figure with a distaste which he tried to hide.

'I would always wish to help my friends,' he said.

Mayland smiled to himself and stood up, slowly uncoiling till he seemed almost the same height as the Prime Minister, who wondered that a few seconds earlier the newspaper proprietor had seemed so small and shrivelled.

'Well, that's it,' he said. 'I understand, Melville. I understand. I'm obliged to you for this explanation – yes, very grateful. I wanted to know the background, and I won't trouble you again.'

'No trouble,' said Melville.

'Oh, I wouldn't go as far as that,' said Mayland. 'No one's without his troubles, least of all a Prime Minister. We'll have to see. . . . It was a great ambition of mine to be a peer – always wanted it when I was in Australia.'

'I'm sorry,' said Melville in a mumble. 'Perhaps next year—'

'Yes,' said Mayland, smiling now as he went towards the door. 'Other times – other people. Thank you, Mister Prime Minister. Very good of you to have taken the time.'

After Mayland had gone, Melville stood at his window watching the manoeuvres of the cars in New Palace Yard. The division bell began to shrill, insistent as a fire-alarm, and from the corridor the policeman bellowed a quadrisyllabic 'Di – vish – i – on!'

Frobisher came into the room, and said,
'Division, sir. Will you vote?'
'Yes,' said Melville. 'How did Mayland look when he left?'
'Well,' said Frobisher, 'he seemed to be smiling.'
Melville straightened his tie thoughtfully.

CHAPTER SEVEN

WHEN the letters between the former Chancellor of the Exchequer and the Prime Minister were published, the Political Correspondents wrote about Lacey as if he were already dead. But whereas obituary notices tend to dilute truth with charity, the comment on Lacey, who in his time had made many enemies with his booming asides in the Smoking Room and his indiscretions at the private dinners with his acolytes in Dining Room A, was uncompromising. 'Vox et praeterea nihil', said one weekly. 'The caricature outlived the statesman,' said another. 'Gone?' said a Government Whip. 'Thank God!'

Even the question 'What's become of Lacey?' lost its interest. He was variously reported as having been seen at the country houses of friends, sinking with his brandy into meditation or slurred monologue, as having gone for a retreat, and as having entered the City. Ormston's return, on the other hand, had been canvassed so widely that his appointment was regarded as natural and his victory at the by-election as inevitable. On a rising political market, his original decision not to serve under Melville had been a reason for regret rather than despair, since after the Party's adequate victory at the General Election, only a few sophisticated commentators wondered what might have happened if Ormston had been second in command. But the more recent decline in the Government's fortunes under Lacey as Chancellor had given rise to a Bring-Back-Ormston Movement among some of the younger backbenchers. Hitherto, Melville had frigidly ignored them, carefully overlooking the Ormstonites when he made a minor Government shuffle earlier in the year. Now, in the reorganization that followed Lacey's departure, he had ostentatiously dropped the Financial and Economic Secretaries – the Chancellor's Castor and Pollux someone had called them – and replaced them at Ormston's suggestion with two well-known Ormstonites.

The summer was particularly hot, and after a flurry of interest in the changes the country settled down to its familiar seasonal interests. A remarkable Australian cricketer, Alan

Cockburn, had made four centuries in four successive innings, and taken possession of the front-page headlines. A British girl had reached the Wimbledon finals. Two British runners had nearly won Gold Medals in a European tournament. And the unemployment figures had shown a slight drop in anticipation of Ormston's policy of reducing Bank Rate. Distracted from politics, waiting impatiently for its summer holidays, the nation absorbed the Parliamentary changes and forgot them.

At the first editorial conference of the Mayland Press after Ormston's appointment and runaway victory at the Wendover by-election, the editor, Colson, said,

'We'll continue with our general support of the Government, putting special emphasis on the part that Ormston's going to play.'

'Why?' asked the Diplomatic Correspondent.

'Because the Old Man says so,' said Colson. He shrugged his shoulders, and added,

'But there's a lot to be said for it. Ormston's Deputy Prime Minister. He's in business again. Melville's taking a chance. What d'you think, Peter?'

'I don't think he's taking a chance,' said Talbot, strangling a yawn – he had been up late dancing with Sylvia at a club in King Charles Street. 'Melville wouldn't have him within a mile if he didn't need him. My guess is that once we've got unemployment below half a million, Ormston will gradually be pushed out.'

As he spoke, he saw the sceptical relaxed faces around him suddenly change, and the editor, who had been sucking his pipe, put it down with an expression at once defensive and deferential. To Talbot's surprise everyone rose, but when he glanced over his shoulder, he rose too.

'No, no,' said Mayland, who had entered quietly on his rubber heels. 'Don't disturb yourselves, gentlemen. I've only dropped in for a few minutes.'

He took a chair near the door, and waited for the discussion to continue.

'We were on general policy,' said Colson.

'Ah, yes,' said Mayland.

'I was saying – there's to be no change. Except that we'll concentrate a bit on the new Chancellor.'

There was a pause.

'Yes,' said Mayland.

'And then,' Colson said, groping for ideas which always deserted him in Mayland's inhibiting presence, 'we'll do something about – the Chancellor and Renewal?'

He ended his statement interrogatively. Again a pause with every face turned to Mayland.

'No,' said Mayland at last. 'We've done enough on Renewal – given it a good send-off – that'll do, I think.'

'Well, now that we've seen Renewal off,' said Talbot, and the news editor turned a giggle into a cough, 'what's our next theme?'

'You're too intellectual, Talbot,' Mayland said sharply. 'On our newspapers, we don't deal in themes. We deal in news. We'll have a word later.'

He sat in silence till shortly afterwards the editorial conference expired, and with relief its members pushed back their chairs and left. Colson, Talbot, and Mayland remained.

'I want the emphasis to be shifted,' said Mayland.

'How d'you mean?' Colson asked, stuffing his pipe.

'I want the paper to concentrate on Ormston. How well do you know him, Peter?'

'Hardly at all.'

'Good. You'll be able to approach him without bias. He's a big man, remember that. You were wrong, you know, Colson, not to have given him more help when Collard was dying – very wrong.'

Colson took his pipe out of his mouth in astonishment.

'But—' he began.

'Never mind "but",' said Mayland, frowning. 'You were wrong as hell.'

'But you yourself—'

'That's all over now,' Mayland continued, waving his objections aside. 'Get Peter to write a piece about him – about his family life. It's very wholesome, I believe. Let's have a few leaders about welcome changes. I want to see his name appearing as the strong man of the Government – the man with the firm grip.'

'I was told the other day,' said Talbot, 'that the P.M. calls him the Bung.'

'The what?' said Mayland.

'The Bung,' said Talbot. 'All the old anti-Ormstonites are

calling him that. It only started the other day. Most curious. It's spreading like a limerick.'

'The Bung,' Mayland repeated. 'That's a very unpleasant description. Nicknames can be very cruel. When I was a schoolboy, I had a teacher who used to call me Mayfly. I never forgave him. He had mean eyes, and was called T. B. Jones. We called him Tibby. Bung! That's very unkind of Melville. But then, Melville's not a very kind man. Perhaps later on, Colson – yes, it'll make an amusing gossip piece for our Charles Chesterfield column. ... The Bung! Yes – full of disagreeable associations. How's the flat, my boy?'

'Oh, it's coming along very well,' said Talbot. 'I'm counting on your coming to the house-warming – just sherry, of course.'

'I've noted it,' said Mayland with a warm smile. 'And by the way, I enjoyed your programme the other night, although a pretty young woman sitting next to me said you're handsomer in the flesh.'

Talbot felt a twinge where the flints on Boadicea's Mount had cut into one of his feet, and said,

'Well, actually, I am.'

Colson grunted, and Mayland said,

'All right, Peter, let's have a good piece on Ormston. A bit of human interest – get a cat or dog in it. And next time, we'll give you a rather bigger picture.'

When he had gone, Mayland turned to Colson and said,

'What do you think of him?'

'Not bad,' said Colson.

'Are they reading his column?'

'Well, yes – but it's chiefly a kind of overshot from his TV. He's good on TV.'

'Is he useful?'

Colson sucked his pipe.

'Yes,' he said. 'He's very useful. He gets everywhere. And he's friendly with Sylvia Melville.'

Mayland sat in an armchair and said,

'That's interesting. When you say "friendly" – what do you mean?'

'Friendly,' said Colson. 'Just that. They go about together. Nothing more.'

'She's a funny girl,' said Mayland.

'Yes, she is. But since she's known Talbot, I'm told she's not as funny as she was.'

'That's just as well,' said Mayland. He looked at his watch.

'Don't forget a picture of a morning coat or two from the Palace tomorrow. The English like them.'

Colson grunted again. One day, he thought, before he resigned, he would do a whole front page on Mayland himself.

Walking down from the top floor, Talbot stopped at the Circulation Department and picked up a lunch edition of the evening paper. He liked its fresh smell, appropriate to the vigour and constant movement in the Mayland Building, which never failed to excite him. He glanced quickly at the cartoon, which showed a cheerful Ormston squeezing into a seat next to a reluctant Melville on an otherwise empty Front Bench. The caption was a quotation from *King Henry IV*, Part I. 'A certain Lord, neat, and trimly dress'd, fresh as a bridegroom . . .'

Talbot read the first paragraph of the leading article, entitled 'Early Days'.

'The reconstructed Government starts with a signal advantage. It now has a co-pilot to meet the emergency caused by a year of drift. To charge a former Chancellor of the Exchequer with the whole responsibility of our present difficulties would be to detract from the part which the Prime Minister has played in the conduct of affairs, both at home and overseas. His energy is undoubted. He deserves the credit which he has won in his successful handling of employers and trade unionists in the recent months of industrial tension. But the flip-side of praise must be censure for his failure to require the necessary measures to close the trade gap and arrest the creeping inflation, revealed in a Commons question yesterday, which confirmed that the value of the £ has depreciated since last year by . . .'

Talbot stopped reading, and left the paper on a table in the entrance hall before he went into the street. The lunch edition was usually a pacemaker for the Mayland Press. If the public caught up with an idea, it was 'on'. If not, it was usually dropped. Its gossip columns also trailed innuendoes, sometimes sensational although disingenuously presented, which could be renounced if they caused too much trouble, or developed if the victim quailed. What Talbot couldn't understand was why the evening paper should attack Melville so sharply when only half

115

an hour earlier Mayland had spoken of support for the Government. Talbot frowned at the sunlight in the street. He had spent several days working on an article dealing with desalination and the United Nations. Melville had made a speech on the subject at the Guildhall the previous week, and grudgingly at first and then enthusiastically, Talbot had re-read it, studied its significance and concluded that there was no single enterprise which could more dramatically bring food and peace to the arid lands of the Middle East. The article which he had written paid tribute to Melville for his advocacy; but if the tone of the leader meant anything it wasn't going to be plain sailing with Mayland.

Walking in the direction of the Law Courts, Talbot wondered if he shouldn't be more neutral about Melville. He could praise the plan and leave out the Prime Minister. But even as he thought of doing so, he felt an impulse of shame. 'The Prime Minister's brave project, as imaginative as the Marshall Plan, but more lasting if it is realized . . .' He liked what he had written. 'To hell with Mayland!' he said aloud, and an approaching typist seeing his lips moving stepped apprehensively off the pavement.

'You're late!' said Sylvia, greeting him on the steps of St. Martin's. Talbot bent forward two inches, kissed her on the cheek, and inhaled her scent.

'I like it,' he said. 'What is it?'

'*Sorcière*,' she replied. 'I got it in New York.'

'Are you having an American day?' he asked jealously.

She put her arm through his, and laughed.

'Yes,' she said. 'I feel happy. I always think it so extraordinary how summer bursts out – even through all that cement.'

They were passing a building site, where side by side with the ruins crumbling under the hammers and drills of a demolition squad, a chestnut-tree, powdered with stone dust, still asserted itself.

'What's that to do with America?' he asked.

'Nothing in particular,' she answered. 'Except that it reminded me of a Museum I knew there – they were rebuilding it, and the trees in the street were always – like this.'

Her voice trailed away, and they walked on in silence till they reached Admiralty Arch.

'Let's walk through the Park,' he said, watching her absorbed face.

'Yes,' she said.

'You look like a girl with a secret.'

'No, there's nothing,' she replied. 'Really nothing at all.'

After a few moments, she said,

'Well, there is something I want to tell you.'

Talbot waited for her to continue.

'I had a phone call this morning – from New York.'

'Oh, yes,' said Talbot. 'And who was that from?'

She hesitated, unwilling to say what he had already guessed, reluctant to make his face deepen in its expression of unhappiness and displeasure.

'I had a call from Cullen.'

She used his surname to lessen the familiarity, to subdue the delight that surged up like water in a lock at the evocation of the face, the voice, the person shut away in the past and now restored to her present. He had telephoned her from New York the previous night when she had come back to her rooms, happily escorted from the theatre by Talbot. ('Will Miss Melville accept a call from Mr. Cullen speaking from New York?' the operator said, and she replied, 'Oh, yes – yes.')

'Where is he?' Talbot asked casually.

'In New York.'

A group of passers-by recognized Sylvia, and muttered to each other as they passed. Talbot bumped into one, and forgot to apologize.

'Rude sod!' said a following voice.

'What did he want?' Talbot asked.

'He's coming to England.'

Talbot put his hand through his hair to occupy a few moments of time 'You'll see him?' he asked.

'Yes – he wanted to see me. That's why he rang.'

'Is that a good reason for seeing him?'

'No.' Sylvia dragged the word out. 'No. I want to see him myself – to see if I want to see him.'

'That's a very good reason,' said Talbot. 'You'll let me know, won't you, when you'll be occupied?'

'Of course,' she said. 'He's arriving on Thursday.'

'Are you going to the airport to meet him?'

He stopped, and faced her hostilely.

'Don't be silly,' said Sylvia, walking on.

'Well, are you?'

'No,' she answered. 'Anyhow, what would it matter?'

They walked into Whitehall without speaking. At the door of No. 10 Downing Street, Sylvia said,

'Now, don't forget. After tea tomorrow by the bandstand. Not the one on the right. The one on the left.'

She took his hand, and he withdrew it.

'I hope you enjoy your lunch,' he said.

The policeman at the door eyed them with curiosity, unable to decide why two such unofficial-looking people should be dawdling as if to say goodbye.

'It's so strange,' Sylvia said. 'This is the first time I've lunched here since I've been back.'

She smiled to him.

'You know, Peter, I'm nervous.'

'Why?'

She lowered her face.

'I always feel so ill at ease with my mother.'

'Perhaps you're at fault,' he said.

'Yes,' she said abruptly. 'Perhaps I am. Goodbye, Peter.'

An attendant opened the door before she could knock, and the policeman, hearing her addressed by name, saluted.

In the evening, after a train journey made irritating by an engine breakdown which added an hour to the time-table, Talbot arrived in his constituency, too late to have dinner in comfort though abnormally punctual for his political 'surgery'. Captain Walker, his agent, was waiting on the platform to greet him with a schedule of his engagements, and complaints about the Executive Committee, and charges of discrimination by the local Press. Talbot listened with half an ear as they walked to the Association's headquarters.

'Have you time for a drink?' Walker asked. He had been waiting a long time, and his thirst showed in his flushed face.

'No, thanks,' said Talbot. 'I think we'd better get on with the interviews. What are they like tonight?'

'Some of the regulars, I'm afraid,' said Walker. 'A few cranks, a housing case, a couple of pension cases, usual sort of stuff.'

'All right,' said Talbot, taking his seat behind the large table in the sparsely furnished room. 'Show 'em in!'

For the next hour, he listened to the problems of men and women, some of whom came in timidly, others arrogantly, some who spoke diffidently, others garrulously, some who were fervent, others evasive, some with genuine grievances, others with bogus claims, all of them exacting attention, seeking an immediate sympathy and comprehension, and all demanding hope. He had already learnt to diagnose from the way in which his constituents came into the room something about the merits of their cases; these were usually in inverse ratio to the brashness of their approach. He also had learnt to identify the paranoiacs by the manner in which they fixed him with their gaze before depositing their heavy dossiers on his table.

The clock in front of him stood at 7.30, and he had made his final notes on what he thought was his last constituent, a widow who was anxious about a pension claim, when Walker said, 'One more,' and ushered in a man who, without removing his bowler hat, pulled up a chair and stared at Talbot. 'See you upstairs!' said Walker cheerfully, and left the room.

Talbot examined the burly figure in front of him, the expressionless but preoccupied eyes and the powerful hands clasped together on the table, and then looked at the door which Walker had closed solidly behind him.

'What can I do for you'? Talbot asked. For about five seconds, the man didn't answer. Then he said,

'You will forgive me if I don't take my hat off. As long as I have it on, I'm inaccessible to them.'

Talbot leaned back in the chair. He had often had similar conversations.

'May I ask your name, sir?' he said.

'No,' said his constituent, looking up suspiciously. 'My immunity depends on my anonymity.'

('That's very good,' Talbot said to himself. 'I must remember it.')

'What,' he said aloud, 'is your problem?'

'I take it,' said his constituent, 'that you believe in spiritual forces.'

'I do,' said Talbot. ('And come to think of it,' he thought, 'I do.')

'You realize, don't you, that some are malign and some benign?'

'Yes.'

Talbot watched his fingers whiten with the effort of concentration. The man's voice became intimate.

'At night,' he said, 'I have to sleep with a head covering to exclude them. My life is a fight to elude them.'

He fell into silence. Talbot waited. The man picked up a heavy metal ruler from the table, and Talbot watched his hands curl around its sharp edges.

'We'll have to do something about it,' Talbot said, and he noticed with displeasure that his voice had risen a few notes.

'I want you to write to the Queen,' the man said firmly. 'We must destroy them.'

He slapped the ruler on the table, and Talbot's papers danced. Upstairs he could hear the Executive Committee assembling, the laughter, and occasionally Walker's voice.

'We must destroy them,' his constituent repeated, his eyes never leaving Talbot's face. Then suddenly, 'You're not in with them, are you?'

'No, no,' said Talbot hurriedly. 'I like your idea of writing to the Queen.'

'But you won't give her my name?' the man said, leaning across the table.

'Better if I don't,' said Talbot. His left hand had begun to quiver, and he put it in his pocket.

'Thank you,' said his constituent, relaxing. 'You see—' he half-removed his hat so that Talbot could see his bald head – 'this makes it easier for them.'

He rose, putting down the ruler, and said,

'I'll come again – when you get the answer from the Queen.'

'I'll let you know,' said Talbot. His constituent shook hands with him till Talbot felt the bones crunching. After he left, Walker entered the room.

'Everything all right?'

'No,' Talbot said, breathing deeply. 'Don't go off and leave me with loonies again.'

'Loonies?' said Walker in surprise. 'One in ten of us is a loony. You depend on them for your majority. . . . Seriously, Peter – they are people too.'

Talbot looked at Walker again – at the mottled face of the confirmed free-loader whom he had always thought of as part of the drab, informal apparatus of a political headquarters – to see if he was in earnest. Walker's face had a dignified gravity which Talbot had never noticed before.

'You're perfectly right,' he said. 'I'm sorry. If that chap comes in again, try and get his name.'

'Two more waiting outside,' said Walker.

Talbot's television fame had attracted an exceptionally large attendance of the Executive Committee. Mrs. Geraldine Rivers introduced him to her twenty-six-year-old daughter Susannah, and Mrs. Morton who took the chair said that the constituency was proud of his outstanding work at Westminster. She mentioned in passing that his weekly column was also 'rather good'. Talbot was warmly applauded for his Parliamentary report, and when the chairman asked for questions, only Hartley Maclean rose.

'Could the Member tell us,' he asked, 'whether in the present state of the Party he's an Ormstonite or a Melvillite?'

'Neither,' said Talbot, rising quickly with his Constituency Smile. 'I'm a neutralite.'

To his surprise, the improvisation was received with ecstatic laughter, and repeated from mouth to mouth at the end of the meeting. It confirmed his view that in politics it is often better to be quick than accurate.

CHAPTER EIGHT

THE ceremonial part of the afternoon was over. Melville and Elizabeth had walked dutifully behind the Queen while the Chamberlains plucked guests fit for presentation from the long hedges of onlookers; and they had taken tea in the Royal Pavilion with the Diplomatic Corps. A breeze had sprung up, blowing away a menacing rain-cloud, stirring the *saris* and making the women hold their hats as they moved over the lawns. The Guards band played 'Oh, What a Beautiful Morning' with a punctilious gaiety, and the guests, flagging from the exertions of following the monarch and queueing for tea, revived like a resting regiment at a bugle-call.

Melville and Elizabeth came from behind the trellis of the Royal compound through the crowd which had gathered at its entrance to glimpse the Royal Family at tea, and which parted as they appeared. The Prime Minister raised his grey hat, the men returned his salute, and Elizabeth smiled amiably all around her. She was wearing a large white hat and a blue dress, and Melville thought to himself that he had never seen his wife look so pretty. She belonged to the small number of women whose faces are unsuited to youth but appropriate to middle age, so that while in their adolescence and early womanhood they seem plain, they grow attractively into their faces. Her light brown hair, now flecked with grey, had a colour which other women of her age tried to achieve with artifice. Her small face, too featureless for her twenties, had remained unchanged with the years; she looked young among her contemporaries. Her figure was distinguished in her forties because while others had thickened or become angular, she had remained with the unremarkable figure of her youth. During the three years of his premiership Elizabeth, despite her official duties, had managed to live a quieter, more subdued life than when he had been Minister of Commonwealth Relations and Colonial Affairs. It reflected itself in her clear eyes, her steady voice.

'What are you looking at?' she asked when they had got away from the crowd.

'You,' he said. 'You're looking exceptionally nice.'

'Oh, no,' she said. 'I always look a mess.'

She began to wipe an imaginary strand from her forehead, and Melville guided her away from the Lord Chancellor whom he saw trying to break out of a small knot of lawyers and their wives.

'Didn't you think Sylvia looked wonderful?' she went on hurriedly. 'I had the most dreadful trouble persuading her to wear a hat, but when she put it on, she adored it. Don't you think blue suits her?'

'Yes, I do,' said Melville.

'And she's been so happy today. So unlike the way she was only a month or two ago. If only she could keep it up!'

Melville gravely raised his hat to a couple of backbenchers and their wives, discouraging any attempt to engage him in conversation.

'Do you think she's in love with that young man Talbot?' she asked.

'I really don't know,' Melville answered. 'Sylvia doesn't consult me on those matters.'

'Of course not,' said Elizabeth, afraid that she had said something to disturb her husband's relaxed mood. 'I wish she would. You've got such excellent judgment.'

'I'm not sure I have,' said Melville. 'Not about Sylvia's young men, at any rate. I'm afraid I've been rather rough with Talbot.'

'You don't like him.'

'No,' said Melville thoughtfully. 'I don't dislike him – he's got ability – but I have the feeling with that young man that he's on the make. Anyone who works for Mayland is automatically on the make.'

'I'm afraid I don't see that,' said Elizabeth.

'Well,' said Melville, 'Mayland pays his people to be his dog-bodies. All he's interested in is power, and he'll use anyone to get it and practise it. Anyone who works for him – even if he has an illusion that he's given a free hand – automatically degrades himself.'

'Do you think Sylvia sees him like that?' Elizabeth asked. She put her question meekly, unwilling to challenge his dogmatism.

'If she doesn't,' said Melville, 'she's – well, more stupid than I think.'

Elizabeth began to laugh, but she saw that Melville was frowning.

'There's a certain pattern of behaviour in ambitious young men that I don't like,' he went on. 'If Talbot had chosen to work for Mayland, I could have forgiven him. But to chase the Prime Minister's daughter on top of it, that's really too much.'

This time he laughed, and Elizabeth joined in, their private laughter drawing the attention and the friendly smiles of those around them till they seemed the radiant hub of a happy circle.

Sir Charles Hamilton-Browne, the chairman of the Backbenchers' Committee, approached with his wife, and the Prime Minister and Elizabeth greeted them. Hamilton-Browne had entered the House at the same time as Melville, but, more of a squire than a politician, he had steadfastly refused office and only reluctantly allowed himself to be elected chairman of the Committee. With a smile of general friendliness fixed on a bucolic face which always seemed inappropriate in the chandeliered corridors of Westminster, Hamilton-Browne was respected without being loved. But at times of crisis in the Party, he was always one of the small college invited to make decisions.

'Joanna,' said Elizabeth eagerly to his wife. 'It's donkey's years since I've seen you. Where've you been?'

'He keeps me in purdah in Surrey,' said Lady Hamilton-Browne, looking affectionately at her husband. 'He only lets me out from six to eight—'

'In the morning, of course,' said Hamilton-Browne.

'—to pick mangolds. It's very hard being a farmer's wife. When are you going to reopen your house in Berkshire?'

'That's for my old age,' Melville replied.

Elizabeth and Joanna began to talk about their friends, and Hamilton-Browne drew the Prime Minister aside.

'It was an uncomfortable meeting, Geoffrey,' he said.

'Why?'

'Well, I thought all that Ormstonite nonsense was over. Gore and his little lot seemed to have settled down in their cave. With Gerald in the Lords, I felt we'd holed up our badger.'

'What happened yesterday?'

'Nothing actually happened. It was the mood. They wanted a Cabinet Committee with Ormston in overall charge dealing with all home affairs.'

'It's approximately what I intended,' said Melville.

'Yes,' said Hamilton-Browne, digging his umbrella uncomfortably into the turf. 'But there's more to it than that. There were some rather critical speeches about you receiving that deputation from the T.U.C.'

'Why shouldn't I have received it?'

'They argued – some of them, anyhow – that you ought to leave the Departmental Ministers some scope – that this was a matter for the Minister of Labour – or for the Chancellor. Ormston told me he'd had a letter from Mayland telling him that he intended to write an attacking leader on the point tomorrow.'

'Why didn't Ormston tell me?'

'He only told me twenty minutes ago.'

Melville straightened himself, and laughed.

'Well,' he said, 'we'll have to carry on in the assumption that an attack by Mayland helps.'

'That's comforting, Geoffrey. But is it true?'

'I don't know,' said Melville more seriously. 'It's good enough to go on with.'

'What's biting Mayland?' Hamilton-Browne asked. 'I always thought you two got on well together.'

'Mayland's had a disappointment,' said Melville.

'I see,' said Hamilton-Browne.

In the centre of the lawn, Ormston and his wife were holding a private court that distracted attention even from the royal progress through the untidy lines of onlookers. Already a national figure, Ormston, whose short and dramatic campaign at the by-election had been reported in detail on television and followed on the front pages of every newspaper, had been promoted into a national idol by his victory, his renunciation of his peerage and his bold return. His melancholy, jowly face had been taken to the viewers' hearts as if he had been a sad-eyed boxer dog with pendent flews. His ambiguities and equivocations, once known as Ormstonisms, began a genre. 'I don't say I am, but I don't say either that I am not, that is to say, not in present circumstances', was his first Parliamentary reply, delivered with his familiar, tight-mouthed expression, which convulsed the House, the Parliamentary Gallery and, in a lesser degree, the nation. What had once seemed inept now seemed endearing. His portentous and muddled pronouncements had now become sibylline sayings. His refusal to serve after his defeat by Melville and his withdrawal from active Party politics, once described as disloyal, were now called dignified, statesmanlike and generous towards Melville, whom he had allegedly declined to overshadow. Lady Ormston, who had reverted to being plain Mrs. Ormston, was somewhat confused by Melville's summons to her husband, especially as she had referred to the new Prime Minister in a careless comment to a friendly journalist as 'a hopeless choice' and to Her Majesty's neglect of her own husband as 'a major bloomer'. She hadn't been quite sure if her husband had slipped on a snake or climbed up a ladder when he told her that he had been offered the Chancellorship. But today, observing with pride how the politicians – Stour-Benson, Haslet, Louise Manley, Forbes, Lockhart and many others – surrounded him with a deference he hadn't known before he went to the Lords, she felt that Gerald had made the right decision. He always did. Deputy Prime Minister. She looked across the lawns at the loyal retinue. Ladies and Gentlemen in Waiting. She caught her husband's eye, and he smiled to her. Prime Minister in Waiting. She liked the idea. Gerald was fifty-nine, not many years older than Melville, but he was very fit. She reflected. Yes, very fit.

Mayland, followed by Hunter and Mrs. Ellen Martin, with her face made up in the manner of the 1920s and wearing a black lace dress, a floppy picture hat and carrying a white parasol, approached Ormston and said,

'My congratulations, Gerald. That was a nice one yesterday. A four through the slips.'

'If they send down fast ones, they must expect it,' said Ormston. 'Morrow should know better than to ask for detailed costs of rocket fuel. They really are inept! Will you be at the third Test?'

'I hope so,' said Mayland.

'I'll try and take a couple of hours at the weekend. Perhaps I can join you.'

'Delighted,' said Mayland. 'But I must warn you – in cricket I'm bi-partisan.'

'Yes,' said Ormston. 'I keep forgetting you're an Australian.'

'Oh, I've been a British citizen for many years,' said Mayland. 'But I still feel sentimental about the past. You got my letter?'

'Yes,' said Ormston, drawing him a little away. 'I must tell you frankly, though you'll understand why I can't say this in public, I very much agree with you. The P.M. said when he came to power that his office would be open to everyone. It sounded all right at the time. Anyhow, there were so many people who felt they had the right to collect.'

'Quite so!' said Mayland. 'Quite so!'

'I feel,' said Ormston firmly, 'that my very first task is to re-habilitate the departments, and break up this over-centralization at Number Ten. Geoffrey's got into the habit of giving too many orders and taking too little advice.'

'He's a very tired man,' said Mayland.

Ormston looked across the lawn to where Melville was standing with Hamilton-Browne, and said,

'One of Geoffrey's troubles is that he's always looking over his shoulder to see who's stabbing him in the back. Politically speaking, he's a bit paranoiac. Just before he was "sent for" when Collard died, he was going about like a man who's having a nervous breakdown on his feet.'

'He's very unpredictable,' said Mayland. 'We'll have to help him.'

'Yes,' said Ormston. 'You put it perfectly. We'll have to give him all the help we can.'

Talbot and Sylvia had joined Mrs. Ormston and her group, and Talbot was saying,

'The only way to meet anyone at this Garden Party is at the bandstand. But it has its dangers.'

'What sort?' asked Mrs. Ormston.

'I had to hear "Oh, What a Beautiful Morning" three times because Sylvia was late.'

'I prefer *Rose Marie*,' said Mrs. Martin morosely.

' "When I'm Calling You"?' asked Mrs. Ormston.

'No, all those whooping Indians,' she answered. 'Whoo-whoo-whoo-whoo!'

'Let's get some tea,' said Hunter, 'before Lyons closes.' He edged her away towards the tea marquees, and Mrs. Martin called fadingly over her shoulder as she went,

'With the totems – and tom-toms – and tomahawks. Whoo-whoo-whoo-whoo!'

'I adore that woman,' said Sylvia to Mayland. 'She's so original. Who is she?'

Then observing the look on his face she remembered, and said to Talbot, 'I must just have a word with daddy. See you later!'

'Impulsive girl!' said Mrs. Ormston. 'She's got Elizabeth's tact and Geoffrey's determination. She'd be quite pretty if only she'd go to a good hairdresser.'

'Do come and dine soon,' said Ormston to Mayland.

The group separated courteously as in a minuet, dissolving into pairs and other figures in time to the music. Talbot walked slowly towards the tea-tent with Mayland, who kept repeating in an emphatic monologue,

'Splendid fellow, Ormston. The right man. Pull it together – that's what's needed. Pull it together.'

After a few weeks in Mayland's entourage, Talbot had learned that his employer in his reveries was best left alone. Even to agree with him invited a challenge as to good faith. And when Mayland's words seemed most fuddled, he still had the capacity for acute thought which would express itself cruelly and destructively to anyone who tried to trifle with him or jolly him along.

'What have you got for us tomorrow, Peter?' Mayland asked, taking off his hat as he caught sight of Lady Drayford. He began to smile his slow cat's smile that expanded gradually under his pouchy eyes.

'I've done a piece on desalination,' said Talbot.

Mayland's smile dimmed.

'On *what*?'

'Desalination – the nuclear project for taking salt out of water. The P.M. was talking about it at Guildhall the other night. In the Middle East—'

'That's no bloody good,' said Mayland in a savage voice, his smile irretrievably dissolved in a scowl. He dug his heel in the turf, and the dust spurted. For a second, his pale, dry skin darkened. 'It's no bloody good. My papers are published for ordinary people living ordinary lives – here in England. They want to read about ordinary things they can pronounce – talk to each other about in their parlours and their pubs. Do you know why the British will never have nationalization?'

His face had become pale again, he began to smile.

'They don't like the word – the sound of it. No Party's ever going to win an election on a slogan with six syllables. They may drag it in later when they're in power. It's an advantage when you're in power. You want to make the people think you're doing great things – so you add a few syllables and make it important.'

'We are in power,' said Talbot. 'It's a most—'

'It's for the Government,' said Mayland. 'Not for us. We're not intellectuals, Peter. We're plain businessmen selling newspapers. I've told Colson. I want a piece on the Chancellor for tomorrow – a good personality piece – seen from the point of view of a younger Member.'

'Do you mean you don't want me to write anything on desalination?'

'I didn't say that,' said Mayland amiably. 'Just keep it for a bit, Peter. And when we do have it in, we'll call it "Bread and Salt" – see what I mean?'

He put out his hand to Lady Drayford, who had been twice intercepted before she reached him, and said,

'You look wonderful, Edwina. How do you do it?'

'Oh, just a lot of hard work on my face in the morning, and a rather good dressmaker. Hello, Peter. Where've you been hiding?'

'Mostly in the Smoking Room and the Library,' said Talbot, his anger with Mayland subsiding.

'You left so suddenly,' she said, undisturbed by Mayland's private smile.

'It was a weekend for leaving suddenly,' said Talbot.

'Poor Henry,' said Lady Drayford. 'Someone told me that he was staying with the Dolans, and one night after everyone had gone to bed, they heard a most terrible sobbing coming from his bedroom.'

'Very unpleasant,' said Talbot.

'At any rate, Rosemary asked Ossian to see what was up. He got inside somehow or another – I think they had to get a spare key from the butler because he wouldn't open up – and there was old Henry, dribbling brandy all over his pyjamas and crying his heart out, saying, "My poor child – my poor child – it's bleeding to death." '

'I didn't know he had any children,' said Mayland.

'That's just the point,' said Lady Drayford. 'He hasn't. Never has. His "poor child" – Ossian got it out of him bit by bit – you can imagine, he was overwhelmed to begin with – his "poor child" was the *Exchequer*. Can you imagine that – the *Exchequer*!'

She burst into loud laughter, in which the other two joined.

'That won't be in his memoirs,' said Mayland.

'No,' said Lady Drayford. 'On the whole, we prefer anecdotes at other people's expense.'

'I've attended to all that,' said Mayland. 'I've bought Lacey's memoirs. He's promised me them for next December.'

Lady Drayford turned to Talbot, and said,

'How's your new flat coming along? Am I invited to the house-warming?'

'It's on the 17th,' said Mayland. 'Of course you are. Isn't she, Peter?'

'Yes, of course,' said Talbot.

Lady Drayford looked into his eyes, and laughed.

Elizabeth was saying in a loud voice,

'But that's exactly what Renewal is trying to do' – and saw that she had been joined by Bishop Turton, who was listening to her with his head on one side while Sylvia stood silently at the edge of the group.

'I don't think it's a matter of legislation. That would be the easiest part of it. I think there must be a new sense of personal responsibility. . . .' She underlined the word 'personal', and the Bishop, leaning forward with his kindly face, smiled till all his large and well-shaped teeth were revealed.

'Yes – yes,' he said in a hollow voice.

'Oh, I don't think you've met Peter Talbot,' said Elizabeth as Talbot joined them.

'No,' said the Bishop, turning to Talbot. 'But I know all about him.'

'Not all, I hope,' said Talbot. 'Do you know Miss Melville?'

'From childhood,' said the Bishop. 'What a glorious day this has been! I—'

The band began to play 'God Save the Queen', smothering his last words as the Royal Family prepared to withdraw and the many thousand guests stood at attention.

Elizabeth was reluctant to leave. This was the first time for three years that she had stood on a public occasion in the presence both of her daughter and her husband. In the dry smell of the lawns, the slow saunter of well-dressed men and women, the light of the sun on the chestnut-trees and the pale stone of the Palace, it was as if there had been no interval of unhappiness, no summers of separation, no clinging to a receding dream.

'It's what the nation needs,' said Bishop Turton. 'Good luck with your work!'

Melville looked at the twin staircases of the Palace, now occupied by bobbing grey hats and multicoloured dresses. It reminded him of the façade of Greystoke, seen from the rose garden, and of the summer evening when Andrew Collard, the old Prime Minister, had lain dying before the Cabinet dinner. Melville and Elizabeth had gone up to his room, where he lay asleep haloed by the bed-lamp. His hands on the counterpane slowly opened and unclenched. His white hair had been neatly combed, and his face, with an earnest and absorbed expression as if wholly intent on matters beyond their concern or understanding, was turned to the wall. Melville had called his name, and the nurse had said,

'He can't hear you. He's far away.'

'Thank you, Bishop,' said Elizabeth cheerfully. 'You must come and see us and talk about it again.'

Then they had walked in the gardens, away from the farewell voices of the others who thought that there was no more to do, away from the starting cars and the swirls of light against the trees under the rising moon and the cold, steel-blue of the lawns. Greystoke, Melville remembered, had seemed like a great cruise ship, with every stateroom illuminated except for the central blackness where the Prime Minister was lying.

They stood in the rose garden by the stone dial, and Elizabeth said,

'He looked so lonely in the huge bed – as if he was an infinite distance away.'

Then she stretched out her hand to a bush, and the yellow petals crumbled.

'It's late for the roses,' she said. 'How awful to die like that – without any family or anyone else near you.'

And afterwards, she said,

'I'll tell you the truth – I'll tell it to you because he's dying, and he asked me here with you – he asked me here with you to face the truth. I'll tell it to you.'

Melville had put his arm around her, cupping the back of her head in his hand.

'You must tell me,' he said. 'You must tell me the truth.'

'I will tell you the truth,' she had answered in a voice that was like a murmur in sleep.

'Is it true,' he asked, 'is it true about you and Robert?'

He remembered that she had paused, and frowned, and then she said simply, 'It's true.'

And he hadn't removed his hand, but he began to stroke her hair.

'All the time?' he asked, looking over her shoulder at the rose garden that was filling the air with its heavy scent.

And she had echoed in a flat voice,

'All the time? No – not all the time. That summer – it was a very unhappy summer. ... He was there – you left him with me – you condescended to me. ... I didn't want him, but he was there all the time – he was there all the time.'

Later she had said,

'Forgive me, Geoffrey.'

And he had answered,

'No, I will never forgive you – neither you nor him. You've taken away all those years. And he was my brother.'

'We'd better go,' said Elizabeth. 'It's been such a lovely afternoon! Are you going back to the House, Geoffrey?'

Her brow was sweating in the sunlight, leaving the scar white where the powder had flaked away. Without waiting for his answer, she turned to greet Sir Gregory Broome who had come up behind them at the foot of the stairs.

'Why aren't you healing the sick?' Elizabeth asked. 'I'll report you to the G.M.C.'

'They'll have a better chance without me,' said Broome.

Sylvia took Melville's arm, and they walked on together, leaving Talbot to walk with Elizabeth and Broome.

'I never could understand,' Sylvia said, 'why you kept that phoney as your doctor. Apart from giving hormones to feeble old men – I'm sure it's unethical – I don't see what he does apart from abortions.'

'For God's sake,' said Melville, affectionately pressing her arm, 'I don't mind you shocking your Aged P., but you'll be had up for slander.'

'I've always loathed his smooth familiarity. I like distinguished-looking men – but a bit rumpled at their grey edges – like you.'

She held his arm tightly as they passed through the crush in the entrance hall of the Palace leading to the cars.

'We could have gone the other way,' he said.

'No,' she replied. 'I love showing you off. I feel happy today.'

He looked at her face, alight with pleasure, and said,

'You're like someone with a secret.'

'I have – I mean, I am. You're the second person who's said that to me today. I don't think I'd make a very good spy.'

'Well, if it's a good secret, it's worth sharing.'

'All right.'

He waited.

'Ask me,' she said.

'I'm asking you.'

'I've got a job – starting the week after next.'

'That's very good,' said Melville cautiously. 'Doing what?'

'It's at Chatham House, on the publication side.'

'But that's excellent,' said Melville. 'Excellent. Why don't you come and live with us? You'll be nearer your work.'

Behind them, they heard Elizabeth's voice, assertive over the voices around them and competing with the loud calls by the ushers for the guests' cars.

'It's surprising,' she was saying, 'that Romney wasn't even an Academician. I was told the other day by the President of the Royal Academy that the most he got – even for those enormous family groups – was only a hundred and sixty guineas.'

'Really!' said Talbot attentively.

'My husband thinks it fantastic,' said Elizabeth.

'The Prime Minister's car,' an usher shouted, and the car crunched over the gravel. Melville said to Sylvia,

'Can we give you a lift?'

'No, thanks,' she answered. 'We're going to walk a bit.'

Melville kissed her on the cheek; then he kissed her again, and drew aside for Elizabeth to enter the car as his detective opened it.

'It was a very pleasant afternoon,' she said when she had settled in.

'Yes,' said Melville curtly, and he looked away from her to raise his hat to a group of people who waved from the pavement outside the Palace.

CHAPTER NINE

AT half-past five in the morning, the roads were empty except for a water-cart that sprayed Sylvia's Mini as she passed it in Holland Park. Two Jamaicans outside the Mango Club, its illuminated sign paling in the early light, turned their heads idly towards the energetic sounds, and then became somnolent again. In the absence of cross-traffic, the lights in the main streets on the way to London Airport were set at green, and Sylvia drove exultantly without interruption, stimulated by the cold air and the feeling that while the rest of the world slept behind barricaded doors and windows, she was awake, free, hurrying at sixty miles an hour and he was nearing London Airport at six hundred miles an hour, losing height through the clouds with the men unshaven, the women combing their hair, all seat-belts fastened, over Ireland, the sea, the pylons, the houses and all the dangerous things between sky and earth, moving to the predestined place where they would meet again.

Since she had spoken to Cullen on the telephone, her heart-beat had quickened, and so it had remained. Tachycardia the doctor had called it in America, and he had given her a prescription. Tachycardia. The rapid heart. The wild heart-beat that was a symptom. She had torn up the prescription. It couldn't have worked. She didn't want it to work. The heart-beat was like a drum-beat, summoning troops of memories, announcing hopes, sending challenges and subduing fears. The drum-beat was a familiar of black nights and the insomnias of her last months in New York. But it was also the accompaniment of joy, the secret, boundless joy which she could always evoke, even in agony. Don – Don – Don. The name itself was a heart-beat – perhaps to no one else in the world but her. Obsessive they had said in New York. But it was real. Don – Don – Don. His name was a pulse, and it was inextricable from the flow of her blood. The heart-beat was love. That was it. Love.

At Chiswick, the night workers were coming off their shift. Some of them, red-eyed and work-stained, waved to her. She waved back, fresh in her blue-patterned summer dress. She glimpsed her fair hair and brown face in the looking-glass, and she was glad of the two afternoons which she had spent with Peter at the swimming-pool in Hurlingham Club. They had been lazy afternoons in the hot sun – oh, no tachycardia, the heartbeat was slow and relaxed – and that was before the telephone call. Peter had swum and she had watched him and liked him. He was uncomplicated, pleasant and ambitious. In his company, she felt at ease, and, looking back on those days, she felt that they were only a preparation, a leave before a return.

At London Airport, as she parked her car, the roofs were dazzling in the already hot sun, and she put on her dark glasses. The tumult of coaches, porters, escalators, open shops, air hostesses, policemen and passengers surprised her. On such a day, it seemed strange that others should be arriving and departing, and that the terminal should serve any other purpose than their own private meeting.

In the main hall she found a group standing in front of the indicator. 536. He had told her his flight number, and her eye searched the left-hand column. 536. Due 07.30 hours. Delay – none. She looked at her watch, and saw that the time was only a quarter to seven. She bought copies of *The Times*, the *Daily Express* and the *Daily Telegraph* from a news stand, and after a moment's hesitation, drawn by a headline, 'A Word to Make News – Peter Talbot, page 15', she bought a copy of his paper too. Then she sat on a stool at the snack bar, where she could have a cup of coffee and watch the progress of Flight 536.

During the night, she had only slept fitfully, afraid that neither the telephone service nor her small alarm clock would wake her up. Now she was afraid that her sleepless night had left her with dark rings under her eyes, and she looked anxiously into her looking-glass. It wasn't bad. She turned to Talbot's article. Desalination. The word spread in heavy black type across the page above a photograph of Talbot looking steadfastly at the reader.

'Do you know this word?' (she read). 'Look at it. You'll know it tomorrow. It's a word that will take the salt from the sea and the sand from the desert. Look at it – because it means something to you.

'There are parts of the world where it costs more to buy water than it costs to raise oil – where men have always killed for water and are ready to kill again. The Prime Minister's project for a Nuclear Desalination Authority has a long title. But its object can be put shortly. Water and power. In the atomic era we can water the desert with de-salted sea water, and set up industries with the by-products – electrical power—'

Sylvia glanced down the page, her eye resting on Talbot's approving references to the Prime Minister's Guildhall speech. Good old Peter. She thought of him affectionately, wondering what he would think if he could see her at this moment after she had said that she didn't intend to meet Cullen. She drank her coffee, and felt hungry. For twenty minutes she ate the rolls she had ordered, and read the newspapers. At the end of that time, the indicator clicked, and she rose to her feet. Flight 536. Delayed thirty-five minutes. Quickly, paying her bill, she went to the Enquiry Desk and asked anxiously whether there was any trouble. The air official telephoned to find out while Sylvia took off her sunglasses and polished them.

'No trouble,' he said, 'just a lot of traffic about, and they're queueing up for orders.'

'Oh, thank you,' she said gratefully, as if he had given her a gift. She had left her newspapers in the snack bar, and she bought another two.

The seller behind the counter recognized her and said, 'These are the latest editions, just up, Miss Melville.'

She put on her dark glasses again, and went and sat on an obscure bench from which she could see the channel through which Cullen was expected to arrive. She tried to concentrate on *The Times* crossword puzzle, but gave it up after ten minutes. Then she opened the other newspaper to re-read a paragraph in Talbot's article about the relative cost of different desalination processes.

She looked at the page, turned over and turned back. The whole article had been 'killed'. Instead, there was a substitute headline, ' "Iron and Velvet", says his wife'. The article was subtitled 'Cynthia Ormston Talks to Ann Ap-Jones'. Sylvia read the article with her forehead puckered. It was what Peter called a Gushpiece, the kind of writing that Mayland's woman editor specialized in, illustrated as usual by its subject in his weekend négligé with a dog and a wife in attendance.

Sylvia went to a telephone booth and rang Talbot.

'Hello,' she heard him say. His voice was irritable.

'It's me,' she said.

His voice became softer.

'Sorry – I've been dealing with a couple of bores who think I like talking in bed. Where are you?'

'At London Airport.'

'Oh.' He paused. Then he added, 'I thought you weren't going.'

'So did I. But I did.'

'I see. Are you feeling lonely or something?'

'No. But I've been reading the papers. I liked your water article.'

'I'm very glad.'

In the middle of his disappointment, he felt warmed by her praise.

'Have you seen it?' she asked.

'Not yet,' he said.

'Well, you'd better be quick,' she went on. 'They've dropped it in the latest editions.'

He said nothing, and she asked,

'Are you there?'

'Yes.'

'What are you doing?'

'Exploding.'

'I thought you would. What happened?'

'I decided I'd be independent. Poor old Colson! We chucked a brick for liberty. What's in instead?'

'A revolting-looking piece on Ormston.'

'That's the one I nearly wrote.'

'Well, be careful, Peter. What's going to happen now?'

'I'll have to talk to Mayland.'

'If I were you, I'd just listen.'

'Perhaps you're right – oh, Sylvia!'

'Yes.'

'Nothing in particular – except thank you for ringing.'

'That's all right.'

'Oh, and one other thing.'

'What's that?'

There was another pause.

'I hope – oh, nothing. Goodbye, Sylvia.'

'Goodbye, Peter.'

Cullen came out of Customs briskly, carrying a grip and two packages.

'They're for you,' he said, handing her the packages as if he had only left her the previous day. She wanted to speak, but instead she stood clutching her parcels while her eyes swam.

'Come on,' he said. 'They've got a special system here for losing your luggage. Let's get going.'

'Don!' she said. 'You look thinner.'

'Good,' said Cullen. 'You look—'

He stopped at the top of the moving staircase, and put his arms around her.

'You look like a summer morning, Sylvia.'

They were being jostled by impatient passengers, and he picked up his grip.

'I've got a lot to tell you,' he said.

'When?'

'All day – all night. Have you any engagements?'

'No – it wouldn't matter if I had. Where are you staying?'

'I haven't thought. Where do you recommend?'

'I'll take you home,' Sylvia said. 'I've got my car. Have you breakfasted?'

'Yes – three times.'

'I'll give you another.'

They drove out of the airport, and Cullen said,

'London! It's like a dream.'

And Sylvia thought, 'He's here – now – here – no longer a dream – here – the familiar, ever-present, hoped-for being – I could reach out my hand and touch him – here at my side on the Great West Road.'

Before he awoke, she sat up, supporting herself on her elbow for almost half an hour as she watched his face at rest. He slept with his left hand beneath his head, exhausted and content, till, late in the afternoon, when the sun drove a shaft through the almost closed curtains, he turned and frowned petulantly in his sleep, and groaned. She touched his mouth with her fingers, and he muttered, 'No.' Then he opened his eyes, and saw her face above him.

'Come here,' he said, and her hair dropped over his face and his naked shoulders like a veil.

'Let's stay here,' he said.

139

'Yes,' she said, smiling down at him.

> 'And whilst our souls negotiate there,
> We like sepulchral statues lay
> All day the same our fortunes were,
> And we said nothing all the day . . .'

'All the day,' he repeated, pulling her beside him. 'Donne understood the lot. Do you think I'd make a good doctor of divinity?'

'No,' she said. And then, irrelevantly, 'Donne's wife died giving birth to her twelfth child.'

'That was too much even for those days,' said Cullen. 'Where shall I take you to dinner?'

'Nowhere,' said Sylvia. 'I've got some food in the fridge.'

She smoothed the hair from his forehead, and said,

'What can I get you, darling?'

'A glass of water,' he replied. She went to pick up her dressing-gown from the floor, but he said, 'No, I like to watch you.'

'You're a disgraceful *voyeur*,' she said.

'Yes,' said Cullen. 'I like to watch the *roulement des hanches*.'

She returned with the glass of water, and sat next to him on the bed while he caressed her arm.

'Tell me—' she began, 'tell me about all the things you've been doing.'

He drank the glass of water, and the two delicate lines between his eyebrows returned. His fingers stopped moving.

'I haven't been doing very much – really nothing at all. I had a very unhappy summer, Sylvia.'

'Didn't you get my letters?' she spoke without looking at him. He hesitated, and said,

'I got them. But I had to make a decision. It was hopeless. I could see – well, there was nothing in it for you – nothing at all.'

'I didn't want anything,' she said as if to herself. 'I didn't ask anything – except to see you – to be with you.'

'It was no good,' Cullen said doggedly. 'No good at all. It would just have dragged on till you'd got sick of waiting for me – sick of those train-rides – sick of all the deceit and hypocrisy and the empty days.'

She shook her head.

'It wasn't like that at all. The days were empty anyhow – all the time from our last day onwards was empty. Why didn't you answer my letters?'

'It wouldn't have done, Sylvia. I didn't want you to answer my objections. It would have dragged on.'

'It did drag on,' she said, lying on her back and taking a cigarette from the filigree box which he had brought from America. He lit it for her, and then lay with his head on her shoulder as she smoked it.

'What did your wife say?' she asked abruptly.

He didn't answer for a few moments, and in the silence she could hear the steady thump of her heart.

'My wife didn't say anything,' said Cullen at last.

'What did you tell her?'

'There was nothing for me to tell her. She knew all there was to know.'

'Did she want to do anything about it?'

'No – all she wanted to do was wait. You see, Sylvia, my wife loves me.'

'That's a complication. And you?'

She sat up suddenly, and faced him like an accuser. He began to smile, but she said,

'Don't laugh, Don. I want to know.'

'I love my children, Sylvia,' he said. 'You know it. I told you so.'

The telephone began to ring, and she said, 'I'm not going to answer it.'

'Perhaps it's important,' said Cullen.

'No,' said Sylvia. 'There's nothing I want to hear.'

'What about our coffee?' said Cullen. 'You make coffee, and I'll take a shower. It'll wake me up.'

'And then?' asked Sylvia.

'Then we'll go back to bed.'

The second time they awoke, it was already night, and Sylvia saw by the phosphorescent bedside clock that the time was two thirty-five.

'In New York,' said Cullen ruminatively, 'it's now about nine thirty-five, and I want supper.'

'You're insatiable,' said Sylvia. 'And I love you. But you're not sleeping enough. Do you know what we'll do tomorrow night?'

141

In the darkness she could feel the slow stir of his body become still, frozen, his arms stiffening around her. The affirmation she intended became a hesitant question.

'Shall we go to the Glyndebourne opera tomorow? It's so lovely there. I managed to get two tickets for *L'Incoronazione di Poppaea*. It's terribly hard to get tickets, but these were returns. If you like, we could picnic by the lake, or we could order dinner in advance – champagne, cold salmon and strawberries. Wouldn't that be delicious?'

She spoke rapidly, as if she feared his reply, and as she spoke Cullen disentangled himself from her arms and switched on the bedside lamp.

'No,' said Sylvia. 'I can't bear that light,' and switched it off again.

She got out of bed in the semi-darkness, and sat by the window, looking out on the deserted and silent streets. She had slept only fitfully but she felt reposed and content. After the panic, security. The nightmares chased away by his presence. She turned her head, like a dog turning to make sure that its master is near, to assure herself that he was still there. But the moments that she spent away from Cullen seemed a deprivation, and she came back to the bed and lay at his side.

At school when the long loneliness was broken by her father's visits, she had grudged the minutes of his talking to her schoolmistress, or the separation at prize-giving, the parents in front, the girls marshalled behind. If anyone spoke to her father and diverted his attention, she felt a nausea which she resented as much as she hated the intruder. But afterwards, she remembered, when they were alone and she could take his hand – his enfolding, dry hand that made her safe – she moved her fingers and still felt it – the world was a happy place. Over the fields away from school and orders and bells, away from the noticeboards and regulations and the hockey voices, there was calmness, her father's voice and hand. Twice her mother had come down. That was too awful. Her schoolgirl verdict recurred. Too awful. Elizabeth had heard of their walks together, and she had insisted on coming. But it was all utterly different. Sylvia had gone ahead while, behind her, she could hear her mother's voice, at first inquiring and then rasping, complaining. The lunch was inedible. The paths were muddy. And, Sylvia, don't slouch when you walk. And her father – patient and at last silent.

'Are you asleep?' Cullen asked.

'No,' said Sylvia. 'I was thinking of the time when I was at school.'

She felt his fingers stroking her face, and then he said,

'Naomi's going to a new school in Virginia in the fall. You remember her, don't you?'

'Yes, I do. Very well. She didn't like me a bit.'

He laughed.

'She probably thought you were a danger.'

'Well, I wasn't.'

'No,' he said, 'no – that's all different.'

'Why is it different?' she insisted, disappointed that he hadn't contradicted her.

'It's different,' he said hesitantly, 'because – well, putting it simply – blood-links are indissoluble. You can divorce husbands and wives – you can't do it with parents and children.'

'Yes, you can,' said Sylvia. 'You can. . . . You've never spoken to me about your parents. Tell me about them. What was your father like?'

'My father,' said Cullen. 'Just think of your own father – then think of the opposite. My father was an immigrant presser. He wasn't called Cullen. All I can say about his English is that it improved. My mother was a very quiet woman who died when I was twelve. She died giving birth to her sixth child. We were a very affectionate family, and my parents skimped so that I could be educated. And that's about it.'

'It's strange,' said Sylvia, 'other people's families. They're so hard to imagine. Do you really think your father was so different from mine?'

Cullen laughed shortly.

'Externally – very. Perhaps in his outlook – I don't know. My father was a great humanist and rationalist, crazy about politics – any kind of politics, state, congress, senate, precinct, community – everything. He was always reading and reading. If he hadn't been a presser, he would have been a Congressman—'

'Perhaps President,' said Sylvia. 'What a delicious thought. "President's son meets Prime Minister's daughter." '

'No,' said Cullen. 'You must brush up on your American Constitution. Foreign-born immigrants aren't eligible for the Presidency.'

'Of course,' said Sylvia. 'You've got to be a true believer to be Prime Minister. How accidental everything is!'

'Part accidental,' said Cullen. 'There are certain taboos in an established order that are relevant to our accidental circumstances, and we can either accept or break them. But in other ways, we decide.'

'Was it an accident or a decision that we spoke to each other in the Museum of Modern Art?'

'A decision.'

'Was it a decision that we are here now?'

'Yes.'

'And what do we do tomorrow?'

'That will be a decision too.'

'Would you like to go to Glyndebourne?'

She heard the curtain flap in the night breeze as she waited for his answer, and opening her eyes she saw that the walls had become a luminous grey in the first morning light.

'I can't, Sylvia,' he said. 'I'm catching a plane at nine o'clock for Paris. I'm going on to Strasbourg. I'm lecturing there.'

'You didn't tell me.'

'No.'

'Let me come. Oh, please, Don, let me come.'

She sat up in pleasure at the new idea, and kissed him on his face and forehead.

'No, Sylvia,' he said. 'I can't.'

'Why not?' she said. 'Why not? I'll be very unobtrusive – I promise I'll keep out of the way.'

'No,' he said in a harsh voice. 'It's impossible. I'm meeting my wife in Paris. She's flying over today. We never fly together.'

'You should have told me,' said Sylvia, her arms still around him. A dream flashed through her drifting mind that she was afloat in a warm sea holding a drowned man. 'It would have been better if you'd told me.'

He tried to turn her face to his, but she said briskly,

'No, Don. I'll make some coffee.'

She switched on the light and they confronted each other with a slight embarrassment as if their faces were more naked than their bodies had been.

'Sylvia!' he said, putting on his dressing-gown.

But she was already in the small kitchen, and he could hear the gas jets kindle with a gentle plop.

They didn't speak during breakfast, and it was only when Cullen was shaved, bathed and dressed, and they could hear the taxi ticking outside in the empty street that Sylvia realized that he had arrived and in a few moments would have gone. The image of the corpse persisted in her mind. The mourners restrained till the coffin's departure. The black mourners turning their faces to the hearse.

Cullen was pale, and he said,

'I love you, Sylvia,' and she didn't answer, but put her face on his shoulder and wept.

'I'll be in touch,' he said, and took her hands from around his waist. The door-bell rang insistently.

'It's the cab,' said Cullen. 'He's getting impatient. Goodbye, Sylvia.'

He opened the door and picked up his case and grip.

'Say goodbye to me,' he said, kissing her wet cheek.

'Goodbye,' she said, and he left, leaving the door open behind him.

When she heard the taxi starting up, Sylvia closed the door carefully, then lay in the hollow of the bed where Cullen had lain. She had forgotten to turn off the gas in the kitchenette, and she could hear its faint murmur, but she didn't want to move. Do you love me? the infant Mozart used to ask his audience before he'd perform. Everyone wanted to be loved before they'd play. It was absurd. What use was it to have love and nothing else? The emptiness was back. The great, terrible nothingness. The awful vacuum.

She wanted to sleep, to escape from the nothing into unconsciousness, away from this room with its dying flowers which his presence had now made uninhabitable. She stretched out her hand into the drawer and took three sodium amytal pills from a phial and swallowed them, choking a little as she drank the water from the glass he had begun. Then she lay with her eyes open.

After a few minutes, she heard a scuffling sound outside the door, and she raised herself from the bed with a sudden hope that Cullen had come back. She went to the door, and opened it, only to find that what she had heard were her newspapers falling from the letter-box. A large headline in the *Daily Express* said, 'Melville for Paris'. She read on. 'The Prime Minister ...

leaving today ... worsening position in South-East Asia ... forthcoming conference ... accompanied by Deputy Prime Minister ... British Ambassador ... blue curtains.'

'Blue curtains,' she said aloud. The Ambassadress was fitting blue curtains in her father's room. This seemed very funny to Sylvia, and she stretched out on her bed repeating the words, 'Blue curtains,' as if they were a talisman guarding her from her terrors.

'Today was the very worst day of my life.' Sylvia began to tremble, and she twisted herself on the bed to fumble through the books and papers at her bedside table.

'Destroy it!' said Dr. Kron in New York. 'You must destroy it!' But she hadn't destroyed it. It lay there hidden away, the neat exercise book of her schooldays that had survived all the later diaries, the cardboard cracked where her father had grasped it. 'Today was the very worst day of my life.'

The diary fell open at the entry June 4th. She began to tremble more violently.

'Today was the very worst day of my life [she read]. He said that he would take me to the cinema if I would take Barbara Solway to Penelope's party. He told me not to come back before half-past five. I took the bus to Kensington with Barbara but Penelope had a temperature, and Mrs. Medlicott said that we had better have some tea and go home. We walked through the Park, but in the end we took a bus back. I knew it was no use going home too early because she was going to have tea with Mrs. Jephcote and Nanny and Solange were going to be out.'

She continued to read the stiff schoolgirl writing, reciting the litany of the day.

'I wish daddy was not away so much. He never has time to talk to me. She didn't give me a key, but I know the way in over the buttress wall that leads to my window. I got in my room and all the curtains were drawn to keep the house cool because she's so fussy. After a while my heart jumped into my mouth because I heard an awful sound of groaning. So I went on to the landing with my knees shivering, and thought I would go to the telephone and dial 999.'

She knew the next paragraph by heart, but she read it as if for the first time.

'The noise was coming from the other bedroom which I had to pass, and the door was half-open, so I stopped for a moment

146

before going down to the telephone. Her head was lying over the edge of the bed, and her hair was hanging down, and she was making terrible choking noises as if she had been running and couldn't breathe. And on top of her something white was going up and down, up and down, up and down, and I couldn't see at first what it was because the curtains were drawn. I was rooted to the floor. My legs were trembling, and it all happened at once. It was like animals fighting. Then, suddenly, she gave a terrible scream, and seemed to heave up in the air, and I saw she had no clothes on at all, and she exclaimed, "Oh, darling, darling, darling." And over her shoulder I could see Uncle Robert's face looking terrible and sweating as if he were dying. And then I must have screamed, because his eyes looked straight at mine.

'After a bit he came into my bedroom, to which I had retired, and told me to stop crying, and said that when I was older I would understand. He sat with me for ages, and gradually I began to stop crying, but the sobbing wouldn't stop. And then I hiccupped a bit, and he laughed. He said I was his very favourite person in the whole world, and I told him that I loved him next to daddy. He said in that case I must never tell anyone, not even daddy, because it would make him very unhappy.

'In the evening we went to St. Giles, where I swore with him on the cross that I would never, never, not even to save my own life, tell anyone what I had seen. Today was definitely the worst day of my whole life.'

That was how it had been, Robert who had been killed in the motor crash. Her mother. And her father with his unhappy face – just before Collard died, before she went away. That had been a dreadful year but it had to be so. And in a way it was an accident because she had almost forgotten it – had forgotten it when she asked her father to look for her G.C.E. certificate in the lumber-room. It was an accident, an accident. She'd known all those years, and hadn't said anything. Nothing at all. And everyone had said, 'How dreadful Sylvia is to her mother.' Her father too.

'Oh Christ,' said Sylvia aloud. 'Oh Christ, let me sleep!'

She took another two sleeping pills, and a few minutes later fell into her darkness.

Through the day that followed, she heard from time to time

the sound of bells as the telephone rang, and sometimes as she rose on the swell of consciousness, she dreamed monstrous dreams. When she woke again, it was night, and she no longer knew what day it was. The room was stifling, the summer heat intensified by the still-burning gas jets. Her head ached and her mouth was dry, and she couldn't orientate herself in the darkness. She groped for a switch, and knocked down a table-lamp. The luminous clock stood at twelve-thirty, but it had no meaning. Night, day – the world was a miasma. She found the switch at last, and as the light came on, the room careened like a ship. She leant against the wall, and gradually the objects began to have a relationship, the floor to become firm and horizontal and time to have a meaning. She turned on a tap in the bathroom, and the sound of water gave her comfort. She put the residue of the coffee on the gas jet again, and watching it begin to bubble, she said to herself, 'I must get dressed. I must talk to someone. If I stay here, I'm going to die.'

She picked up the telephone, and dialled her father's telephone number. The night-duty officer, bored at first, became attentive as soon as he realized who she was.

'The Prime Minister, Miss Melville,' he said, 'is away – in Paris.'

'Yes,' she said in a flat voice. 'Yes – he's always away.'

'Well, not always,' said the duty officer, laughing politely. 'Would you like to speak to Mrs. Melville?'

'No,' said Sylvia, and hung up. Of course he was in Paris. She knew it. But she had to hear that he wasn't there, that he couldn't help her, that she was alone. Try Talbot.

'Peter,' she said when he answered the telephone.

'Good Lord, Sylvia,' he said, 'where on earth are you? I've been trying to get you all day.'

'Peter,' she said, 'I feel terrible.'

'You sound it,' he answered.

'I think I'm going to die,' she said.

'Don't be ridiculous,' said Talbot, his voice sharp and urgent. 'Where are you?'

'I'm at home.'

'I'll come and talk to you if you like.'

'No,' she said, 'no.'

'What are you doing?' he asked. 'You sound muffled.'

'I've wrapped myself in a sheet like a shroud. Donne – do you

148

remember Donne? – he wrapped himself in a sheet and had himself painted as a reminder of mortality.'

'Don't be so damned morbid,' said Talbot.

'No,' said Sylvia, throwing off the sheet. 'Look – I'm out of the shroud. I'm naked. I'll come and call on you naked.'

'Don't be silly.'

'Why not? You are an old prude. I'll take you for a drive – a lovely drive right out to Glyndebourne.'

'Why Glyndebourne?'

'Why not? There's lovely music there – wonderful. Music at night.'

There was a pause.

'Sylvia – you don't sound very well.'

'And you sound like a stupid bastard. I'm coming to take you for a drive.'

She opened the roof of her car, and with a scarf wrapped round her head drove fast through the late-night traffic. Coming from a side road into Bayswater Road her car hit the side of a van. The damage was considerable, but as the driver, though unhurt, was abusive, she prepared to drive away. When the policeman asked her for her particulars, she told him to talk more politely. At the police station, they kept her waiting in a stuffy charge-room, and she dozed off. After a police-woman awakened her, she answered a number of questions, peculiar questions that had to do with arithmetic and spelling, and was cautioned and told that she would be charged with driving under the influence of drink or drugs.

Later on, Gregory Broome called for her and she met her mother somewhere, and fell asleep.

CHAPTER TEN

'DOCTRINE tempered by heresy,' said the Ambassador, 'is a great French quality. It's the strength of the Church in France – and of the Communist Party too.'

'I don't think it's as simple as that,' said the Prime Minister. 'France is the country of permanent revolution. That's why it's also a country of paradox – conservative statesmen with radical policies.'

'That's really what I mean,' said the Ambassador easily, adding to Melville's glass from the whisky decanter. 'Inflexible dogma flexibly applied. Mediterranean theory and Northern pragmatism.'

'Chastenet didn't give much away this evening,' said Melville.

'But very accommodating when he got his marching orders from the Chief. That's the trouble. He makes them look like boys – all of them.'

'I think,' said Melville, 'that in politics there's a kind of national masochism as well as national sadism. At the moment, the French are going through the first condition. They've had too many weak governments. They enjoy a firm hand.'

'And the British?'

Melville laughed, and emptied his glass before replying.

'They're having a pronounced sadistic phase. It's a useful democratic disturbance – rather like a fever in certain diseases. It's uncomfortable but cathartic. Every now and again, a large section of the British public decides that it hates the sight – I mean literally, the sight of their political leaders. It's infectious. Spontaneously, everyone – the country, the Press, TV – get flushed with fury as soon as they see us.'

'But it's only an attack.'

'Oh, of course. When they've given us a good tanning, they suddenly relent – especially if they think the other lot are going to raise their taxes or take away their savings.'

'We're only an hour away here,' said the Ambassador, 'but

it's hard to get the feel of things. What do you think of the situation?'

Melville laughed again.

'Well,' he said, 'it's much easier to control events in South-East Asia – and God knows, that's almost impossible – than in Britain.'

'I thought Gerald was in great form when he was talking about N.A.T.O. support costs to Chastenet. They like a bit of Gallic logic coming from an Englishman. And I don't think his row with Izard will do him any harm at home.'

'No,' said Melville, rising and going over to the window overlooking the courtyard. 'What time is it, Philip?'

'It's late,' said the Ambassador, contorting his jaw behind Melville's back to stifle a yawn and then stroking his short moustache to make the camouflage certain. The Conference had begun with a three-hour session before a dinner at the Embassy and had ended with a second three-hour session and an extra hour spent in drafting the communiqué. The Ambassador had known Melville for many years, but he couldn't help noticing how Melville had changed since he had been Prime Minister. He was more difficult to talk to, unwilling to sit in a chair and engage in detailed conversation, occasionally distracted as if he wished he were in another place talking to someone else. Greyer – that was inevitable. And without his old gaiety. Pamela had been very hurt that he hadn't noticed the blue curtains. Pity. He had only two more years in the Service; the Lords beckoned him; and he was anxious to please.

'A little more whisky, Geoffrey?'

'No, I don't think so,' said Melville slowly, still looking out of the window. 'I'm very happy. I'm always very happy in Paris. I'm only sorry that in the last few years I haven't been able to see it without being whisked away in an official car with hordes of those extraordinary motor-bike acrobats.'

He touched the brocade curtain, and said,

'I've very pleasant recollections of this room, Philip.'

And he remembered how when he had been a very young Member of Parliament he had stood at that same window talking to the Ambassadress, who was asking him about his constituency and his Committee interests in the House. But as she spoke, she idly stroked the bulbous tassel of the curtain, resting her beautiful face against the thick cord till in confusion before her steady eyes he mouthed an excuse and withdrew.

'It's always been a pleasant post,' said the Ambassador.

'I was thinking of the time when Collard was still P.M.,' said Melville. 'We were all in the room – Curwen, poor chap, died on the way to the States, Grindley – he's gone too, Ruth Alford – used to be such a pretty girl – she's now a tight-lipped old harridan.'

'Oh, come,' said the Ambassador.

'All right,' said Melville, 'a very sour, middle-aged woman – all that lovely hair – it's very sad.'

'You're getting elegiac,' said the Ambassador. 'It's late. What time will you be leaving tomorrow?'

'As early as possible,' said the Prime Minister. 'I'll deal with the boxes first. Yes, Frobisher?'

Frobisher came in with a note which the Prime Minister glanced at indifferently.

'Why on earth does he want to bother me at this time of night?' he asked.

'He's on the phone now, sir, in your room,' said Frobisher. 'He told me it was very urgent.'

'Sir Gordon Taylor is a splendid chap, but a waffler and a bore,' said Melville.

'Isn't that a qualification for the appointment?'

'I suppose it is,' said Melville. 'That and the sort of priggish good looks that go well under a wig. Gordon's got all that it takes to be a fine Attorney-General. He could do perhaps with a little more intelligence. Good night, Philip.'

The Attorney-General's voice from the other end of the line was clear.

'How are you, Geoffrey?'

'Tired.'

'All go well?'

'Yes.'

There was a pause and Melville waited for the Attorney-General to continue.

'Are you returning tonight?'

'Of course not. I'm coming back tomorrow.'

'I see.'

Melville sat on the edge of his bed, and began to take off one of his shoes.

'Did you ring to ask me how I am?'

He was becoming irritated with the Attorney-General's velleities, and wanted to tell him to get on with it or get off the line. Instead, he patiently untied his shoe-lace, and let the other shoe drop to the carpet while the Attorney-General whirred like an old-fashioned gramophone about to give voice.

'I'm afraid, Geoffrey,' he said at last, 'I've got something rather difficult to tell you.'

Melville paused hopefully. He had been dissatisfied for a long time with the Parliamentary performances of the Attorney-General who, despite his knowledge of law, had always been uncomfortable in exposition. He had also blundered badly in connection with an appeal to the Privy Council by an expatriate Englishman and he had mishandled an application for Habeas Corpus. Melville put his feet on the bed, and lay back with the telephone to his ear. If the Attorney wanted to go, so much the better.

'It's about Sylvia,' the Attorney-General said in a firm voice as if he'd made up his mind.

'What's that?' said Melville, sitting up abruptly.

'Sylvia,' the Attorney repeated, his tone now matter-of-fact. 'I had the D.P.P. on to me a few minutes ago.'

The familiarity with which he used the initials exasperated Melville.

'What's the Director of Public Prosecutions got to do with Sylvia?'

'Well, I'm afraid Sylvia had a traffic accident.'

'Is she hurt?'

'No – not in the least.'

'Was anyone hurt?'

'No, a lot of damage to a van.'

'Then why—?'

'I'm afraid, Geoffrey, she was taken to the police station – she's there now – they're proposing to charge her with driving under the influence of—'

'Utterly ridiculous.'

'Well, Geoffrey, nothing's ridiculous. We both know it.'

'This is ridiculous. Quite ridiculous.'

Melville stood by the bedside in his stockinged feet, and saw his reflection multiplied like a visual pun of his words in the long wardrobe mirrors.

'The D.P.P. has asked my guidance.'

'She's at the police station?' Melville asked.

'Yes.'

Suddenly Melville recognized that the Attorney-General was asking for advice as well as giving him information.

'Get Gregory Broome to see her – get him down there at once. Sylvia's been ill. She almost never has anything to drink. You'd better not tell her mother – it's better that you don't.'

'She's been told, I'm afraid.'

'Sylvia's been ill, Gordon. If she had an accident, it's because she was ill. Get Broome down there to examine her.'

'I think her mother had better arrange that.'

'Yes – yes. Do it straight away. Poor Sylvia. She's been ill.'

'Yes – I understand. I'll speak to the D.P.P.'

'I have every confidence, Gordon, that you'll do whatever is necessary and right.'

'Naturally. I'm sorry about all this, Geoffrey. You understand my position.'

'Of course I do. See that Broome gets there. Will you ring me back?'

'In an hour.'

'Good night, Geoffrey.'

'Good night, old chap.'

Lidgett, the Night Editor, telephoned Colson to ask his advice.

'He's sure of it,' he said.

'When will it be coming up?' asked Colson sleepily from his bed.

'Tomorrow.'

'Well, trail it – just call it an incident wherever it was.'

Ten minutes later, Lidgett phoned again.

'Something funny,' he said. 'Can't get anything out of them at all at the police station.'

'Well, that's that,' said Colson. 'Now we can all go to sleep.'

'Yes,' said Lidgett. 'It's funny all the same. He saw her at the station – says he saw her entry. Copeland's one of our best lads.'

'The old man will give him a medal. Is he absolutely certain?'

'Absolutely. He says he saw the entry. What happened was that Copeland saw Sylvia, and said to the station sergeant, "You know who you've got? You've got the Prime Minister's daughter." '

Colson, who had been talking in darkness, sat up and switched on the light.

'The sergeant got the vapours, and referred it, as he put it, to his superior. It went all the way up, I believe, to the D.P.P. It's no joke booking the P.M.'s daughter on a "drunk in charge".'

'Very embarrassing,' said Colson.

'Yes – it's very strange, though. They won't talk about it.'

'It's a bit dicey, Bill. I'd better have a word with Mayland. Hold it a few minutes. Has anyone else got it?'

'No – Copeland was doing his night-shift. If we hadn't been looking for it, we wouldn't have got it.'

'I'll talk to the Old Man. Ring you back.'

The morning edition carried a short piece in heavy type entitled: '3 a.m. News. *Sylvia Melville in Car Crash*. Sylvia Melville, 23, was involved in an incident with a van in the early hours of this morning. Her red Mini was damaged, but she escaped injury. Police inquiries are proceeding.'

When Sylvia failed to arrive and didn't answer his telephone calls, Talbot assumed that she had changed her mind, disconnected her bell and gone to sleep. He was serving on the Committee dealing with the Travel Agencies (Registration) Bill, and after a late breakfast provided by Mrs. Rogers, the daily who looked after his new flat, and a long talk with the decorators who had painted his study in a shade of grey which he disliked, he hurried off to the House of Commons in the small sports car he had recently bought out of an increased overdraft. At the back of his mind, he felt an unformed anxiety. He might have been reassured if he had been able to talk to Sylvia, but as he drove into New Palace Yard he saw from Big Ben that he was already late, and decided that he would telephone Sylvia before going on for the weekly luncheon with Mayland.

Sitting in the Chamber, he found it difficult to concentrate on the list of amendments in front of him. Martin Holgate, a Queen's Counsel with a sonorous voice, was engaged for the Opposition in an abstruse analysis which fell meaninglessly on his ears.

'Clause 22 of the Bill has to be read with Clause 21(a) which provides for a period of not less than twenty-eight days . . .'

And the Attorney-General, uncertain and indecisive.

'I must concede that Clause 22 gives a period of twenty-eight days from the date of service. . . . But the delay must be kept to a minimum, otherwise the intention of Clause 22(a) will be defeated.'

Talbot turned his head to a large Victorian composition on the wall called 'The Burial of Harold'. The lead-coloured figure at the centre went well with the dirge-like voice of the Attorney-General, and Talbot occupied himself with a seagull which was sunning itself on the other side of the glazed Gothic windows. In the ill-ventilated Committee Room, the light tropical suits which some Members wore and the rattle of the old-fashioned fans set in the glass enhanced the atmosphere of heat. Talbot began to think of his holidays, and whether he would accept the Pattersons' invitation to spend the recess – August at any rate – at their villa in Beaulieu. He liked sailing, and they had promised him a lot of it. Sylvia had once told him that she had sailed at school. Perhaps they could meet there. He didn't want to make any arrangements till he knew what she was going to do. There was, of course, the Deauville weekend that he had gone on last year, when a Parliamentary team of golfers and tennis players and yachtsmen had met a counterpart team of *députés*. He was going again this year with Patterson. Strange how Mayland had his knife into Morrow. He'd sent a couple of journalists over, ostensibly to cover the sports meeting, but actually to keep track of Morrow. They hadn't done very well. 'Lost much?' one of the journalists asked Morrow at the Casino after the gala dinner. 'No – only a pound or two. I'm going to bed.' The next day the Mayland gossip story read, 'Shadow Minister Loses at Roulette. Takes to his Bed.' Talbot smiled to himself. Mayland, he thought, would only take his knife out to make the blood flow more freely.

Talbot began to doodle. This wasn't his subject, and he had been indignant at being appointed as a make-weight for the Committee. Lawton, the junior Government Whip next to him, was equally bored, and Talbot noticed that the energetic notes he appeared to be making consisted, in fact, of his correspondence. Lawton caught his eye, and smiled.

'It's the only time I get,' he said. 'How's Sylvia?'

'Sylvia – oh, she was in very good form when I last saw her.'

'You saw the papers this morning?'

'No – anything special?'

'She seems to have had a tiff with a lamp-post last night.'

Talbot looked at his Whip with distaste.

'What do you mean?'

Lawton pointed to the Stop Press column in the paper beside him, and Talbot read it quickly. The Committee was preparing to 'divide', and the Clerk began to call the roll-call of names. They sounded muffled. Mr. Nathan – Aye – Mr. Norton – Aye – Mr. Oswald – No – Mr. Outram – Aye – Mr. Paine-Everett – Aye – Mr. Parsons – No – Mr. Phillipps – No – Sir Gerald Porter-Browne – Aye – Mr. Reston – No – Mr. Salter – Aye – Mr. Talbot—

That explained it. She'd had an accident on the way to him, and he'd turned over in bed. Nothing. Just turned over and gone to sleep.

'Mr. Talbot!' the Clerk repeated.

'Talbot!' said the Whip.

Talbot looked up hurriedly and said, 'No.'

'Mr. Tilling,' the Clerk continued with his roll-call.

'That was pretty gratuitous,' said the Whip hostilely to Talbot.

'What was?' Talbot asked.

'And bloody offensive,' the Whip added.

'What are you taking about?'

'Your vote – voting against us.'

'Did I?' Talbot asked abstractedly. 'I'm sorry. You'll have to excuse me.'

He rose, and the Whip said,

'Where are you off to?'

'I've got something I have to attend to,' said Talbot.

'The Chief will have to be told, Talbot. You realize that?'

'Yes,' said Talbot. 'Yes.'

He pushed back his chair, and clambering over the Whip's legs, went out into the Committee Room Corridor. He bought himself a cup of coffee from the trolley, and stood uncertainly in front of a telephone booth, wondering where to begin his inquiries about Sylvia. As he had expected, she was out when he telephoned her at home. At Number 10, a secretary said, 'We have no information about Miss Melville's whereabouts.' He then rang Colson, who said,

'No, we don't know where she is. I've got an idea she might be in the country. ... We've got three leads on the story.'

'What story?'

Colson chuckled.

'Well, between you and me and the National Press, the Old Man wants to blow the thing up.'

'In what way?'

'He's got an idea that the P.M. got into the act.'

'How could he? He was in Paris.'

'Don't be daft. There are telephones, Peter. The story is that the D.P.P. asked the Attorney-General for advice. The A.G. then got on to the P.M., who says "Scrub the charge!" '

'What charge?'

'Drunk in charge.'

'That's absurd. I spoke to Sylvia about ten minutes before all this happened. She sounded perfectly normal.'

'Well, where was she off to at that time of night?'

Colson sighed, and added,

'It's no good, Peter. Mayland looks as if he's got a hate coming on. See you at lunch.'

Budd greeted Talbot coolly as he entered the dining-room at Mayland House. Budd in possession of the floor allowed no one to encroach on his territory. With his legs planted apart and holding a gin and tonic in his hand, he was describing to Mayland, Colson and Hunter exactly how he had tamed an ambassador who had failed to give him due consideration when he had called at his embassy. While Mayland was observing Budd like a boxing manager delighting in his new 'boy', Colson and Hunter were listening to him with a mixture of deference and dislike. They knew Mayland's importations into the board-room, and had learnt over the years to dislike them. Talbot hadn't expected to meet Budd, with whom he had often exchanged jibes across the floor of the Chamber, and he knew that he wasn't going to enjoy the afternoon.

'You know each other, of course,' said Mayland when they were sitting down. 'What do you think of the Paris Agreement, Tom?'

'Well, if you ask me—' Budd began, and for five minutes explained why the total cost of military support in Western Europe would be increased by the decision, and why Ormston had been a fathead to 'carry the can' for Melville, who'd got away with things too many times. He told an anecdote about Melville, who just before he became Prime Minister had said at Lancaster House to Lady Drayford that 'he wanted the African to be his brother, not his brother-in-law', and how that had nearly caused M'landa to break off relations, and how in the riots that followed dozens of Africans had been killed.

'I don't like Melville,' he said. 'When he was younger, he'd say anything for a laugh or a woman's compliment. I honestly don't know how Elizabeth puts up with him. Now, there's a woman!'

'Yes – charming woman,' said Mayland. 'Come on, Tom. We've been leaving you behind.'

Budd applied himself to the *blanquette de veau*, and Talbot said,

'I think the Paris Agreements are first-class, but I wouldn't expect Budd to agree. He's anti-Europe anyhow.'

'Anti-your-kind-of-Europe,' Budd said.

'And Ormston's and Melville's,' said Talbot. 'You say you're internationalists, but you don't like shaking hands with foreigners.'

'I like choosing them,' said Budd, swallowing a glass of Haut Brion at a draught. 'But when it comes to a showdown, I prefer my own kind. The trouble with you, Talbot, is that you don't drink in pubs. It's the trouble with Melville, too.'

'I don't think we ought to talk of pubs in front of Government backbenchers,' said Mayland, taking a large second helping of the *blanquette*.

'Why not?' Talbot asked casually.

'It's a very curious situation,' said Hunter.

'It's one of the things that appear and disappear, and you don't know what you're left with,' said Colson.

'Well,' said Mayland, pushing his plate away as if the effort of digestion and concentration was too much. 'What's the position – as of now? Give us the hard story as you told it to me this morning.'

'The hard story,' said Colson, 'is that there isn't going to be one. The charge has been withdrawn on the orders of the D.P.P.'

Talbot took up his glass, and swallowed a mouthful of claret quickly. That was an enemy disposed of. It would have been unpleasant if there had been any truth in the story which he'd heard reported in the Smoking Room before leaving for the luncheon that Sylvia was 'up' for being 'drunk in charge'. The whole thing was absurd, in any case. He'd never known her drink too much.

'Who gave the orders to the D.P.P.?' asked Mayland, his lips scarcely moving.

'That we don't know,' said Colson. 'But Melville certainly spoke to the A.G. that night.'

'The Attorney-General?' Mayland asked sharply. 'How do you know?'

'I spoke to Elizabeth Melville,' said Colson. 'I know her quite well. I tried to check – explained that we only wanted the facts. She said Dr. Broome – beg his pardon, Sir Gregory Broome – had seen Sylvia at the P.M.'s request – the Attorney-General had given her a message from Melville.'

Budd leaned forward with his arms folded on the table.

'Do you mean to say the P.M. asked the Attorney-General – it's quite fantastic!'

'We're just neutral in all this,' said Mayland, 'but it seems very strange to me that the Prime Minister should have dabbled in a matter affecting the judiciary – even if the case is a trivial family affair.'

'Just *because* it's trivial,' said Budd, his face flushing, 'just *because* it's a family affair. Who does Melville think he is?'

'I can imagine,' said Mayland calmly, 'that he was upset about his daughter being charged with being under the influence of drink or drugs – it sounds so unpleasant. I can't really blame him on a personal plane. You yourself, Tom, as a father—'

'That's not the point,' said Budd. 'It's a cardinal principle. The executive mustn't interfere with the judiciary.'

'I do think,' said Mayland, lighting a cigar and then offering one to Budd, 'that we ought to get some facts on this. You've reached a full stop, I believe.'

Colson grunted.

'Something may turn up.'

'I suppose,' said Mayland thoughtfully, 'that the House is really the place—'

'To be perfectly frank,' said Budd, 'when I got your invitation this morning, I was just preparing to put down a Private Notice Question.'

'Well, my dear fellow,' said Mayland, smiling, 'it isn't too late.

We mustn't prevent you. What sort of thing did you have in mind? I know how quick off the mark you are when there's a job like this to do.'

'I thought,' said Budd, 'I'd try and get permission from the Speaker to ask the P.M. in what circumstances the Attorney-General intervened to quash a charge, particulars of which I have sent him, laid against – well, a person in charge of a vehicle involved in an accident – whenever it was yesterday.'

'Interesting question,' said Mayland cheerfully. 'It should clear the air a bit. The whole of Fleet Street is thick with various versions of how Melville sat on the A.G. from Paris. Burnt up the wires, they tell me. He'll probably get the A.G. to answer.'

'Probably,' said Budd, setting his porcine face in a determined manner. 'But it'll set the ball rolling.'

'We'll give it a push,' said Mayland.

After Mayland had shaken hands with Budd at the door and closed it behind him, he returned to his chair, and said,

'Strange how every Parliament has its Budd. Truffle-diggers. You've got to have the nose for it.'

'Somebody one day ought to do a job on Budd,' said Colson.

'There's no hurry,' said Mayland. 'It's useful to have fellows like that who can sniff out trouble and get at the facts. Great thing not to be sensitive in politics!'

'Budd's all right,' said Colson. 'He'll kick you in the face and say it's in the line of duty. But you just tread on his toe!'

'Well, what do you think of all this, Peter?' said Mayland. 'You've been sitting there like a plaster cast.'

Talbot shrugged his shoulders.

'I really think there's nothing in it,' he said. 'It's all so trivial – like "Magistrate fined for speeding – forty shillings in his own court." Budd's going to get a thick ear.'

'Yes,' said Mayland reflectively. 'Yes. But it will be interesting to see how it develops. She's a charming girl, Sylvia. A bit withdrawn. Gave her mother a bit of trouble when she was young. Have we ever done a piece on her, Frank?'

'Not really,' said Colson. 'Odds and ends here and there.'

'Well,' said Mayland, standing and bringing the conference to an end, 'I think we ought to have something about her in tomorrow's paper.' He picked up an apple from the dessert bowl, and began to toss it from one hand to another. 'People, Peter –

that's what other people like to read about. None of those long headlines' – he had begun to smile, but the word 'desalination' flashed across his mind, and he scowled – 'I want a strong piece on Sylvia Melville. You know her pretty well.'

'Yes.'

'Good – about six hundred words – "The Sylvia Melville I Know" – and a good big photograph. Right, Frank?'

'O.K.'

Mayland began to walk to the door, but Talbot stepped in front of him.

'I'm sorry,' he said.

'What about?'

'I'm sorry,' Talbot repeated. 'I can't write about Sylvia.'

Colson and Hunter waited while Mayland's frown deepened before slowly lifting.

'Why not?' he asked.

Talbot hesitated.

'I wouldn't want to exploit my friendship with her,' he said at last.

'What else?'

'I don't like Sylvia being used as a stick to beat her father with.'

Mayland took a chair between his hands, and rocked it backwards and forwards, humming as he did so.

'Frank,' he said without looking up, 'you heard this man refuse to do his job.'

'Yes,' said Colson miserably.

'You will sack him on the spot, and tell him to leave the building at once.'

'Well, Mr. Mayland,' Colson began, but Mayland, still rocking the chair, said,

'Just do as I tell you.'

'It's all right, Frank,' said Talbot, his face pale. 'I've got the point.'

He shook hands with Colson, who moved his lips unhappily as if about to say something, but Mayland went on, his voice now rising,

'And one other matter. How much does this fellow owe us, Hunter?'

'We advanced him £2,000 for rent and fittings for his flat,' said Hunter in a factual, accountancy voice.

'On recall.'

'Ten days.'

'That's in the agreement?'

'Yes.'

Thrusting his hands in his pockets, Mayland turned to Hunter and said,

'See that he pays up in ten days.'

'I'll need a bit longer than that,' said Talbot.

'Ten days,' said Mayland, 'or you're in trouble.'

As Talbot closed the door behind him, he heard Mayland's voice, at once satisfied and contemptuous, saying,

'Quite useless. The fellow was a mistake.'

BUDD's failure to get permission from the Speaker to raise the Melville affair on a Private Notice Question seemed to dispose of the matter, although for the next two days he could be seen in the Members' Lobby before Prayers, standing in his favourite posture below the bronze statue of Lloyd George, accosting Lobby Correspondents and complaining that he had been ill done by. For the most part, the journalists dismissed his protests as yet another of 'Old Tom's grievances'. But a public opinion was being formed by the downward percolation of gossip from Fleet Street, Parliament and the Inns of Court. A happy photograph of Sylvia, arm-in-arm with Cullen in Central Park outside the Tavern-on-the-Green, was published in the Mayland Press. The Sunday gossip-writers began to interest themselves in the social structure of American campus life. And a number of limericks began to circulate. With the help of an ingenious Press Secretary at No. 10, Elizabeth Melville kept Sylvia's whereabouts secret.

On the Monday following Budd's unsuccessful attempt to put his question, *The Times* carried a short letter, made particularly striking by its place at the top of the page, its double headline – 'A Constitutional Question – Principles Re-examined' – and its widely spaced print. Lord Blaxton, who wrote it, had been the Chairman of a number of Royal Commissions, and was always in demand when those in power wanted either to shelve a policy by submitting it to his detailed scrutiny or to endorse it with his prestige. Occasionally, however, inspired by his family's long traditions, he would emerge spontaneously, either in the Lords or in *The Times* (after discussing the matter with a few intimates, among them an Archbishop), to offer a few thoughts on the state of the nation.

'Sir [his letter read],

'There is a consensus of opinion in Britain that to subject justice to the arbitrary play of politics would be to undermine the foundations on which our own system of justice stands.

For many centuries we have been zealous for the independence of the judiciary in all matters, great or slight.

'I am, therefore, impelled to urge that the present unhappy situation, the subject of much distasteful rumour, concerning an alleged political intervention in the province of the judiciary, should be disposed of by Parliamentary debate at the first opportunity.

Yours sincerely,
Blaxton.'

The letter was reproduced in the late editions of the Mayland Press and in the afternoon papers, which also carried a small paragraph reviving a dismissive description of Blaxton by Melville when he was Secretary of State for Colonial Affairs. 'The machete man of the backwoodsmen' he had called him after a debate in which Blaxton, supported by some never-heard peers whom he had whipped up for the occasion from their sisal estates, had attacked him for his African policies. Later, Melville had apologized. He had attributed too much vigour to Blaxton. 'The backwoodsman of the machete men' was what he meant, he explained.

Talbot read the letter while he was waiting to see his bank manager in Park Lane. He had arrived early for his appointment, and watching the casual procession of clients banking and collecting money, and seeing the clerks behind the grille unwrapping what seemed to him huge wads of notes, he thought of his cairn terrier sitting patiently at his feet at home during meals. For the last few days, he had been adding up sums. The agents of the landlords had refused curtly to refund any part of the money which he had advanced for rent and fittings. The decorators had agreed to stop work, but reminded him that their terms were monthly, and that they were committed for the French fabrics which he'd ordered with Sylvia.

Sylvia he'd found was now staying with her friend Mary Simpson, who had a cottage near Aylesbury. She wouldn't take telephone calls, and he'd have to go and see her. But first, there was the obsessive question of the money.

A smiling girl clerk, very pretty, he noticed, opened the counter and beckoned him in to the manager's office. Hayward. A friendly name. His own hands were a bit moist, and he rubbed them on his grey suit. More friendly smiles. He liked Hayward.

They'd lunched together, and spoken about politics and sailing and at the end of it, Talbot had felt that everything he said was either witty or penetrating. Hayward had laughed and agreed so much.

Now, facing the window behind Hayward's head, he felt less fluent, less cogent, less scintillating. Hayward's face, he thought, didn't look so amiable in shadow.

'I want to raise £2,000 – well, say £1,800 – in the next few days,' he said.

'You owe the bank nearly £1,500 already,' said the manager, examining the papers in front of him. 'Most of it's unsecured – and based on my own judgment. Have you any security?'

'No,' said Talbot, leaning back in the chair. 'Only my capacity to work.'

'That,' said the manager, 'is a potentiality, not a security. Would you think it inquisitive of me to ask what you want the extended facilities for?'

'Yes, it's to repay a loan from Mayland. He's just given me the sack.'

'I see,' said the manager in the controlled tone of a doctor whose patient has just described the symptoms of a devastating disease. 'We'll have to think about this. You see, Mr. Talbot, it's never good business to lend people money to repay other people's loans.'

'No,' said Talbot. 'I never imagined that. I'm in a difficulty, and I want to get out of it.'

'Won't they extend your loan?' the manager asked.

'No – and if I know Mayland, what he'd like to do is to bankrupt me.'

'Oh, no,' the manager protested. 'My dear fellow – your friends wouldn't allow that – the Whips – can't you raise a personal loan or get a guarantor?'

'I might. But it's a matter of time. I've got about six days left, and so far – I haven't tried anybody I know well, and I can't try any of the businessmen I've had political dealings with – so far it's a blank. When you talk to them of money, they just evaporate.'

'Have you any insurance policies?'

'Only the one you're already holding.'

'Very awkward,' said the manager. 'In my job, I'm tied down by Head Office – and I'm already over the top with you.'

'I'm sure' – Talbot heard his voice using the formula – 'if I have the loan for a few days, something's bound to come along.'

'Of course,' said Hayward, rising, his smile returning. 'Of course it will. And when it does, come and see me and we'll see how to make the best use of it.'

'But—'

'In the meantime,' said Hayward briskly, his fresh, open-air face glowing, 'I'll try and keep Head Office at bay for the next couple of weeks.'

He shook hands, and a few moments later Talbot found himself standing in the sunshine of Park Lane.

Monday. Saturday and Sunday didn't really count. On Friday, people went to the country. Monday, Tuesday, Wednesday and Thursday. The car would be going back tomorrow. Five hundred deposit, less the deduction. Three fifty. That left sixteen fifty. Talbot walked slowly down the street, absorbed in his arithmetic and cutting the Tunisian Ambassador, whom he had dined with only the previous evening.

He sat in his drawing-room in one of the armchairs which had been included in the fittings, and made an inventory of the articles in the half-furnished flat. If he was lucky, he would be able to raise £300 for the lot, and that would take time. Besides, he'd need some furniture wherever he lived. He studied again the list of appointments he had made – British Council, Rediffusion, J. Walter Thomson. On the assumption that he got a contract – could one borrow money on the security of a contract? But he'd have to get a contract first. He went into his uncurtained study, and looked across the roofs at the complex architecture of houses, spilling their drainpipes like viscera, and at the geraniums withering in the hot afternoon. That was how he felt himself – degutted and shrivelled. Sixteen fifty. Sixteen million. He'd lost count.

He took up the telephone, a cream instrument to tone with the grey walls, and dialled his mother's telephone number. She usually played canasta in the afternoon with a faithful group of friends, but her telephone was private, standing on an occasional table next to the armchair in her bedroom. He knew that it would take her at least two mintues to answer, but after the first burr he became anxious in case she wasn't there.

'Hello, who is that?'

The familiar thin voice at last.

167

'Mother – it's me.'

'Oh yes, dear, how are you? Why aren't you at the House of Commons?'

'Well, I don't sit there all the time. How are you?'

'Not too good, I'm afraid. I've got a most frightful pain right down my left leg. I think I'll have to see a specialist.'

'What about someone locally?'

'Oh, they're no good. I wish you could find time to ask someone about me in London. You're always asking the Minister of Health questions about other people.'

'Yes, but—'

'I realize you're awfully busy, and I'd do it myself if I could. Perhaps when I come up for your party—'

Talbot sat on a decorator's table.

'I'm afraid, mother, the party's off.'

'That's a pity. I've bought a new dress. Harrods sent me three on approval, and I bought a blue one – rather extravagant, I'm afraid.'

'Well, I hope you enjoy it. The party's off because I can't really afford the flat.'

He could hear his mother's quick breathing.

'Yes,' she said. 'Everything's so expensive. Thank you, dear, for ringing.'

'There's something I wanted to ask you. I think you've got an insurance policy.'

'Well, of course I have. Why do you ask?'

'I was wondering, mother, if you would use – or rather let me use your policy – I think it's worth over £1,000 already at redemption value – as a security for a loan I need.'

He heard her change the receiver from one hand to another.

'I – really, Peter – that's rather a surprising thing to ask. You know I'd do anything for you, but don't you think – the insurance after all is my own security – I'd hoped before next year when the policy matures to get away somewhere warmer – you know I'm not very well.'

'Yes – I see that, mother,' said Talbot. 'I only need the money for a few weeks.'

'That's just it, darling. If you only need it for a few weeks, wouldn't it be better to get it somewhere else? Let me see! Have you tried your bank?'

'Yes.'

'That's very awkward. I really don't know what to advise you. Listen, darling. I can't talk now. They're all in the other room screaming for me. I hope everything goes all right. If there's anything I can do to help—'

'No, don't worry. There's nothing I really want. Look after yourself.'

'And you, dear.'

As soon as he put the receiver down, he raised it again and dialled the number of Lady Drayford.

'Edwina!' he said cheerfully.

'Peter, darling!' she replied with her emphatic casualness. 'Where've you been? Not a word since the Garden Party and all these fantastic happenings. I looked for you at the House the other day, but you weren't in your place. Why are you so neglectful?'

'I've been too busy—'

'Yes, I know – all those pretty girls at Sallah's dinner party. But you watch out – polygamy in the Middle East doesn't extend to strangers. Why don't we have lunch together soon?'

'That's why I was ringing. But I want to see you sooner than that.'

'When – now?'

'No – this evening.'

'I can't. I'm dining with the Rossdales. But afterwards – I know the rule's been suspended and you'll be sitting till after midnight. Say I pick you up at midnight exactly. Wouldn't you like that?'

'Yes. Where's Edward?'

'In South Africa. Midnight?'

'All right. Midnight. Thank you, darling.'

Talbot put down the receiver with a sense of relief as if the hope and the fulfilment were one. Edwina. The night at Hedley House with its shames and dissatisfactions was no longer vivid in his memory. All that he recalled was her resolute, masterful voice, mocking, unimpressed and making decisions. Talbot stretched his arms, and looking around the room again, decided that if he was lucky, he might be able to have his party after all.

When he arrived at the House of Commons, the Opposition Party meeting had just ended, and Members in twos and threes were making their way down the stone staircase from Committee Room 14 to the Smoking Room and Tea Room.

He had stopped to talk in the Lower Waiting Hall to a Lobby Correspondent who was asking with an allusive discretion what had happened at the meeting, when Armstrong accosted him and drew him aside.

'What's old Geoffrey been up to?' Armstrong asked bluntly.

Talbot leaned against the podium of Oliver Cromwell's bust, and said,

'Nothing, Owen. Nothing at all. They're gunning for him, that's all.'

'He's got a lot of enemies – on your side too.'

'Mostly on our side,' said Talbot. 'What are your chaps going to do about it?'

'Sorry,' said Armstrong. 'I can't tell you that. But I wouldn't like to see Geoffrey in trouble – not that kind of trouble – not over a thing like that. If I had a daughter, I'd do the same.'

'He hasn't done anything,' said Talbot doggedly. 'Nothing at all.'

'You'd better look at the tape,' said Armstrong. 'I think Ormston's shopped him.'

They walked round the corner to the tape machine outside the Smoking Room, and while it stuttered out the Stock Exchange prices and company changes, they read an earlier sheet which someone had marked with a jagged pencil.

12.15 p.m. *Chancellor and the Public Administration.* Speaking at the annual conference of the National Union of Public Employees at Weymouth today, the Chancellor of the Exchequer, the Rt. Hon. Gerald Ormston, said that the separation of powers was and remained one of Britain's great constitutional principles. It had enabled a Civil Service to emerge which in all its branches was the envy of the world. It would indeed be an unhappy day if it were ever thought that either for Party or personal reasons there could be any blurring over of the well-defined distinction between legislature, executive and judiciary. It was outrageous that an innuendo had been made that all was not well with our well-tried system. In the absence of proof to the contrary, he had no reason to believe that there was any reason for the imputation that the Government had not in every particular upheld the fundamental principles on which our constitution securely rested.'

'That doesn't seem too bad,' said Talbot, peering over Armstrong's shoulder.

'No,' said Armstrong. 'But look at it again. It's a typical Ormston let-out. Look at that "no reason to believe".'

Budd approached them and said to Talbot,

'Like to sign a Motion?'

Talbot looked at him frigidly and said,

'What's it all about?'

Budd unfolded a large sheet of paper, and said,

'It's a Motion I've drafted asking Melville in the interest of public policy to make a statement on the circumstances in which a charge preferred against a certain person on July 12th for being drunk or under the influence of drugs when in charge of a car was withdrawn by the decision of the Director of Public Prosecutions acting under the orders of the Attorney-General.'

Talbot glanced at the piece of paper and handed it back to Budd.

'No, thank you very much,' he said. 'I don't like scavenging.'

He turned round and walked towards the Central Lobby, where he was to meet an American couple called Nelson, with their two children, on behalf of a colleague who had been delayed in his constituency.

'Cocky bastard,' said Budd, watching him go. 'What about you, Owen?'

'No,' said Armstrong. 'You know the Party decision. Why the hell can't you wait for Yates' question?'

'Because I put mine down first,' Budd said blandly.

As Armstrong hobbled off to the Tea Room, Budd planted himself with his feet apart at the entrance to the Smoke Room.

In the Central Lobby, where visitors were already beginning to assemble, Talbot stood for a few moments watching the Nelsons as their heads swivelled round in an inspection of the carved bosses on the roof and the Venetian mosaics. They all looked delighted – the slightly stooping, early middle-aged bespectacled lawyer, his wife with her skirts a little too short, and the two small boys of about twelve and ten staring entranced at the statues in the niches and the panel of St. David with a dove on his shoulder and two angels in support.

Talbot, preoccupied by arithmetic, regarded the family with

dislike. But when Eric Nelson looked down and their eyes met, he hurried forward smiling to greet them.

'Well, this is most kind of you,' said Nelson in an amiable tone. 'We know how little time you've got, especially on a day like this.'

'Oh, it's always very much like this,' said Talbot, shaking hands with each of them, including the two boys, who were called Joseph and Michael. 'Harry asked me to tell you how heartbroken he is at not being able to meet you, but he was kept in his constituency.'

'We thought,' said Mrs. Nelson, 'that we walked into a sort of crisis.'

'What made you think that?' said Talbot.

'There's something in the *Herald Tribune* about your Prime Minister having some problems about his daughter, and the Leader of the Opposition, Mr. Yates, going to talk about it this afternoon.'

'Just gossip,' said Talbot.

When taking constituents over the House of Commons, he had three speeds; the first for parties of schoolchildren and their teachers, a shuffle with pauses for rounding up stragglers. The second was for welcome visitors, with whom he enjoyed a slow dawdle through the corridors. And the third was a brisk jog-trot for visitors not of his seeking who, he felt, regarded the Palace of Westminster merely as a tourists' *corvée*. He put the Nelsons in the third class, and set off rapidly with them through the House of Lords in the direction of the Royal Gallery. The family walked ahead of him like a platoon, Nelson hand in hand with his wife and the two boys walking decorously behind them.

In the Royal Gallery, Talbot waved towards the murals as they passed and said to the taller boy, 'That picture on the right shows the meeting of Blücher and Wellington at Waterloo in 1814.'

'1815,' said the boy unsmilingly.

Talbot looked round in time to hear the boy's mother's contented murmur to Nelson. From the Royal Gallery they went back to Westminster Hall, and stood together at the top of the stairs looking up at the vast hammer-beam roof and from there to the great bare Hall with its grey flagstones.

'It's so cold and empty,' said Mrs. Nelson.

'But full of history,' her husband added. 'Full of ghosts.'

'Where are they?' said the little boy bravely as the light streamed through the memorial window on to the glistening plaques set in the floor.

'They come out at night,' said Talbot. 'Have you ever heard of Oliver Cromwell?'

'1599 to 1658,' said the older boy.

Without waiting for Mrs. Nelson's proud sigh to exhaust itself, Talbot said,

'They dug up his body in 1661 and stuck his head on a pole in the roof of the Hall.'

'Where?' said Joseph.

'Right up there,' said Talbot, pointing. 'And down there's where our kings lie in state when they die.'

'What kings?' asked Michael.

'Lots of them,' said Talbot generally. He reduced the speed of his tour. He had begun to like the self-contained warmth of the family. What at first had seemed laughable, now seemed enviable. They had been married for twenty years, the Nelsons told him. The wife never answered without looking to her husband for approval, nor he without seeking her reassurance.

'You had your revolution three hundred years ago. That's why you British are so settled and calm,' said Nelson.

'I hadn't thought of it that way,' said Talbot.

Towards the evening, Talbot's anxieties, which had been appeased by his decision to meet Lady Drayford, began to rise again. He dined in the Members' Dining Room, taking his usual place at the table for eight near the window, but the conversation, cautious and half-hearted in its references to Yates' Private Notice Question, only added to his unease.

Earlier in the day, the Leader of the Opposition had asked the Attorney-General in what circumstances he had quashed a criminal charge already sanctioned by the Director of Public Prosecutions against an individual, particulars of whom had been delivered. The Attorney-General had replied that no charge had been sanctioned, and that in those circumstances the first part of the question didn't arise. Budd had got up in the general uproar that followed and made some reference to the Prime Minister's duty to declare his interest in the matter, but although Melville had risen to reply, the Speaker had ruled Budd out of order on the grounds that the question of the Leader of the Opposition referred only to the Attorney-General. Budd had tried to move the Adjournment of the House under Standing Order No. 9, arguing that there was an urgent question of public business to be discussed, namely the Prime Minister's intervention in a matter affecting the judiciary. Later, amid shouts of 'No, no', the Speaker declined to accept the Motion. He wouldn't, he said, offer his reasons other than to say that the terms of the hon. Member's Motion weren't sufficiently specific. Melville sat with his arms folded, saying nothing, but acknowledging with a nod Yates' statement that the Opposition would revert to the matter as soon as possible.

At Talbot's table no one had mentioned Sylvia's name. But he knew that as soon as he left, Whoberley, who knew of his friendship with her, would certainly do so. Talbot finished his Stilton, drank the rest of his glass of Beaujolais, and went into the Library to relax in one of the large armchairs in the Silence Room before meeting Edwina. The restless thought of Mayland kept him awake. Despite his anger with him and his sense of relief as if at an escape, Talbot in his memory kept seeing Mayland in friendly situations when he offered him drinks, contracts, loans, introductions. His reason rejected the false *bonhomie*. But the cordial image persisted until he picked up an evening paper discarded on the Library floor, and read the headline, 'Renewal Calls for Clean-up'. The National Organizer of Renewal, Mrs. Susan Bolding, had issued a statement calling for a re-examination of public standards which wouldn't shrink from an inspection at the top. Talbot could hear Mayland's voice dictating the manifesto, and he threw the paper on the floor in distaste. Through the Library windows, he could see the night sky turning a purplish-mauve over the river, and he went down to the Terrace to wait for Edwina.

The Terrace was crowded with Members and their guests, sitting at tables or sauntering between the House of Lords and the Speaker's House. The lamps over Westminster Bridge bloomed yellow against the dusk, but the Terrace itself was in darkness, except for the lights that filtered from the corridors and Committee Rooms. Occasionally a familiar voice established itself over the murmur of conversation, and the sound of glasses on the teak tables. Talbot leaned with his back against the parapet, waiting for Edwina to appear.

As midnight approached, the Terrace began to empty and a sudden mutter of thunder made a group of women in light-coloured hats rise like disturbed moths. From the Members' Bar came a burst of laughter, and Talbot walked towards it, eager to lessen his feeling of exclusion.

'Where are you going?' said Lady Drayford, detaching herself from the company of two Opposition backbenchers who, she had decided, were promising young men.

'I didn't see you,' said Talbot. 'I was going to get a drink.'

Big Ben began to chime, and Lady Drayford said,

'I can't stand that terrible row. Come and have a drink with me.'

'Where?'

'At home.'

Talbot hesitated.

'It's all right,' said Lady Drayford. 'There are no more votes tonight. The Chief Whip told me. Let's slip out through Speaker's Court.'

Talbot walked reluctantly with her. He wished he'd had his drink. She had taken his arm in Parliament Square, and as they strolled through the empty streets and she talked about a villa which she had taken in Italy and about a charity ball over which she was presiding and about her difficulties with I.T.A., his firm decision to ask her for a loan which earlier on had seemed to resolve his problems shrank impotently. When she adjusted a sagging geranium in the window-box before turning the key in the lock, Talbot was already beginning to bid her good night. But she pushed the door open, and said,

'I've an excellent rule with my staff. Nobody visible after midnight.'

She switched on the light, and Talbot looked with pleasure at the Loiseau, a painting of a village under snow, which had charmed him on the other occasions he had lunched with Lady Drayford.

'Get yourself a drink,' she said. 'I'll have a large gin and tonic.'

Talbot prepared the drinks while she studied a series of notes left by her staff.

'Edward's coming home on Saturday week,' she said. 'Do you think we'll have a new P.M. by then?'

She sat on the sofa by the window, but Talbot remained standing.

'I hope not,' he said. 'I like Melville.'

'He doesn't like you,' Lady Drayford said flatly. 'He told me so.'

Talbot half-smiled.

'I'm an unpopular chap,' he said. 'With Mayland as well as Melville. So I might as well take my pick.'

'I'm sorry about Mayland. Come and sit over here. He told me.'

Talbot came and sat next to her.

'You're too chivalrous. What's the point of it? Melville's going anyhow.'

'I doubt it,' said Talbot. 'He's not going to run because Mayland says "Boo".'

'It isn't that,' said Lady Drayford, her face darkening in recollection. 'Melville's a coward. I know him very well.'

'Were you ever his girl-friend?'

She sipped her drink.

'Not exactly. Just a skirmish. But it wasn't that. You know about him and Elizabeth.'

'No – what?'

'If you don't know, it doesn't matter.'

Talbot looked at her flushed face, and realized that her last drink was topping up several that had gone before.

'He's got no guts,' she went on. 'Why didn't he give Mayland his peerage? Because Mayland had a little black mark in Australia a hundred years ago. But what does he do when Sylvia, that little pecksniff, gets into trouble? He tells the A.G. to revise the law.'

'I don't believe it,' said Talbot.

'That's because you're such a prig yourself. Why don't we go to bed? Get me another drink.'

Talbot took her glass, and refilled it. Then he returned to her and said,

'Edwina, there's something—'

'I've known hundreds of politicians,' she said. 'I'm sorry for you all. You've got to put on one show in public and another in the backroom – Melville, Yates, the whole lot of you.'

She finished her drink fast, and her eyes brimmed, reddening her lids.

'It's disastrous to fall in love with a politician. You might as well fall in love with a papier-mâché mask. You look for the person – and it's all hollow. God, how I used to love that man Yates!'

'That's a new one,' said Talbot.

'No, it isn't. I adored him – despite his ghastly wife and revolting children. I adored him. He'd hold me in his arms, and I'd feel his fingers counting out on my spine the paragraphs in his next speech.'

'And now?'

'Oh, it's all over – all finished. I once met him on a train going to a Party conference in Llandudno. His nose was running. He complained all the way about the cold, and when he got there he complained about the draughts in the hall. Conferences are great romance-killers.'

'Do you miss him?'

'No – only the feeling I had for him. Let's go to bed, Peter.'

Talbot rose, and said,

'Edwina, dear, there's something important I want to ask you.'

'Tomorrow.'

'No, now.'

She looked up at him, and he saw that her face and shoulders had become mottled with heat.

'You know,' he went on, 'that Mayland's given me the sack.'

'Yes – you asked for it.'

'I owe him £2,000.'

'It's better to owe than to lend.'

'I'm being serious, Edwina. He's going to issue a writ if I can't raise the money by Monday.'

Lady Drayford reached for a cigarette from the box on the table.

'Have you tried your bank?' she asked without meeting Talbot's eye.

'Yes,' he said. 'It's no good.'

'I am sorry,' she said. 'Tried Pickton – McRourke – Hahn – they've all got money?'

'I asked Pickton. It discouraged me from trying anyone else.'

She lit a cigarette, and said,

'I wish I could help you, darling.'

'I don't want to borrow from you.'

She looked up quickly and suspiciously.

'What *do* you want?'

'I wonder, Edwina' – this time he didn't look at her. Instead, he walked to the window where the lawn curtains were billowing in the night breeze – 'I wonder if you'd guarantee the money at my bank for a couple of months.'

'Of course I would,' she said lightly. He turned to her hopefully. But she added, 'Unhappily, darling, I can't. I'm all trustified. Didn't you know? Apart from my income, it's all – well, I can't touch a thing.'

'But if you went to my bank manager, Edwina – with your credit – and said you'd act as a guarantor—'

She put down her glass and stood.

'No, don't go on, Peter. You'll embarrass yourself and me. I can't do it. That's the end of it.'

They faced each other with dislike, he for the rebuff he had received, she for the rebuff she had given. He began to say, 'When you were in—' but she interrupted him, and said,

'Don't say it, Peter. We'll both be sorry. One thing has nothing to do with the other.'

He left his scarcely begun drink, and said,

'I had no intention of saying it, Edwina. I never even thought it. Thank you for the drink.'

He noticed that the flushes on her shoulders had changed their pattern. Mayland and Edwina. He had scored a double.

But in the street, his debt returned to sit on his mind like an Alp.

CHAPTER TWELVE

FORBES turned to Ormston, who had sat silently for the last twenty minutes as the discussion proceeded, and said,

'Would you like to comment, Gerald?'

Ormston, pallid against the black which he wore in summer and winter, didn't answer for a few moments. Then he said slowly,

'You asked us here to your house, Howard, not to form a cabal but as friends – friends in the Government, who are worried – I think that's the word – about the country as well as the Party.'

There was a mutter of assent from the eight men who sat grouped closely in Forbes' study in Eaton Place.

'Health,' Ormston went on, 'Works – Agriculture – Education' – his glance traversed the faces – 'Private Members too – Patrick, Herbert – you're all concerned about the rumours that have been flying about. We needn't pretend to ourselves that Yates doesn't know about our anxieties.'

'He called us "a disorganized hypocrisy" at Nottingham this evening,' said Patrick Stephens, a young backbencher. 'It was on the News.'

'We'll get a lot more of that,' said Ormston.

'And some of it justified,' said Forbes. 'If no one else will say it, I want to say that Geoffrey's been reckless with the Party's reputation.'

'It's the Attorney-General's reputation in the first place,' said the Minister of Health.

'What time's Gordon coming?' asked Ormston.

Forbes replied, 'He said he'd be here at 10.30 after the House rose. But I'd just like to read *The Times* leader for tomorrow. It's called "On Whose Orders?" and it's a sizzler.'

He read, ' "The position of the Director of Public Prosecutions, his actual powers, rights and duties, and the relations between him and the Law Officers of the Crown, are far from clear, and it is to these points that we should like to see inquiry directed.

The office of Director of Public Prosecutions exists only by virtue of Acts of Parliament, the first of which was passed in 1879. His duty to institute prosecutions is very vaguely indicated in the Act of 1879, more specifically in the Act of 1950. He is to do so 'under the superintendence of the Attorney-General', but whether he is legally bound to do whatever the Attorney-General tells him we do not know.

' "The whole, as nearly as possible, of the criminal law ought to be substantially known to those who administer it and capable of ascertainment by anyone who wishes to know what it is. It would be much to the public advantage if an authoritative answer could be given to some such questions as the following: How does the Director of Public Prosecutions usually become aware that an indictable offence is supposed to have been committed? In what sort of cases, if any, does he take action independently of the Attorney-General? In what sort of cases does he (a) seek or (b) receive from the Attorney-General instructions to prosecute or not to prosecute? When he receives such instructions, is he legally bound to obey them or is he (a) entitled or (b) bound to exercise any judgment of his own? Has the Attorney-General legal power to put a stop to any criminal prosecution (a) by the Director or (b) by a private individual, before it has reached the stage at which the issue of a writ of *nolle prosequi* becomes appropriate?" '

He took a breath, and looked around to see if he was holding his audience. Satisfied, he went on,

' "There is one more person whose duties and rights concerning the withdrawal of prosecutions might be ascertained with advantage, and that is the magistrate. Has a magistrate any duty of preventing or any right to prevent the withdrawal of a prosecution?

' "These are questions which fall to be answered, and when answers are given, it will then be for Parliament to ask on whose orders a prosecution, made apparently with sufficient reasons, has lately been withdrawn." '

While Forbes was reading, the Attorney-General had entered, and stood at the back of the group. Ormston saw him and said,

'Come and sit down, Gordon, and tell us what's been happening.'

The Attorney-General stretched his legs wearily as he took the chair nearest to the fireplace, which Stephens had surrendered to him. He waved towards the Press cutting in Forbes' hand, and said,

'All that's out of date. The Opposition have put down a Motion of Censure.'

'What sort of Motion?' Ormston asked quickly.

'On you – me – all of us. It's for next Monday.'

'Where's Geoffrey?' Ormston asked.

'He's busy with his personal problems – he's gone off to the country.'

There was a silence broken by an angry outburst from Forbes.

'That's really what I've been saying,' he said. 'It's an extraordinary situation that Melville ought now to be getting ready for the Conference on South-East Asia. Instead of which, he's haring off somewhere or other to settle his family affairs – and landing the Government with a nasty vote of censure in the bargain.'

'What do you think of it?' said Ormston to the Attorney-General.

'It's very unpleasant,' said Taylor, frowning into a mid-distance. 'But I mustn't anticipate the debate. I wrote to *The Times* yesterday – you saw the letter. I said quite simply that I will answer in the proper place – and that is the House of Commons.'

'I'd better tell you, Gordon,' said Forbes, 'that in the present state of the Party, there may well be abstentions. Apart from what some of us may feel about the thing on principle, Mayland's running his own campaign. I needn't tell you that. He's got out a Melville dossier, and he's passing it around, using Budd as his messenger-boy.'

'What's he saying?' the Attorney-General asked, his face controlled.

'He's saying,' said Forbes, 'that you sent for the D.P.P. and went with him to the P.M.'s room – that you spent an hour there, and that next day at the hearing the case against Sylvia Melville was withdrawn.'

'Mayland's got his interpretation wrong,' said Taylor.

'He's saying that you're being chivalrous – and that the responsibility is the P.M.'s.'

Ormston stood up, and said,

'Gordon was perfectly right when he said the Motion of Censure is against us all. We've got to deal with one thing at a time. If we don't face Yates and his gang as a united Party – even on this – they'll hack us to bits. I think this is an issue on which we're backing the Attorney-General quite apart from Melville's own involvement.'

There was a chorus of 'Hear, hear.'

'I'm afraid,' said Ormston, 'that the credit of the Party is involved in this. We've got to defend it. Then, if we need our own inquiry – inside the Party – we can undertake it, and Melville will no doubt have his own case to put.'

Forbes pushed back his chair, and said,

'I don't think we ought to break up before thanking Gerald and the A.G. for coming tonight. As Gerald said at the start – we're not a cabal, although I suppose that's what the anti-Ormstonites call us. We're here because – well, we love our Party, and we don't want to see its face smeared by the innuendoes and rumours that are in circulation now. I've been in four Parliaments and two Governments, and I hold the view that the Party's reputation has never been so compromised as it is today. But this is only part of it.'

He produced a benzedrine inhaler from his pocket, and took a deep breath through one nostril.

'I think we ought to go into this debate determined to win, but at the same time recognizing that, in a sense, even with a majority of votes, we still will have lost something.'

'What?' a voice asked.

'Public confidence,' said Forbes. He faced Ormston directly. 'I think we should go into the debate remembering that we have a first-class Deputy Prime Minister who some of us think should have been P.M. last time.'

There was an outburst of 'Hear, hear,' and clapping. Ormston stood without moving, looking at the ground. At last, with a smile flickering at the end of his lips while his eyes remained melancholy, he said,

'We can leave that thought till after the debate. For the moment, we must apply ourselves to backing up our friend, the Attorney-General.'

Sir Gordon Taylor smiled, and patted Ormston on the shoulder. He'd always liked him – a simple, straightforward man, so unlike Melville.

On Friday morning, the Prime Minister drove with the Chief

Whip to Chequers, where Elizabeth had already gone. He had arranged for a number of Ministers to come down for the week-end for a discussion on economic policy and the strategy of the debate. In front of him his detective, Pritchard, sat next to the chauffeurs, two solid figures, unchanging and phlegmatic, guardians of his routine.

'Ormston won't be coming down,' said Scott-Bower.

'I'm not surprised,' said Melville.

He gave a quick glance at the headline 'Midnight Meeting of Ministers', by the Political Correspondent.

'I imagine he leaked this,' said Melville.

'No,' said the Chief Whip firmly. 'No. Whatever you can say of Gerald, he wouldn't do that.'

'Wouldn't he?' said the Prime Minister, pressing the button to raise the glass partition in the limousine. 'Gerald's the first to "Convey a libel in a frown And wink a reputation down." His trouble is he won't come out with it.'

'I don't think it's that,' said Scott-Bower, filling his pipe. 'Gerald's trouble is that he was never sure in his forties whether he wanted to be Prime Minister, Speaker or Chairman of Barclays Bank. They all need different qualities, once you accept that to be an Old Etonian is a good starting-point for all of them.'

'Not for me,' said Melville.

'It's what some of them don't like in you,' said the Chief Whip.

They drove on without speaking till they reached the Amersham road when Melville said, as if continuing his train of thought,

'What's new in all this is that Gerald's now got a campaign manager.'

'Howard?'

'Yes – Howard Forbes. I wouldn't be at all surprised if that piece didn't come from him. He never forgave us for not giving him Health. Tell me, how would you like a Department?'

Scott-Bower reflected.

'I've got out of the habit of speech,' he said. 'Whips develop a psychogenic dumbness.'

'That needn't be a handicap in a Department,' said Melville smiling. 'I'd like to bring in some of the younger men as

Parliamentary Secretaries – Potter, Hazel, Parfitt. I'd like to give the Opposition something new to look at.'

'After Monday, I think,' said the Chief Whip. 'Let's get rid of that first.'

He lowered a side window, and the air from the beechwoods at the roadsides blew into the car.

'It's the only time of the year that I like Chequers,' said Melville. 'I must try and get you to play tennis this weekend.'

'You'll have to try harder than last time,' said the Chief Whip. 'I haven't played for twenty years.'

Their conversation halted. Scott-Bower had wanted to ask Melville whether he had heard from Sylvia, but, whenever he approached the subject, the Prime Minister's face had hardened as if the Chief Whip were about to commit a breach of intimacy.

'On Monday,' said Melville, 'the Attorney-General can open, and I'll wind up. Could I see the Motion again?'

'It's here,' said the Chief Whip, taking the pale green Order Paper from his brief-case. 'It's quite simple – "That the conduct of Her Majesty's Government in relation to the withdrawal of proceedings against Miss Sylvia Melville is deserving of the censure of this House." '

Melville took the Order Paper in his hand, and examined it with an alienated curiosity. He had held such a Paper a thousand times in his hands, and seen his name attached to Motions on hundreds of occasions. He had himself been the author and the Government the subject of a dozen Motions of Censure. But his name and Sylvia's seemed misplaced. The Motion with the names of Yates, Davies, Henley, Price and McNeale in support was like a dream in which words attached themselves to inappropriate objects. He handed the Paper back to Scott-Bower, and said,

'It looks strange. What are they saying in the constituencies?'

'Well,' said Scott-Bower in a professional voice, 'I've been inquiring from Central Office, and the Whips have been doing their stuff. The general view is that all this is going to come to the boil this weekend. I don't think that Budd's supplementary did us any good – the one to the Postmaster about you having a private line from Paris to the Attorney. But there's another aspect of the matter, Geoffrey – and you'll allow me to be perfectly frank. Some of our Party workers will booze their heads off on occasion, but they don't like to think of the P.M.'s daughter being charged with drunkenness or whatever. On the other hand, if she is charged, they like to gossip about it.'

'Yes,' said Melville.

'The other point is, I think, less clear. Some take the view that if you did order Gordon to withdraw the prosecution against your daughter, you did what most fathers would have done if they could. Others are a bit more purist.'

He turned his head towards Melville like a slowly swivelling turret of guns.

'Speaking for myself, Geoffrey, there's only one thing I want to ask you. Perhaps I should have asked you three days ago. Did you order the A.G. to withdraw the prosecution?'

Melville returned his glance, then looked away.

They were approaching Great Missenden, and the Chief Whip knocked the ash from the bowl of his pipe.

'I think you'll have to be more precise on Monday.'

'We'll have to see,' said Melville.

For the rest of the journey neither of them spoke.

Later in the afternoon, Sylvia arrived at Chequers, brought there in Melville's car from Mary Simpson's house. She was wearing a blue cotton dress, and she had tied her hair behind her head in a pony-tail with a black bow. Melville was waiting at the door for her, and she said, 'Hello, father,' and kissed him on the cheek.

'I'm so glad you could come over,' he said in an easy voice as if he were greeting a neighbour. She looked pale, and her eyes were dark, and he said,

'I thought you might like a stroll up to Beacon Hill with me.'

'I'd love it,' she said politely. 'Will we need your detective?'

'I think we can dodge him,' Melville said.

They could see Thornton, the Home Secretary, approaching with Elizabeth along the forecourt, and Melville said,

'Let's take the path.'

As soon as they were out of sight of the house, Sylvia, who had been walking in silence, said,

'Daddy – I'm sorry. I'm afraid I've got you into a mess.'

Melville looked at her unsmiling profile turned to the ground as if indifferent to the horizon that widened as they slowly climbed, and said,

185

'I'm not in a mess.'

'I mean the Motion of Censure.'

'That's a commonplace. It's what Prime Ministers are there for.'

She shook her head.

'No, you can't jolly me along. I've caused you a lot of trouble. I didn't mean to. I'm sorry.'

He took her hand, and they walked without speaking till they reached a grassy point overlooking the Vale of Aylesbury.

'Look at that,' said Melville, sitting down. 'It's really a most splendid view. If we lived on the Continent or in America, it'd be a sort of registered panorama with special parking and Coca-Cola stands.'

Sylvia knelt beside him, but turned her face away from the scene towards the lapel of his tweed jacket.

'You've got a ladybird,' she said, and he went to brush it away, but she said, 'No, it's lucky,' and took it on her finger. 'Look,' she said, 'it's beautiful. Perfect. Without a problem.' She put the insect on a blade of grass, and after a long pause said to her father,

'What shall we talk about now?'

'Is it hard to talk to me, Sylvia?'

'Yes – in a way it is. Have we ever talked about anything but things? You don't realize it, but you've never talked to me about anything that matters.'

'Like politics?'

'No, not politics.'

'What then?'

She put her face in her hands, and looked bleakly at the sun-filled landscape.

'I don't know,' she said. 'All I do know is that when I was young – when I was a child – I used to ache and yearn for you to talk to me, but you were always so busy – with your work, your old business friends – mother too.'

'Why didn't you talk to me?'

'Oh, I used to. I tried. Often.'

'What did I say?'

'Nothing at all. You'd just kiss me.'

Sylvia lay back and looked up at the sky.

'And then I went through a long, long adolescence with a secret.'

Melville raised his knees, and cupped his chin as he listened to her young, clear voice.

'It was very hard to be fourteen and fifteen and sixteen and know something terrible, that you've sworn not to tell, that no one would believe if you told. And all the time you're blamed for feeling it. Yes, that's exactly what happened. . . . The wonderful things everyone called me – an unnatural daughter! It sounds like the title of a Restoration comedy.'

She sat up, and said, 'When mother said—'

'I don't want to talk about her,' said Melville. 'I don't, Sylvia.'

'Oh, yes,' she said, sitting at his side. 'Don't you think that today's a special day for talking?'

'Why today?'

'Because we are alone together – do you realize this is the first time we've been alone together in the open air since I left school? Please talk to me.'

'What do you want me to say?'

'I want to know about you and mother. You were about to be Prime Minister. You stayed with her—'

'There's nothing more to say. You know it all.'

'No, not all. That scar on her forehead that she keeps touching.'

Melville lit a cigarette before he answered.

'Why do we want to dredge all that up?'

'Because,' Sylvia replied, frowning, 'I want to understand what's happened to me. Tell me about the scar.'

'We all have our private ways of punishing ourselves,' said Melville. 'That was hers.'

'Well, tell me.'

He pulled at a tuft of grass before answering. Then he said, speaking rapidly,

'One night, I asked her about Robert – she got hold of a – one of those cut-glass powder bowls – she used to have one on her dressing-table – and she dashed it against her forehead.'

Sylvia put her hand to her own head, and Melville said,

'I sent for Broome – she was bleeding rather badly – and then later on – why should we talk about this, Sylvia? It's a very beautiful day – it's all over – finished – everything's healed up – scar, pain, everything.'

'Then why,' Sylvia asked, 'do you never smile?'

'Smile?' Melville repeated. 'I smile all the time. My TV smile is famous. Look!'

'Yes,' she said tenderly, putting her hand on his. 'I'm looking It isn't a smile at all.'

'Yes, it is,' he said, taking both her hands. 'It's a real smile, but a different smile. What's gone is gone. It can't come back But there are other things – new things – some of them just as good.'

'But the arm you lose. Sometimes you feel it as if it's still there. When you ache for someone, and you know that nothing will do instead—'

'In time,' said Melville, 'you may find it hard to believe, but in time – if you're patient – you make peace and all the pain you've had becomes a form of immunization.'

'I'm not immunized,' said Sylvia. 'Not at all. Not one bit. I'm not sure of anything any more.'

Melville raised her chin so that she looked him in the face.

'Why do you think that's an exceptional condition? Why do you think it's so good to be sure?'

'Because until I am, I won't be able to sleep.'

Melville rose, and taking her hand, raised her to her feet.

'We'd better get back for tea,' he said.

'It must have been a very unhappy time for her,' said Sylvia 'All those complications – and then him dying – and I suppose knowing that I knew – and all the time wondering.'

'Yes,' said Melville. 'Poor Elizabeth!'

When Chequers came in sight, Melville said to Sylvia,

'I want to talk to you later about what happened the other night.'

'Of course,' she said. 'I'll tell you everything.'

'How would you feel if your father left the Commons and became an Earl?'

'I hope I'd get over it.'

'And could you bear to live with your family for the next few months?'

'I wouldn't have the courage.'

She laughed and hugged him with both her arms around him.

'Be careful,' he said, 'the staff hardly know you.'

At midnight, Frobisher gathered up the abandoned papers left on the trays in Melville's study, and said,

'You must be tired, sir.'

'No,' Melville replied. 'I'm going to stay up a bit longer and try and get on with my speech.'

Frobisher said good night, and Melville, after turning off the main lights in the room, sat at his desk.

'The separation of powers', the last words he had written, seemed to him meaningless, their sound and shape remote and unrelated to the theme for the following day. The sentences of the handwritten page in front of him became like the paint on a picture when removed from its significance. He tried to give them sense, but the weary day with its desperate arguments, now about the balance of trade, now about foreign investments, and now about the Attorney-General, obtruded themselves, became commingled and left him exhausted. He rested his head on his hand, and stared at the Jacobean panelling of the wall in front of him. Finally he decided that he would wait for morning, rise early and with a clear mind compose an orderly speech.

He had sat for about twenty minutes, half-dozing in his chair, when Elizabeth entered.

'I don't want to disturb you,' she said.

Melville looked up, and said, 'You're not. I was thinking that if you look long enough at a word it becomes just print.'

'You've been working so hard lately,' Elizabeth said. 'When I heard them talking about cyclical recovery, and Euro-currency, and boom distortions, my head started swimming.'

Melville, who had risen as she came in, said, 'So did mine.' He offered her a chair, but Elizabeth said,

'No, thank you very much, Geoffrey. I'm going to bed soon. Are you worried about tomorrow?'

'No,' said Melville. 'There's nothing I regret.'

Elizabeth adjusted the shoulder strap of her evening dress, and Melville thought again, as he had thought whenever he saw Elizabeth's shoulders, that they were beautiful. She looked up at him half-shyly, and said,

'What are you looking at, Geoffrey?'

He patted her face, and said,

'I was looking at you. You made the Cabinet look very drab at dinner.'

Elizabeth laughed. 'Well, they are drab. I don't think the

country would ever tolerate anything but a drab Cabinet. The last time it had a twopence-coloured Cabinet Minister, they found him altogether too much. They like to feel their rulers are respectable.'

Melville turned to his desk and started to put his papers back into the file. Elizabeth followed him with an anxious expression, fearful that she might have said something to displease him. But Melville suddenly smiled, and said,

'I had a pleasant walk with Sylvia. We had a very happy afternoon.'

'She couldn't have been sweeter when she got back,' said Elizabeth. 'You know how bored she is with all the odd jobs and openings that I have to do. And today she actually asked me about the National Conference of Women Voluntary Workers that I'm speaking at in the Central Hall on Wednesday. You must take her for walks more often. She obviously loves it.'

Melville put his portfolio under his arm, and said,

'When she starts working at Chatham House, I'm going to ask her if she'll come and see us more often. I think if we gave her a room – not actually to live in, but as a sort of dropping-in place where she could keep her books and have people in for drinks – it might encourage her to come and see us.'

'That would be lovely,' said Elizabeth. 'I want to get her some new clothes too. She can look so pretty. She looked sweet this afternoon, standing in the sunlight on the lawn. If only we could keep these beastly photographers from spying on her and following her around. I was told that Mayland got one of his photographers to take a room opposite Sylvia's and that he's been taking photographs from there with an infra-red camera. That's how they got the one of Sylvia with a suitcase the other day.'

Melville shook his head.

'Mayland dresses himself up as a champion of causes, but all he really does is pursue private vendettas which he then sells to the public as holy wars. There's no one too weak for him to kick if it'll help his purpose. Ne doesn't give a damn about the executive interfering with the judiciary. All he's concerned with is exercising his spite.'

'Why is he so vindictive towards you, Geoffrey?' Elizabeth asked. 'He's always been so particularly nice to me.'

Melville looked at her eyes, already reddened through lack of sleep, and said,

'I'm never quite sure, Elizabeth, whether you're excessively simple or excessively subtle. Assuming that you're excessively simple, let me tell you that the traditional way for inferior men to wound those they hate is to – to be amiable to their wives.'

She opened her mouth to speak, but closed it again.

'Good night, Elizabeth,' said Melville curtly.

As she opened the door, a telephone began to ring. Melville saw that the sound came from the outside telephone and not from the private telephone, and he said to Elizabeth,

'Will you please answer?'

He stood with his hand on the door-knob, watching the expression on her face slowly change as she listened to the voice at the other end of the line.

'Yes,' she said faintly. 'I'll come straight away.'

'What is it, Elizabeth?' Melville asked impatiently. She had put the receiver on the desk instead of on its bracket, and its burr filled the room like the sound of a trapped insect.

'It's Sylvia,' she said.

'What about her?' Melville asked roughly, taking hold of her wrist.

'I must go over and see her,' said Elizabeth.

'Why? What's the matter?' Melville insisted.

Elizabeth looked at his expression, and made an effort to compose herself.

'She's been taken ill,' she said. 'I'd better go and see her.'

'How ill is she?' Melville asked.

'I don't know,' she answered. 'I want to go over and see if I can help.'

'I'll come with you,' said Melville. He ordered the car, and to the surprise of the petty-officer in the Stone Hall, one of the WREN staff detailed for the weekend, they left without bidding her good night.

Dr. Lebourne was waiting when they arrived at Mary Simpson's cottage. They went into the living-room and stood by the chintz-covered chairs while Lebourne, with Mary Simpson, white-faced and desperate at his side, told them what had happened.

'I think,' said Lebourne, a tall man who looked more like a

farmer than a physician, 'that Sylvia couldn't sleep, and that when she awoke from her first sleep after having her normal dose of sleeping pills, she was a bit fuddled and took a couple more.'

'But she must have taken ten,' said Mary Simpson, correcting him. 'At least ten. There were ten in the bottle before she went to bed.'

'How do you know?' Melville asked sharply.

'Because they were mine,' said Mary Simpson. 'She told me that she'd forgotten her sleeping pills, so I gave her some of my own sodium amytals – the blue ones. She must have taken at least ten.'

'A very easy thing to do,' said Lebourne sonorously. 'Very natural if you wake up feeling a bit confused. Now, Miss Simpson, I think you'd better go to bed while I talk to Mr. and Mrs. Melville.'

'I'm sure I won't be able to sleep,' said Mary Simpson, straightening a picture of a hunting scene. 'I'm sure I won't.'

'In that case,' said Lebourne firmly, 'you'll just lie in the dark and think. A snooze is as relaxing as sleep.'

After she had left, Lebourne said to Melville,

'Perhaps we can sit down for two minutes. Your daughter's resting, and I'd like to offer you an opinion.'

They sat in front of him docilely, while Lebourne cleared his throat.

'Sylvia,' he said, 'swallowed about twenty-five grains of sodium amytal. If she'd swallowed more, she might by now be dead. She didn't swallow more because there were no more in the bottle to be swallowed. But it's also possible that this wasn't a genuinely suicidal attempt' – he paused while he observed the effect of his words on Melville, who lowered his head and rested his chin on his intertwined fingers – 'it may have been hysterical.'

'What does that mean?' Elizabeth asked.

'It means,' said the doctor, 'that perhaps she wanted attention rather than to end her life.'

'Why should she—' Elizabeth began, but her voice trailed away and she was silent.

'How is she now?' Melville asked.

'She's drowsy,' said Lebourne. 'I had to give her a stomach tube. It's unpleasant and exhausting. If her attempt was hysterical, I think she won't want to swallow pills again. But she might. She ought to go into hospital.'

Melville hesitated.

'I ought to say, though,' said Lebourne, 'that the minute she goes into hospital, however trustworthy our medical staff are, the news is bound to leak out. There are too many people involved. Ambulance men, porters, doorkeepers.'

'Is there any danger in keeping her here?' Melville asked. 'If you had nurses and so on?'

Lebourne stood massively above them like a dispenser of life and death conscious of his power, magnified by his capacity for decision beyond the authority of the Prime Minister. He pondered, and they waited.

'I think we'll see how the night passes,' he said. 'I'll stay with her and I'll try and get a nurse from Aylesbury. But it might be difficult.'

'I could drive over and pick her up,' said Elizabeth.

'We'll have to see,' said Lebourne.

'Can we go up and talk to her?' Elizabeth asked.

Lebourne hesitated. 'I don't think that you should, Mrs. Melville.'

'Why not?' Elizabeth asked.

Lebourne again hesitated. Then he said tenaciously,

'I think you'd better not. I think it might be best, Prime Minister, if you saw her alone.'

The doctor had left the door of Sylvia's room open, and only the light from the passage filtered into the room. Melville entered quietly, and stood for a second while his nostrils quickened to the persistent smell of vomit. Gradually his eyes became accustomed to the light, and he began to identify the contours of the room.

He sat at Sylvia's bedside for ten minutes, listening to her drowsy half-moans, and then he put his hand on the moist arm which she had flung over the sheets.

'Sylvia,' he said quietly. She stirred, and opened her eyes.

'They're doing terrible things to me, daddy,' she said. 'Why don't you take me away from here?'

'Go to sleep,' said Melville.

She rolled her head on the pillow, and said, 'I don't want to sleep. What are you doing here?'

He tried to answer her, but he felt his throat tightening and he said nothing. She heaved herself up and leaned forward as if about to be sick. Melville looked helplessly around him, and she muttered,

'Don't get panicky. I'm not going to be sick again. Oh, God, I feel awful!'

'Tell me what happened,' said Melville. He stood up and switched on the light.

'Yes,' she said. 'Put on the light. I want you to see how squalid I am – how squalid everything is.'

His sudden anger disappeared, and he went back to the bed and took her hands in his.

'What is it, Sylvia?' he said. 'Why do you want to destroy yourself – all of us?'

'Destroy myself?' she repeated. 'I don't know. I don't understand anything any more.'

'But you must know,' he insisted. 'Why do you want to punish us?'

'Punish you?' she said, lying back and staring at the ceiling. 'I don't want to punish anybody but myself.'

'But why?' said Melville. 'You haven't done anything. Why do you feel guilty?'

'I wanted life to be a certain way,' she said, 'and when I was a child I dreamed and hoped it would be always the same – with mother, you – our family. But it didn't turn out like that. Things happened differently. We became like sleepwalkers.'

'I did what I had to,' said Melville.

'It was all pretence and compromise,' said Sylvia. She became drowsy again and he watched her sleeping. When she awoke, it was as if there had been no interval.

'All of it was pretence and compromise,' she said.

'But all living is based on compromise,' Melville said quietly. 'We can believe in absolutes, but people must make concessions – all the time. They must forgive each other. And sometimes themselves.'

'I made concessions,' Sylvia said. 'All my life at home was a concession. I had to live with her, and I loved you and knew how she'd destroyed you.'

'You must go to sleep,' he said.

'Yes,' she said. 'I'll sleep. . . . Don't go away.'

After a few seconds, she said,

194

'I wanted you to know. . . . That's why I asked you to find my certificate. I left it there deliberately.'

His face didn't change as she opened her eyes and looked at him.

'Do you hate me?' she asked.

'No,' he answered. 'I love you.'

He kissed her face and drew the curtains. For a few minutes, he stood contemplating the silent landscape faintly lit by the morning moon. Then he turned and said, 'Will you come back with us tomorrow?' She didn't answer, and when he returned to the bed he saw that she was asleep.

CHAPTER THIRTEEN

'ALMIGHTY God, by whom alone Kings reign and Princes decree justice, and from whom alone cometh all counsel, wisdom and understanding: we thine unworthy servants here gathered together in Thy Name do most humbly beseech Thee . . .'

Melville, his head bowed, facing the wall with the handful of Members assembled for Prayers, listened to the Chaplain's voice, orotund and mellow, flowing through the echoing Chamber.

'. . . and laying aside all private interests, prejudices and partial affections . . .'

The solemn words rose from the litany as if embossed.

'. . . in true Christian love and charity one towards another, through Jesus Christ our Lord and Saviour. Amen.'

Melville's lips moved in accompaniment to the murmur of amens around him. He folded his arms as the Chamber began to fill with Members who had been waiting in the Lobby for Prayers to end, and the Gallery with visitors being directed to their places by the attendants. On some of the Government Benches, prayer cards reserving places were strewn like visiting cards. And Melville, looking around, thought that at a public execution there still would be those who would reserve their places in exactly the same way.

After a night without sleep and a morning of work he felt exhausted, and he shut his eyes for a few moments as the Minister of Housing and Local Government rose to answer the first question about how many slum houses were demolished in Leicester during the period 1951 to the latest available date. Melville had chosen to spend the hour before the debate at Prayers and Question Time in order to avoid the need to make an entry amid cheers and counter-cheers. That was the custom of gladiatorial debate, and he didn't want to challenge the ovation which he knew that Yates, the Leader of the Opposition, would receive.

The Chief Whip entered from the Lobby side, and took his corner seat on the Front Bench next to the Prime Minister.

'I've just had a message from Ormston,' he said. 'He's flying over to the International Monetary Conference at Brussels this afternoon.'

'Very discreet,' said Melville, studying his Order Paper.

'I don't think it will help us,' said the Chief Whip.

'We'll see,' said Melville. 'How are the abstainers?'

'I've had most of them in my room,' said the Chief Whip. 'If there are more than ten, it'll be uncomfortable.'

'For them, I hope,' said Melville, still smiling. He stretched his legs on to the table, and gave a quick glance around the Chamber. To the left of the Hansard reporters, he could see the Lobby Correspondents, indifferent to the monotonous recital of Questions and the pricking Supplementaries, as they observed the demeanour of the two Front Benches. Roger Cornforth, the Shadow Home Secretary who was going to open for the Opposition, was already in his place, self-absorbed with his familiar and unchanging expression of malevolence, a permanent prosecutor. Yates, the Leader of the Opposition, hadn't yet arrived, but in front of the Despatch Box there was a small area of green leather kept open on the congested bench to await his arrival. As the Questions succeeded each other, only the Speaker, the immediate questioners and the Ministers replying occupied themselves with the subject, a private conclave in the assembly of Members, who from the floor of the House kept glancing at the clock, or from the upper galleries where their numbers overflowed peered impatiently into the well of the Chamber as into an arena. The East and West Galleries quickly flowered with the hats of Members' wives.

'The *tricoteuses*!' said the Attorney-General, who had taken his place next to Melville.

The Prime Minister didn't answer. He had seen Elizabeth come with Sylvia into the West Gallery, noticed the whisper and movement of heads as the attendants guided them, each with an Order Paper, to the places next to Mrs. Speaker in her Gallery; and when Elizabeth looked over the brass rail to look for him, he gave her a quick smile.

The Parliamentary Secretary to the Minister of Agriculture was saying, '. . . the yield next year will be doubled,' and a great swell of 'yah-yah-yahs' rose in approval from the Opposition benches. The Parliamentary Secretary, gratified, glanced up from his brief to acknowledge the applause, but the cheers were for Yates, who picked his way slowly and delicately over the legs of his colleagues to his place in front of the Despatch Box. He looked across at Melville; and then in a symmetrical gesture stretched his legs till they rested on the table.

As the clock hands quivered towards three-thirty, the murmur of conversation rose steadily till at last it became a sustained background to the voice of Miss Muriel Beddows, the Parliamentary Secretary to the Minister of Pensions. Her virile contralto, amplified and vibrant though it was, still failed to penetrate the blanketing clamour.

The Speaker rose sternly, and the uproar diminished before his frown.

'It would be an advantage,' he said, 'if hon. Gentlemen would allow the hon. Lady to hear what she is saying.'

There were laughter and silence. The hon. Gentleman the Member for Walthamstow East asked in what circumstance Mr. R. Borden of 123 Clipper Road was refused a disability pension, and the Parliamentary Secretary told him. The Clerk read the Orders of the Day, and at three-thirty-seven Roger Cornforth rose to an ascending volume of cheers from the Opposition to move the Motion of Censure.

'Mr. Speaker, sir,' he began, leaning over the Despatch Box, 'I beg to move that the conduct of Her Majesty's Government in relation to the withdrawal of proceedings against Miss Sylvia Melville is deserving of the censure of this House.

'I cannot conceal from the House the sense of responsibility which I feel in moving the Motion which stands in my name on the Paper. It is a serious Motion, not only because of its immediate consequences, but because of the effect which what we do today will have on the administration of the law in this country. Many matters of controversy will be raised in the course of this debate, and there will be certain differences of opinion, but I will venture some propositions which, I think, will gain the assent both of the Prime Minister and of the hon. and learned Gentleman the Attorney-General. These propositions are as follows: If the administration of the law were to become subject to any considerations of expediency, then justice as we have known it in this country—'

'Oh, come off it!' a Government backbencher called out in a loud voice, and his interruption was challenged by a roar of counter-cheers from the Opposition benches. The Speaker rose, frowning, and waited for the din to subside.

'I think it would be as well,' he said, 'if I make it quite clear at the beginning of this debate that I intend that all who take part in it shall have a proper hearing.'

Cornforth gave a slight bow to the Speaker, and went on.

'I was saying that if expediency is to take precedence over law, then justice as we have known it for centuries will disappear. Civilized communities can only enjoy full liberty if the executive is excluded from interference with the mechanism of the administration of justice. It is for that reason that the very salutary rule has been observed in this country that the Attorney-General, in forming his opinion on matters of prosecution, is entirely free from any influence whatsoever. No case is too trivial to illustrate this point, no intervention by the Government too unimportant for this House to ignore it.

'Let me say at once that if we move a Vote of Censure directed against Her Majesty's principal Minister, the Prime Minister, we are addressing ourselves to a specific matter rather than to the general matters for which the Prime Minister has been censured, not so much by ourselves as by his honourable friends assembled so faithfully around and behind him.'

There was a burst of laughter and cheers from the Opposition back benches.

'No,' Cornforth went on, smiling, 'if we were seeking merely to criticize the Prime Minister for his shortcomings as Prime Minister, there would be many on the benches opposite who could do, and indeed often do, our work equally well.'

Melville sat looking stonily ahead of him.

'But today,' said Cornforth, 'we are concerned with a specific allegation, that a charge was made and then, on the Prime Minister's personal intervention, withdrawn. It is for us a particularly sad circumstance that we will have to touch on matters affecting the lady who is named in the Motion. On personal grounds we must regret it. It cannot be other than painful to concern ourselves with a matter of public interest which at the same time affects, most intimately and deeply, the private life of one of our colleagues and his family. And yet, the principle which we raise today is such that even if it requires this illustration, we cannot shrink from the task of providing it.'

He paused, cleared his throat, and poured himself a glass of water from the carafe next to the Despatch Box.

'The burden of our indictment today,' he went on, 'is that the Prime Minister, having been informed through the Attorney-General, who in turn had received information from the Director of Public Prosecutions, who in turn had learned of the matter from the Commissioner of Metropolitan Police, who in turn had learned of the matter from an inspector at a police station – the Prime Minister having learned that Miss Sylvia Melville was arrested on a charge of driving a car while under the influence of drugs or drink then ordered the appropriate authorities to drop the charge.'

From the Opposition benches came a collective, menacing growl.

'You will see from the chain of events that all of the gentlemen I have mentioned are linked in the decision which brought about the withdrawal of the charge. But it will be my purpose to apportion responsibility, and to show that those who carried out orders are less guilty than those others – the Prime Minister and the Attorney-General – who made the decisions.'

Incisively, with his finger stabbing in the direction of Melville, Cornforth went through the chronology of Sylvia's accident, her dispute with the driver, her arrest and the charge while the House listened in a tense silence.

'Perhaps at this stage,' said Cornforth, 'I may say a word about the relationship of Press and Parliament since it is so relevant to the matters before us. It is a singularly fortunate circumstance that after the charge was made two reporters, Mr. Copeland and Mr. Cowley, were present and by their vigilance took note of the succeeding events. Indeed, had it not been for their alertness and the due sense of responsibility of their editor – and hon. Gentlemen on this side of the House will know that we at least have no reason to feel any particular tenderness or sympathy for the Mayland Press – the matter might have dissolved into the oblivion which the Prime Minister clearly intended.

'Let me say at once that I am not here concerned with the merits of the indictment against Miss Melville. Nor am I without sympathy for the right hon. Gentleman in his personal dilemma. Indeed, who is there who could feel anything but understanding for a father faced with the decision – in constitutional if not technical effect – of prosecuting his own daughter, or alternatively of saving her from distress? Nor am I so' – he groped for the word – 'so ungenerous as to suggest that the Prime Minister was caring for his own situation in the matter.'

There was a loud groan of disapproval from the Government benches, and Cornforth, recognizing that he had made a tactical error, hurried on.

'No,' he said, 'my case is a simple one – an irrefutable one. It is that the Prime Minister told the Attorney-General to take "whatever action is necessary" – those are the words which the right hon. and learned Gentleman has himself admitted – to have the charge against Miss Melville withdrawn. And I would bring to the attention of the House one further and, I believe, conclusive item of information – and I have the hon. Gentleman's authority' – he extended his hand towards Budd – 'to indicate my source that on the day the charge was withdrawn, the Director of Public Prosecutions, Sir Leslie Beagley, arrived at the House at 3.47 in a taxi-cab—'

He waited for the effect of his statement to establish itself.

'—went straight to the Prime Minister's Private Secretary, was taken straight to the Prime Minister's room, and there' – he raised his voice and slapped the flat of his hand on the Despatch Box – 'spent thirty-five minutes with the Prime Minister and the Attorney-General. One hour later, the charge against Miss Melville was withdrawn.'

From behind him came a chorus of 'A – a – ah's', a gasp of indignant surprise.

The Opposition spokesman waited for Melville to react, but he continued to make notes on his writing-tablet, his head down, his face impassive.

'The right hon. Gentleman doesn't dispute the facts,' he said, and waited again.

Melville went on writing as some of the Government supporters waited for him to comment.

'In that case,' said Cornforth, 'there seems little to add.'

For another ten minutes, he went on to speak of the relationship of the executive and the legislature, the Prosecution of Offences Regulations, 1946, and the circumstances in which the Director of Public Prosecutions is appointed by the Home Secretary with the concurrence of the Prime Minister and after consultation with the Attorney-General.

'Sir,' he ended, 'my duty today is a disagreeable one. But if I have to dispose of the Prime Minister's credit, it is also to save the reputation of a man, the Director of Public Prosecutions, who cannot today speak for himself. He acts, it is true, under the general superintendence of the Attorney-General who should defend his actions. But what we have today is the spectacle of an Attorney-General and a Prime Minister both hiding behind the quasi-judicial position of the Director of Public Prosecutions in the exercise of his discretion to prosecute. That is a shameful thing, discreditable to the right hon. and learned Gentleman, discreditable to the Government, but above all discreditable to the Prime Minister, himself at the heart and centre of the attack on the system of law which it is his duty to defend. That is our indictment. That is why we hope that this issue will be elevated above the contest of Parties, and that the vote of censure will be a vote against anyone who seeks to tamper with the law which we all should exist to serve.'

He sat down, and the cheers around him rose in a tumult.

'That was a hell of a good speech,' Forbes murmured to his neighbour, Anthony Griffin, the Minister of State at the Foreign Office.

'Good debating speech,' said Griffin non-committally. He preferred to watch the course of proceedings before taking sides.

'Well, this *is* a debate,' Forbes said acidly, and thinking that Griffin wouldn't be long for the Ministerial life in a new dispensation, turned to add his cheers for the Attorney-General, who was heaving himself up like a reluctant and outweighed boxer climbing into the ring.

From the beginning of his speech, it was clear that Sir Gordon Taylor would forfeit the sympathy of the House. Beginning with a historical survey in which he referred to the Communal Courts, the Hundred Moot and the Shire Moot of the Saxon kings, he went on to speak of the practice under Edward III of sending the king's judges on Assize as Commissioners for Gaol Delivery and Oyer and Terminer. Then he spoke of the origin of the Director of Public Prosecutions, of the Departmental Committee of 1883 under the Home Secretary, Sir William Harcourt, which inquired into the office of the Public Prosecutor. As he developed his historical exposition, the House, at first somnolent, became restive. Some Members left ostentatiously for tea, the Chamber thinned, and still the Attorney-General forged on with an analysis of the Criminal Justice Act, 1925, and the Criminal Justice Act, 1948.

Suddenly Yates rose and said, 'I don't want to interrupt the right hon. and learned Gentleman in his legal ramble. Will he now tell the House in simple language accessible to laymen in what circumstances a prosecution can be abandoned once begun?'

Yates sat back, and folded his arms while the Attorney-General rose again, and straightening his tie as if he had been assaulted, replied in a hurt voice,

'I was coming to precisely that point. Cases in which a prosecution is dropped are reported to the Director so that he may consider whether a prosecution is *bona fide*, or alternatively whether the public interest requires that the prosecution should proceed, notwithstanding that the prosecutor may wish to discontinue.'

Yates rose again.

'Would the Attorney-General now come clean with the House? Did the Director of Public Prosecutions make a decision to withdraw the prosecution over the head of the Commissioner of Police? And if so, did the Attorney-General and Prime Minister assist him in his decision?'

The Attorney-General pondered for a moment while rumbles of agreement with Yates passed through the House.

'It is the duty,' he said at last, 'of the Attorney-General as it is of the Director of Public Prosecutions, to exercise his discretion in a quasi-judicial way as to whether or when he must take steps to enforce the criminal law. It has never been the practice in this country – and I hope it never will be – that suspected criminal offences must automatically be the subject of prosecution. Under the tradition of our criminal law, the Attorney-General and the Director of Public Prosecutions only intervene to direct a prosecution when they consider it in the public interest to do so.'

Several Members, including Budd, rose to interrupt from the Opposition benches, and at first the Attorney-General declined to yield, but in face of the shouts of 'Give way!' he resumed his seat, and the Speaker called 'Mr. Budd!'

'I am obliged,' said Budd in his hoarse voice, clutching his

203

papers under his arm. 'Will the right hon. and learned Gentleman now give us a straight answer? Did he or did he not – in what he calls his quasi-judicial position – instruct the Director of Public Prosecutions that it would be in the public interest, as well as his own, to carry out the request of the Prime Minister not to—'

The end of his sentence was lost in the roars of approval and disapproval from the opposing benches. The Attorney-General, reddening, said,

'That is a typically offensive innuendo by the hon. Gentleman, supported by nothing except—'

'The facts of the matter!' a Scottish voice called, and the Attorney-General stood confused and ruffled, his own succeeding words drowned in laughter. For the rest of his speech, after the failure of his improvisations, he returned to his brief, reading it steadily and only departing from it to advise his interrupters to await the Prime Minister's winding-up. He ended with the words,

'This is a debate which transcends personal reputations. It is concerned with the principles of law. When I decide on what is the public interest, I have the advice of the Director of Public Prosecutions and very often of Treasury Counsel as well. In informing myself, I may consult colleagues from the Prime Minister downwards – and as the late Lord Simon once said, the Attorney-General would be a fool if he did not.'

'You did and you're still a fool!' the anonymous Scottish voice called out, and the rest of the Attorney's speech collapsed in guffaws and ribaldry. When he sat, his face suffused and sweating, to a patter of faithful cheers, none of his colleagues offered him the conventional congratulations.

'There are some speeches,' said Sir Stewart Craig, an elderly Member who had once been Minister of Works, 'too bad even for jeers.'

'Yes,' said Talbot, sitting at his side below the gangway, 'I'm always making them.'

He jumped to his feet with about seventeen other Members to catch the Speaker's eye. The speaker said in an emphatic voice,

'Mr. Appleton!' – and Tom Appleton, a Durham coalminer, began a calm, slow-spoken analysis of the unequal proceedings of the law in different parts of the country and in different social strata. His speech was unsensational, and the Chamber slowly emptied except for those who hoped to take part in the debate, including Melville himself and Yates, with a number of Whips on both Front Benches in support.

For the rest of the afternoon and evening, Talbot tried unsuccessfully to get called. The hours passed, he thought, as in a long play, interrupted by the exits of the audience in the intervals after the chief actors had spoken their curtain lines. He felt sorry for Melville, alone and unbending on the Front Bench, the protagonist and the accused; and he wondered whether the Smoking Room gossip earlier in the afternoon that at least twelve Members would abstain mightn't after all be an understatement. He felt sorry for Melville and sorry for himself. He had decided as a last resort that he would approach Edgar McCrindley, a leading industrialist in his constituency, in the hope of borrowing the money that he owed to Mayland. But the thought of doing so gave him a sense of nausea.

The Speaker had called Budd, and watching his tapir-like nose twitching at the edges as he accumulated innuendoes and imputations against Melville, referring to previous Parliamentary debates in volumes carefully tabbed, and quoting from law books with the satisfaction of an autodidact, Talbot began to feel in his hatred of Budd an anodyne self-hatred. This, he felt, was the image of himself. Budd, fed and flattered by Mayland, his vanity provoked and incited by a bogus friendship which would use him and discard him – Budd was his *alter ego*. And Talbot wondered to himself whether, if he had the chance all over again, to write the article on Sylvia as Mayland had ordered, he would do so. He decided firmly, 'Never – not in any circumstances', and feeling better addressed himself to the pleasure of loathing Budd.

'Yes,' Budd was saying, 'I accept that it's my job to do the chore properly of preparing for a debate in which I'm going to make charges. When I bite, I bite hard. I don't let go. And the Prime Minister knows it.

'If he thinks I'm going to apologize for studying who goes in and out of his room, he's got another think coming. I love this House. I don't want its practices and traditions to be abused. And when I come here, and say that it was reported to me how and when the Director of Public Prosecutions was sent for by the Prime Minister, I believe I'm doing my duty as a conscientious Member of this House, responsible to his constituents.'

The nasal, plangent voice went on and on with intermittent hoarseness, and Talbot wrote in a careful Gothic script on the back of his Order Paper, 'Sanctimonious bastard'. When Budd ended his long and devious speech, Talbot tried for the last time to catch the Speaker's eye. On this occasion, the Speaker looked him straight in the face, and called out, 'Mr. Cordery!'

Talbot subsided with a scowl, tore up his notes, and after a calming few minutes rose, bowed to the Speaker, and made his way out into the Aye Lobby. He had failed to make or declare his position. He had decided in those minutes not to try and borrow money. His debt to Mayland crushed him with apprehension. He knew Mayland's vindictiveness, and he was certain that before the next day was over, the writ would be issued and he would himself be pilloried as a defaulter if not a bankrupt.

He greeted a group of his colleagues, refused an invitation to have a drink in the Smoking Room and hurried on to the Members' Lobby with the intention of leaving the House and returning for Melville's winding-up speech and the Division. He envied the serene, unconcerned faces of the Members who were standing about discussing the progress of the debate.

'Bad luck you couldn't get in,' said one of them.

'Doesn't matter a bit,' said Talbot, and as he spoke he felt that he was dealing in an untruth. The time for politeness was over. Tomorrow he would himself have to face the possibility of seeing his photograph and his name in the Mayland Press, with the typical hint in the captions that he was a man who didn't meet his obligations. He felt that everyone who nodded or smiled to him – policemen, attendants, and Whip's messengers – were greeting him under a misapprehension, that his claim to their courtesy was a fake, and that all that was left for him was to slink away like some nocturnal animal at daylight.

He pushed the heavy doors leading from the Members' Lobby to the corridor linking it with the Central Lobby, and as he did so he came face to face with Mayland, Hunter and Mrs. Martin. Taken by surprise, he made as if to pass them without recognition. But Hunter intercepted him and said, 'Hello, Peter.'

'Talbot?' Mayland inquired, and Talbot noticed that he had difficulty in recognizing him even through his thick glasses.

Talbot stopped and shook hands with Mrs. Martin and with

Hunter, who had put his hand out with a neutral and noncommittal expression.

'We were talking about you,' said Mayland, his dry, lined face creasing into a grin. 'Hoping you'd get into the debate.'

'Too much opposition,' said Talbot. 'But I must admit I didn't expect you to like what I was going to say.'

Mayland laughed.

'That's all right. I never mind a good bit of mutual sandbagging. In fact, I enjoy it very much. It gives life to politics. What do you think of the debate, Peter?'

Talbot replied, 'I don't think it's going very well for the Government. Perhaps when Melville replies—'

'Well, never mind about that,' said Mayland as if he were no longer interested in the subject. 'I've good news for you, Peter – great news.'

Talbot raised his head, which had begun to droop during the conversation. A small hope had begun to burgeon in his mind that perhaps Mayland in his present manic mood might have decided to issue a statute of oblivion which would release all his debtors from their obligations. It passed like a dream through his mind as he stood in the corridor, and when he looked at Mayland's face, his upper lip drawn back into a kind of rictus which exposed his yellowing teeth, the hope persisted.

'I've great news for you, Peter,' said Mayland.

'Well, thank you very much,' said Talbot. His voice had become deferential, and he hated this deference which had taken possession of him.

'Well,' said Mayland with a short, happy laugh, 'tomorrow morning Mrs. Martin and I are going to announce our forthcoming marriage.'

'At last,' said Mrs. Martin.

'Yes,' said Mayland. 'I call her "my eyes".' And his smile faded.

Talbot looked from one to the other, and then towards Hunter, unable for a moment to assemble his thoughts or to express his feelings.

'I'm so pleased,' he said at last, changing in his mind from pity to amusement and fury at his disappointment. 'Congratulations. Congratulations, Mrs. Martin,' he said, and shook Mrs. Martin's hand. When he came to Mayland, who was still standing with a preening expression on his face, he said,

'Congratulations, Mr. Mayland. I'm so pleased. But I've got one bit of bad news for you. I'd better tell you here and now that I can't pay the £2,000 tomorrow.'

'What £2,000?' said Mayland, his expression changing.

'The £2,000 I borrowed when I began to work for you,' Talbot said in a mumble. A group of Members and their wives were passing, and he was embarrassed by the possibility of their overhearing his conversation.

'My dear fellow,' said Mayland, 'because I sack you it doesn't mean I hate you. Hunter, what's all this about £2,000?'

'It's due,' said Hunter curtly.

'Well,' said Mayland easily, 'give him a year to pay. You mustn't be so hard on these young men, Hunter.'

'But you said—' Hunter began.

'Never mind what I said,' said Mayland, taking Mrs. Martin's arm and beginning to move towards the Central Lobby. 'The trouble with you, Hunter, is that you take things too literally.'

In the Central Lobby where all the benches were occupied and the policemen were calling out the lists of unavailable Members, Talbot, like a man who has been told by his doctor that he is free from some terrible disease that he feared, stood for a few seconds while Mayland fumbled for his direction, asking Mrs. Martin where the exit lay. Then he turned to Talbot and said,

' "Take therefore no thought for the morrow; for the morrow shall take thought for the things of itself." '

Talbot escorted them as far as St. Stephen's Hall, and watched Mrs. Martin holding Mayland by the arm and helping him carefully down the stone steps. Then, unconscious of anything but his liberation, he hurried down to the Members' Bar, where he ordered himself a large whisky and soda.

Later in the evening, Talbot went to the Library and finding himself a table in the empty Silence Room, sat for a few moments looking out of the window at the sky reddening over the river with the onset of the July dusk. The day had been hot, but he had scarcely been aware of it in the air-conditioned Chamber. Some Members, he noticed, wore light-weight suits, relics of Parliamentary delegations to Africa and Asia. They didn't seem exotic; appropriate rather to the Palace of Westminster as the residence of some imperial numen.

Talbot listened for a few moments to the chugging of river-boats, the splash and wash of their passage and the distant voices of the guides calling out from their decks. Then he took a sheet of paper with the House of Commons crest from the holder in front of him, and wrote:

'My dear Sylvia,

'I'm writing you this note in the Library after trying without success to reach you in the country. I saw you in the Gallery, and I am sending you the letter by messenger.

'You were looking rather pale, and I do hope you're well. But anyhow, you're there, and after all the bothering things that have been happening, I feel relieved. I'm sure all will go splendidly (despite the A.G.'s speech), and Yates and Co. will end up with a black eye.

'But that isn't why I'm writing to you. I've been thinking for a long time in an obscure way which has become clearer to me as I've gone along that, politically speaking at any rate, I've got into a track that I don't want to be in, that I haven't been able to get out of and that's leading me to a destination where I never wanted to go.

'I went into politics because I believed that it was the way to do and speak about the things I believed in. I won't try and define what I've become. I will only say it's not what I hoped to be.

'Tonight I made an important decision – for me at any rate. I've decided not to stand at the next Election, but to try and get an academic job at an African university – to try it out for several years, and then perhaps, with a background of experience, return to the House, if I can, and speak from knowledge.

'You see, I'm not giving up this place because I don't like it. On the contrary, I've never known or hope to know any political institution more worth while or that anyone could be prouder to belong to than the House of Commons. But I think I got off on the wrong foot. I want to make a new beginning, and this is how I hope to do it.

'Why, you may wonder, am I telling you all this? The answer is . . .'

He heard the clacking of the annunciator from the next room, and, seeing that it was nine o'clock, knew that Yates had begun his winding-up speech.

'. . . the answer is,' he went on writing, 'that somehow or other, I feel that, tonight especially, you will understand what I feel and what I mean when I tell you that despite everything I feel hopeful and optimistic about the future.

'I have thought a great deal about you, Sylvia, and if by any chance you could see me next week, perhaps we could hear the Brahms on Thursday at the Festival Hall and have dinner afterwards – I should be very happy. Perhaps you'll drop me a note here or ring me.

Yours ever,

Peter.'

He sealed the letter, and strolled slowly and contentedly through the deserted corridors and the Members' Lobby to the lift leading to the Galleries. As the lift door opened, he could hear Yates' voice amplified and resounding through the crowded Chamber.

'For Miss Melville,' he said to the attendant. And he stood, half-hidden behind the Strangers' Gallery, watching the bent backs of the spectators in the West Gallery as they peered intently at Yates.

The Leader of the Opposition was speaking emphatically, confident that he was dominating the House, secure in the unchallenged facts to which he kept recurring.

'No,' he said, 'there can be no dispute that the Director of Public Prosecutions was sent for by the Prime Minister.'

It was the *leitmotiv* of his speech, and each time it recurred the backbenchers accompanied it with an ascending roar of cheers.

'Why the devil doesn't Geoffrey say something?' said a Government Member who had come up behind Talbot.

Talbot didn't answer. The note had reached Sylvia, and when she saw his writing he had seen the half-smile on the face which he knew that he loved.

Yates ended his speech triumphantly.

'Yes,' he said, 'the Prime Minister has forfeited the confidence of this House, and in what might be called a political death wish, he has involved his colleagues with him. I am conscious that tonight on the benches opposite, old friends may become separated – perhaps even estranged. The Chancellor of the Exchequer has prudently found another engagement abroad more important than the defence of his leader. He always reminds me' – it was a throwaway line, and Yates' eyes were mischievous – 'of the old advertisement "Why wait to inherit?" The Chancellor has already pledged his hoped-for legacy – some might think prematurely. We on this side are not the only Shadow Cabinet. The Chancellor's only problem will be what to do' – Yates moved his hand over the Government Front Bench – 'with those discarded heirlooms.'

Melville looked back at him unsmiling.

'But however that may be,' said Yates, 'for the Prime Minister himself this is settling day.' His voice rose accusingly. 'He has shown himself unworthy of the great office he occupies. He has put his personal interest before his public duty, and tampered with the law. I ask all the hon. Gentlemen on every side of the House if they value what we all have always held to be the most precious – if they cherish the law that in turn safeguards us – I ask them to declare themselves and come with us into the Lobby tonight.'

He sat down, wiping his forehead, while his nearest colleagues leaned over to clap him on the shoulders. His speech had been an outstanding success both in its matter and in the assured way in which Yates had settled down after his first few sentences like a batsman who has taken the measure of the bowling.

While the rolling cheers for Yates were spending themselves though still being revived in ripples by some backbenchers as if demanding an encore, the Prime Minister rose slowly to the contrapuntal applause of those beside and behind him, a defiant affirmation of solidarity, only broken by the closed expressions and folded arms of a group of Members below the gangway.

'Cheer up, Forbes!' an Opposition Member called out, and Melville waited for the guffaw to subside.

'Mr. Speaker, sir,' he began quietly. And the House became silent, with every eye in the Chamber and in the Galleries turned towards the Prime Minister's face, made even paler than usual by the concealed lighting reflecting itself from the green leather benches. Melville paused for a moment to take in the figures sitting in the gangways near the Speaker's Chair and standing at the Bar next to the Serjeant-at-Arms and looking down from the Members' Upper Gallery.

'We have come,' he began, 'to the end of a long and thought-ful day in which we have heard speeches, some compelling, many of them powerful, but all inspired by a concern not for Party advantage but for the very rule of law which is the common concern of every Member of this House.'

There was a mutter of agreement, and Melville raised his voice slightly, already confident that he had established a proper tone for the debate.

'Within a few minutes' time,' he said, 'I will address myself to the claims of the Motion of Censure in order to rebut them. But before I do, let me say this. If there is any fault in this matter, then I agree at once with the right hon. Gentleman who moved the Motion that the responsibility is mine.'

'The whole lot of you!' Yates interjected.

'Oh, no,' said Melville quickly. 'It is the essence of the Censure that I as Prime Minister intervened in order to distort and frustrate the aims of justice.'

He half-turned to his own supporters, and said,

'Let no one attribute responsibility in this matter to anyone but myself. When the time comes for this Motion to be voted on, I only ask those to come into the Lobby with me who have faith in my integrity as a statesman – no, as a man entrusted with a high office from which any dereliction is a total one. I will honour those' – his voice was challenging – 'who believing that I failed in my duty, will support their belief with their voice and vote. I will respect those who, unable to make up their minds, will continue to sit on those benches for everyone to see their agony of doubt – or perhaps' – he gave a quick glance over his shoulder – 'their petrifaction of intellect.'

There was simultaneous laughter on both sides of the House.

'But what no one of integrity should tolerate tonight is the ignoble attitude of those who, willing to ambush but afraid to confront, will skulk somewhere in the Library when the Division Bell rings, or who after their incitements from the back of the crowd, absent themselves on some pretext from our proceedings.'

Someone said 'Ormston!' The name was repeated loudly on the Opposition benches and became a hiss that mingled with the cheers from opposite.

A Lobby Correspondent noted, 'Melville has shown right at the start of his speech that he's standing no nonsense from

Ormston. He's making the debate a vote of no confidence in Ormston as much as a vote of confidence in himself.'

'Sir,' Melville went on, 'we have seen in recent days a number of very curious combinations directed towards the downfall of the Government – the hon. Gentleman' – he waved towards Budd – 'whose constituency I've forgotten for the moment, in close alliance with a newspaper whose energies, however erratic, have been applied in the past to promoting causes very different from those which the hon. Gentleman's constituency sent him to Westminster to support.'

Budd stood up to interrupt, but Melville waved him away.

'The hon. Gentleman has had his say,' he said. 'And I have only another twenty-two minutes.' Then, facing Budd unsmilingly, the Prime Minister added, 'I understand that the hon. Gentleman has hired his services as a political consultant to the Mayland Press. He will no doubt have future opportunities of publishing his views.'

'Did you know about Budd?' Yates asked Crowther, without turning his head.

'No,' said Crowther. 'The point is that Melville knows.'

'At this stage,' said the Prime Minister, 'I want to talk about the part played by the Mayland Press in provoking the libel which has led to this Vote of Censure, and perhaps I may be permitted to offer a parenthesis, relevant to this subject, on the relationship of Press, Parliament and – if the neatness be forgiven – the People, a theme which I will later illustrate with the experience of my own daughter.

'There was a time,' he went on, 'when I held the view that the British Press was the best in the world. Today, I would modify that opinion, and say that the British Press *includes* some of the best in world journalism – and also some of the worst. It is the honourable function of the journalist to preserve for the written word the liberty which we in this House attach to the spoken word, to write truth as he sees it just as we speak truth as we see it. The Press provides a legitimate commercial service in spreading truthful information. It is fitting that those who serve should be rewarded. Yet if ever we reach a stage in Britain when the written word becomes a commercial token irrespective of its content – where men can *trade* in the debasing lie, the debasing slander, and the perverted confession, then indeed the title "the freedom of the Press" will acquire a different meaning from the one we have known – then indeed it will mean a Press no longer serving a high purpose but a Press prostituted for gain and indifferent to its moral and social function. And if such a Press becomes so powerful, so concentrated and monopolizing in its resources that it abuses its power, it is time that this should be said here in the House of Commons. And this I do tonight.

'In the last twenty years the debasement of the Press can be summarized in the word "hypocrisy". I mean by that the profession of virtue in order to mask vice, as for example in the Sunday pornography, bought at high prices from the vicious yet pretending the moral that vice doesn't pay, ostensibly displayed for condemnation yet presented to titillate and excite. The pornography which has been so freely thumbed in the moral campaigns of its retailers' – Melville's obvious allusion to Renewal was greeted with a murmur of 'Hear, hear' – 'is of small significance compared with the greater evil by which a section of the Press with great power has elevated materialism into the most desirable goal of our society, while at the same time claiming to pursue idealistic ends.

'Sir,' said Melville, turning to the Speaker, 'I will not dwell on the private vendettas of the Mayland Press which have been elevated into public causes. I will deal straight away with the scurrilous charge that I tried to deflect the course of justice; and I will show its unworthy origin and its ignoble course.'

He paused and leaned over the Despatch Box.

'The accident in which my daughter was involved was reported in the Press because of the vigilance of two reporters. Who were these gentlemen? Perhaps I can enlighten the House. They were two men especially assigned as part of a team of four reporters or, more accurately, informers, delegated to keep an around-the-clock watch on the activities of my daughter – to spy on her, to photograph her – indeed, they engaged a room for this, opposite her residence.'

Yates rose in the hush that followed, and said,

'The Prime Minister is making a grave allegation.'

Melville resumed his seat while Yates continued.

'He is saying, as I understand it, that the object of this – pursuit – was to discover his daughter presumably in discreditable circumstances. Will he offer any evidence to that effect?'

Melville rose again, and said,

'I will lay on the Table a photostat of an instruction and the affidavit of one of the gentlemen involved in this matter in support of what I have said. I will also present to the House a copy of an instruction to a New York correspondent asking him to assemble details of my daughter's private life during her years as a student in the United States.

'Sir,' Melville went on contemptuously, 'to some the persecution of a young woman by a vast organization may seem unsavoury in any circumstance. When it is related – as related I must say it is – to the private disappointments of a newspaper proprietor who has sought to injure the reputation of a daughter in order to destroy a father, it must seem a particularly gross and odious action. But when it is recklessly exploited in order to bring down a Government, then I say that all of us – Government and Opposition alike – must feel the gravest anxiety that a wilful man, possessed of great power, should be able to inflict so great a public mischief.'

'What about the D.P.P.?'Budd called out savagely. And there was a chorus of support from the Opposition benches. 'Yes, tell us about the D.P.P., never mind about Mayland.' Budd rose, but Melville refused to give way. For a few moments the two men stood together in an uproar from both sides and shouts of 'Give way!' and 'Sit down!' At last the Speaker rose, and said, 'The right hon. Gentleman has possession of the House,' and Budd reluctantly took his seat again. But when Melville went to continue, the din surged up again. 'Answer! Answer! What about the D.P.P.?'

'I will most certainly answer,' said Melville. 'That is the centre of our rebuttal.'

He picked up his notes and faced Yates, but as he did so a jagged pain tore like a great rending through his chest and over his shoulder and left arm, a suffocating pain that took his breath and raced through his gums.

'Answer!' the incantation began again.

'Answer! Answer!'

He could see the faces, the open Hogarthian mouths and hear the merciless demand.

'Answer! Answer!'

But he couldn't answer, and leaned over the Despatch Box.

Then the agony ebbed, receding till all that was left was the after-pain in his chest and teeth. He took a sip of water from the glass in front of him, and heard the Chief Whip's urgent whisper,

'All right, Geoffrey?'

'I was about to say,' Melville went on, and the faces which had become like a photograph on which the emulsion had run gradually returned into focus. 'I was about to say,' he said, and from the Opposition came a single sympathetic and perceptive cheer as he slowly resumed his speech, 'that the visit of the Director of Public Prosecutions to my room is the essential element in our rejection of the Motion of Censure.'

His voice became stronger.

'Yes,' he said, 'I did say to the Attorney-General when he spoke to me by telephone to Paris, "Do what is necessary." What could that mean in the context? It meant "Do what is right and proper in the honourable discharge of your duties." What happened then? When I returned to London, the Attorney-General informed me of the D.P.P.'s intention not to persevere with the charge. It was not for me to inquire into the merits of the charge. That surely was for others. But I had a responsibility – yes, indeed – to ensure that if the charge was not continued, there should be no other reason than the D.P.P.'s objective legal decision with the concurrence of the Attorney-General.

'To those who have steadily asked the question today "Did I send for the D.P.P.?" I now give the answer "Yes". Yes, I did. Was the purpose to order him to discontinue a prosecution? The answer is "No". I sent for him in order, in the presence of the Attorney-General and my Private Secretary, to obtain from him the assurance – which was minuted – that his decision was made wholly and entirely in discharge of his quasi-judicial function, exercised in the case of my daughter as it might be in the case of any other person in this realm.'

The House had become silent.

'Sir,' said Melville, the palms of his hands on the Despatch Box, 'I have nearly ended.' He looked up at the clock, which stood at 9.54. 'The debate and the day which is drawing to a close have permitted us all to look inwards at our consciences. A Motion of Censure is in a sense a capital charge. A Government is on trial, and what is true of the Government is doubly true of myself who am on trial as an individual as well as a Prime Minister. There can be no half-measures in your decision

– no tones of black and white – no degrees of guilt and innocence – no verdict of guilty with extenuating circumstances. I stand before you now, conscious of the rectitude with which I and my colleagues have acted' – the cheers rose solidly behind him – 'certain that my care for the honour and greatness of Parliament is as substantial as that of any Member of this House—'

The cheers swelled again.

'—determined to uphold the dignity of the Commons as the grand forum of the nation, and confident – confident' – he turned to right and left to include all his backbenchers in his survey – 'that tonight we will go into the Lobbies as a united Party, rejecting an odious and unjust aspersion and reaffirming our own will and fixed purpose to lead the nation as successfully in the future as we have done in the past.'

The cheers broke out in a storm as he sat down, and continued to roll on while the Speaker was putting the Question.

'As many as are of that opinion say "Aye" ' – the Opposition roared 'Aye'. 'The contrary "No" ' – in a great counter-roar the Government supporters shouted 'No'. 'I think the "Noes" have it,' said the Speaker. And the Opposition challenged the decision with another loud 'Aye.'

'Clear the Lobby!' said the Speaker.

'Clear the Lobby!' echoed the doorkeeper. And the Division Bells began their urgent clamour in every part of the House.

'Well done!' said the Chief Whip to Melville, and then he looked at him again. 'Are you sure you're all right?'

'Yes,' said Melville, summoning a faint smile. 'Yes, I'm all right. A bit tired. That's all. Any abstentions?'

The Chief Whip looked over his shoulder.

'I don't think so,' he said with a quick grin. 'Not even Forbes.'

CHAPTER FOURTEEN

AFTER the division, the Smoking Room quickly filled with Members having a final drink. In the far corner to the left Yates, undisturbed by the failure of the Censure Motion, was already surrounded by his regular group of intimates – Lippincott, a Queen's Counsel with a voice like a cement-crusher, explaining in loud tones the need to reform the Prosecution of Offences Regulations, Garvin, a Scottish Member who was chronically aggrieved about the breakdown of trade talks with China, Bellamy, anxious to impress on his leader the need to rebuild the National Gallery, and Brangwyn, who had many years ago been almost appointed Speaker and had preserved the deportment of the narrowly missed office. After the day's excitements, they were uninhibited and relaxed, and even when Melville came in with the Chief Whip, they scarcely turned their heads.

Melville walked slowly to his favourite place at the end of the sofa near the Dispense, and as he did so he was greeted cheerfully by those he cared to notice. There was, he observed, a scattering of Ormstonites, not seated together as they had been during the debate, but distributed as if taking protective cover.

'Splendid speech, Geoffrey,' said Forbes, looking up from his whisky and soda. 'Absolutely superb!'

Henry Lacey, who was sitting with him, added his melancholy and resonant voice to the congratulations.

'Yes, Geoffrey,' he said, 'you had Yates over a barrel. What a pity Gerald wasn't here to see it!'

'He'll read about it,' said Melville.

And Lacey, nodding his heavy head, said,

'No doubt! No doubt!'

Melville took his seat and the steward brought him his usual drink, a whisky and water. Within a few minutes, a number of Junior Ministers joined them.

'Extraordinary thing,' said the Chief Whip. 'Our majority went up to twenty-nine. We'll have to look into it.'

'I think some of the Opposition abstained,' said a young Member. 'I saw at least four on the Terrace who didn't vote.'

'The House is a very surprising place,' said the Chief Whip. 'All that fever – and you'd think it had never happened. Is Elizabeth waiting for you?'

'Yes,' said Melville. 'I asked her to stay on. It's a pleasant night. I think we'll walk back together.'

He finished his drink, said good night to the Members around him, and as they made way for him, he stepped carefully over the legs of those still drinking, and then went towards his room, where he had arranged to meet Elizabeth and Sylvia.

It had been a very long day, and when he reached the Library Corridor he paused for a few seconds. A trace of the constricting pain that he had felt during the debate had returned like a ghost of itself, and disappeared; but the memory made his arms tremble, and he rested against one of the Members' Lockers.

'All right, sir?' the policeman at the Library door asked.

'Yes, quite all right, thank you,' said the Prime Minister. He smiled, and walked on down the empty, dimly lit corridor.

Room Number One. Prime Minister. He put his hand on the brass knob of the oak door, and waited for the thumping of his heart to subside. His forehead was sweating, and he wiped it with the back of his hand before opening the door.

Inside, Frobisher was chatting to Elizabeth and Sylvia as they stood by the window watching the cars shuffle and the taxis arrive in New Palace Yard. Sylvia broke off the conversation as soon as she saw him enter, and went forward to kiss him on the cheek.

'You were marvellous, daddy,' she said, 'absolutely marvellous.'

'Splendid speech, sir,' said Frobisher.

'Thank you,' said Melville. 'I won't keep you, Eric. Your wife was complaining to me at lunch the other day that she never sees you.'

'Shall I—?'

'No,' said Melville. 'I think we'll walk back together. Pritchard can follow us.'

'In that case,' said Frobisher, 'I will bid you good night. I thought everything went off well.'

'Very,' said Elizabeth enthusiastically. 'Good night, Eric.'

From outside they heard the long cry, relayed from policeman to policeman, of 'Who goes home?' and almost simultaneously the light in the Clock Tower was extinguished. Melville gathered up his papers, and after a few minutes he said to Elizabeth, 'I think we can go.'

They had to pass through the Chamber, empty now and with its doors flung wide open, to reach the Central Lobby, and Melville, hesitating at the Speaker's Chair, said to Elizabeth, 'Look at it. It's like a battlefield.'

Order Papers were scattered over the floor and benches as if after acts of violence. Specially rolled squibbets lay across the red border of the carpet like discarded weapons.

'We're the survivors,' said Elizabeth; and Melville, glancing at her triumphant face, said grimly, 'Yes.'

The Central Lobby was already in darkness except for the small lights which transformed the Gothic walls into mysterious cathedrals in a different possession. A policeman murmured 'Good night,' and they walked without speaking through the shadows of the narrow St. Stephen's Hall, past the statues of Clarendon and Hampden, Walpole and Chatham, Pitt and Fox, who, with his fist clenched, seemed to resume an interrupted speech, like some figure in a waxworks after the doors have closed.

Sylvia clung tightly to Melville's arm as they entered the vast, engloomed Westminster Hall, their footsteps echoing over the flagstones under the vaulting roof as if they were being followed.

'It's frightening here at night,' she said. 'All those dead kings on their catafalques – and generations and generations of Members of Parliament – and Charles the First on those steps.'

She looked towards the plaque in the floor, expecting at any moment a spectral court to appear around them.

They heard the hurrying sound of footsteps, and Pritchard, the Prime Minister's detective, joined them.

'Sorry, sir,' he said. 'I didn't realize you were walking.'

He fell in behind with Elizabeth, and Melville walked ahead with Sylvia.

'What happened,' she asked, 'towards the end, when they were shouting "Answer"? I could have brained Yates. You suddenly went terribly white, and stood there without speaking.'

He didn't answer, and Sylvia said, 'Is there anything wrong, daddy? Please tell me. I'm so worried about you. You looked awfully ill in the debate.'

They had reached New Palace Yard, and Melville saw her face in the yellow light of the lamps.

'There's nothing to worry about,' he said. 'You're not looking well yourself. Will you come and stay with us for a little?'

She hesitated, and said, 'Yes – for a little.'

Sylvia stood for a few moments looking at the dark building, inert, a dead silhouette against the sky.

'I always find it so sad,' she said, 'when they cry "Who goes home?" and the House closes down.'

'It isn't really sad,' said Melville. 'The doorkeeper always calls out "Usual time tomorrow."'

'I like that,' said Sylvia as they moved across the courtyard. 'Usual time tomorrow! It's nice. It makes me feel optimistic.'

When they reached Number 10 Downing Street, the policeman on duty saluted, surprised to see the Prime Minister on foot, and Melville thanked Pritchard for accompanying him.

'Come, Sylvia,' Melville said.

Sylvia hesitated, and answered, 'Only for a little.'

'Yes,' said Melville gravely. 'Only for a little.'

Elizabeth looked up at the mauve, star-filled sky, and, taking a deep breath, said,

'What a wonderful night this has been!'

The door opened, and Melville stood aside to let his wife and daughter enter.